SURRENDER TO
THE SCOT

Books by Emma Prince

Highland Bodyguards Series:

The Lady's Protector (Book 1)

Heart's Thief (Book 2)

A Warrior's Pledge (Book 3)

Claimed by the Bounty Hunter (Book 4)

A Highland Betrothal (Novella, Book 4.5)

The Promise of a Highlander (Book 5)

The Bastard Laird's Bride (Book 6)

Surrender to the Scot (Book 7)

Book 8 (Vivienne and Kieran's story) coming mid-2018!

The Sinclair Brothers Trilogy:

Highlander's Ransom (Book 1)

Highlander's Redemption (Book 2)

Highlander's Return (Bonus Novella, Book 2.5)

Highlander's Reckoning (Book 3)

Viking Lore Series:

Enthralled (Viking Lore, Book 1)

Shieldmaiden's Revenge (Viking Lore, Book 2)

The Bride Prize (Viking Lore, Book 2.5)

Desire's Hostage (Viking Lore, Book 3)

Thor's Wolf (Viking Lore, Book 3.5)—a Kindle Worlds novella

Other Books:

Wish upon a Winter Solstice (A Highland Holiday Novella)

To Kiss a Governess (A Highland Christmas Novella)

SURRENDER TO THE SCOT

Highland Bodyguards, Book Seven

EMMA PRINCE

Surrender to the Scot (Highland Bodyguards, Book 7)
Copyright © 2018 by Emma Prince

For Scott. Always.

Chapter One

Late April, 1320
Northern England

There was no denying it. Elaine Beaumore's friends —her *only* friends—were boring.

She propped her elbow on the wooden counter dividing the cloth shop's front display from the reams of colorful material in the back, resting her chin in her hand as Judith droned on about a new shipment of brocade.

"...first glance you'd call it ruby, but of course it's truly more of a burgundy." Judith dragged her shears across a length of brown-dyed wool that was decidedly less interesting than the silks she and Julia had been eagerly anticipating for months.

"And wait until you see the threadwork on it, Lainey," Julia, Judith's twin sister, added, deftly scooping up the bolt of wool and carrying it to the back of their father's shop.

"Aye, it's enough gold to make my—"

"—head spin."

The twins had a habit of doing that—cutting each other off and finishing each other's thoughts. It happened more whenever they spoke about some new silk or velvet their father had ordered. Naught made Judith and Julia more excited than cloth.

Elaine made an interested noise, but she was saved from having to comment because Julia had already reemerged from the back. She and Judith suddenly fixed her with an assessing look, their identical brown eyes sharp and their brown heads tilting at the same angle.

"You would like it, Lainey," Judith said. "The needlework is very fine. Mayhap for a—"

"—wedding dress," Julia continued. "You'll need something nicer than what you normally wear. But then again, the color—"

"—is all wrong for you." Judith waved vaguely at Elaine's head. "What with that copper hair, burgundy would be—"

"—a disaster."

Elaine realized she'd been grinding her teeth. Judith and Julia were the only girls in the village her age, and despite the fact that she was a lord's daughter and they merely the daughters of a cloth merchant, Elaine had sought their friendship.

She didn't begrudge the twins' overfamiliarity with her, or even their criticisms of her appearance and her penchant to dress plainly. There was a time when Elaine had even looked up to Judith and Julia, for they'd taught her how to weave scraps of silk ribbon into her hair and had always told tales of the latest fashions from the French court.

Nay, she was used to overlooking their informality and their cutting remarks. What she found she could no longer swallow was the triviality of their endless chatter.

She straightened from the counter abruptly. "I just remembered—I have to go...help my father with...something."

The excuse was laughably thin, but neither twin seemed to notice. They merely blinked at her, then turned their attention back to folding the length of wool they'd just cut.

"That brocade is supposed to arrive within the sennight," Judith commented as Elaine turned to leave. "We can take your measurements and then you'll be sure to have—"

"—a gown fine enough to be wed in!"

Elaine shut the shop door on Julia's words. There was another topic of conversation the twins had fixated on—Elaine's imaginary wedding. A month past, she'd told them that her father had broached the subject of finding a suitable husband for her. The twins had been oblivious to the tightness of Elaine's voice as she'd spoken and had jumped straight into planning a grand event in their minds. Never mind the fact that Elaine's eyes burned with the threat of tears every time she thought of it.

Marriage. That meant the rest of her days spent tucked behind stone walls, the lady of some manor or other. It would be a quiet life, no doubt. A safe life. A boring life.

Though the spring day was mild, Elaine's cheeks felt cool as she strode away from the shop. She realized belatedly that a few tears had slipped out. Annoyed, she dashed them away with her palms.

She'd long disliked the fact that she was quick to tears, for it seemed to confirm what everyone already thought of her—that she was an overly sensitive girl who had to be handled with care. And because of that, only the most inane topics—ribbons and gowns and how to dress most becomingly for the exact shade of her hair—should fill her life.

Letting a frustrated breath go, she pointed herself toward the stables at the edge of the village, just below the rise atop which Trellham Keep sat.

"Milady," Jacob, one of the stable lads, said as she stepped inside. He set aside a piece of leather he'd been oiling. "A saddle on Gertie for you?"

"Aye, thank you." Her rides were becoming a frequent enough occurrence that Jacob hardly needed to ask anymore.

Elaine cast her gaze about the stables, a thrill going through her to find that none of Trellham's guards were inside. With the village only a long stone's throw down the hill from the keep, she was allowed to walk there by herself, though Finn Sutherland, her stubborn mule of a brother-in-law, had instructed the guards not to let her ride without an escort.

It had been four quiet, peaceful years since Elaine's sister Rosamond had been kidnapped by those working against the alliance between their father, Lord Henry Beaumore, and the Scottish King Robert the Bruce. Finn had saved Rosamond—and stolen her heart, leading to their joyful union here at Trellham.

In truth, Elaine loved Finn, for he made Rosamond unfailingly happy, but her Highland brother-in-law could be just as bad as her sister when it came to being overprotective.

Northern England—including Trellham Keep— was securely in Robert the Bruce's hands now, and none dared to challenge him. Elaine would be forever grateful to the Bruce for bringing peace to the Borderlands. She'd grown up in a time of war and uncertainty, and these last few years had been blessedly calm. Still, it meant that her rides through the countryside were her only excitement—and that Finn needn't have ordered guards to accompany her.

Even as Jacob slipped the bridle over Gertie's head, Elaine swung up into the saddle, uncaring that riding astride meant her blue woolen skirts hitched up to reveal her tall boots.

"In a hurry, are you, milady?" Jacob asked, lifting the reins around Gertie's alert ears and handing them to Elaine with a knowing smile.

She'd done this before—slipped out of the stables without an escort—but never had she made it more than a few breathless moments before they caught up to her. She accepted the reins and clicked her tongue, guiding Gertie toward the open stable doors. "How far do you think I'll get this time?"

"Oh, at least to the copse of trees in the western valley, milady," Jacob replied.

With a flashing grin over her shoulder, Elaine squeezed her knees into Gertie's flanks and snapped the reins lightly.

The dappled gray mare needed no further encouragement. Elaine had selected her for her lean strength and eagerness to run. The animal longed to tear across the rolling landscape just as badly as Elaine.

As they darted around Trellham's base, she heard a shout go up from one of the keep's towers. The guards had spotted her, then.

Though they were good, honest men, Elaine couldn't help resenting them, for they were a constant reminder that Finn, Rosamond, and her father still thought of her as a child that needed constant watching. Elaine was a woman grown at nearly nineteen—old enough for her father to raise the topic of marriage—yet her freedoms were as narrow as a reed.

But at least she had this moment. She urged Gertie on, and the ground beneath them turned to a blur of spring-green grasses. As the copse at the bottom of the valley came into view, Elaine dared a look over her shoulder. Four guards barreled after her on big, powerful steeds, but to her surprise, they were only just descending from Trellham's hilltop.

Elaine leaned back over Gertie's neck, letting the wind rip at her hair and sting her cheeks. Her eyes burned with exhilaration as she shot past the copse and up the other side of the valley. When she crested the next rise, a thrilled laugh rose in her throat.

But as Gertie careened down the back side of the slope so fast that her hooves barely touched the ground, the mirth died inside Elaine like a doused fire.

She wasn't alone.

A rider had just dipped through the valley floor and was headed up the slope toward her. A man Elaine didn't recognize.

Her elation shattered as a sharp lance of fear stabbed her. She reined in hard, but Gertie's momentum and the slanting ground beneath them meant the horse couldn't stop her descent into the valley—right toward the strange rider.

Gertie's hooves showered clumps of grass and dirt as she at last scrambled to a halt only a few paces from the man.

"Easy there," he said, lifting a palm as if he could halt her horse with just his hand.

Elaine's panicked gaze landed on that big, callused hand. Then again, mayhap he could. He was a fearsome sight. Seated atop an enormous roan stallion, he towered over Elaine, but as her eyes swept over him, she knew it wasn't just the horse that made him seem overpowering.

His dark brown hair was held back from his face, revealing features chiseled from granite. Thick stubble the same color as his hair dusted his angular jaw. The severe line of his lowered brows matched his flat, hard-set mouth, yet his lips were surprisingly full. Beneath those dropped brows lay sharp chestnut eyes that seemed to bore straight into her.

"Are ye all right, lass?" he asked, his dark gaze searching.

Elaine's fright must've been written clearly on her face. She'd never had any skill at hiding the emotions that so easily bubbled to the surface.

Distantly, she registered that the man had spoken in a Scottish accent—and not just Scottish, but the same curling burr as Finn's. He was a Highlander, then. Aye, he wore a plaid belted around his hips in the Highland style, though she did not recognize the red and yellow-slashed pattern.

We are allies, she told herself, desperately trying to check her terror. *He is a Scot, and my family is loyal to the Bruce*. Still, kilted Highlanders did not normally ride alone into Northern England—unless they were lawless men, beholden to no one and out to take whatever they could.

Elaine's hands tightened on the reins as she attempted to urge Gertie backward away from the man. "I...you are..."

The man's gaze shifted to something over her shoulder. Before she knew what had happened, he'd closed the distance between them and clamped a hand around her waist. Suddenly she was being lifted off her horse and onto his. She connected with the hard, warm wall of his body. The air rushed from her lungs at the coiled strength there.

Even as he settled her across his lap, one arm still gripping her waist, he drew the long, deadly-sharp sword from its sheath at his hip.

Too shocked to scream, Elaine's eyes widened on the

glinting blade the man held before them both. Her gaze snagged on a motion at the top of the ridge. All at once, she knew why the man had dragged her so abruptly from her horse.

The four guards from Trellham had crested the ridge and were barreling toward them, swords drawn at the sight of their lady in the arms of a rogue Scotsman.

Oh God, nay.

Elaine had wanted adventure. She'd wanted excitement. And now her foolishness would end in catastrophe.

Chapter Two

Jerome Munro's arm tightened around the wide-eyed English lass in his lap. If he'd spotted the brigands chasing her a few moments earlier, he would have shifted her behind him in the saddle to free up both hands, but as it was, he would have to face the four bastards one-handed.

It was better than the alternative—simply continuing on his way to Trellham Keep and letting the lass fend for herself. Damn if he didn't like the diversion from his mission, but he was a Highlander, which meant he couldn't stand aside and ignore injustice.

Or a terror-filled pair of bonny blue eyes.

The way the lass had come tearing into the valley a moment before had nearly made him reach for his sword right then, but it had been the look of fright on the lass's delicate features that had sent the warning bells ringing in his head. When her four pursuers had topped the hill above them, he'd acted on instinct to protect her.

Jerome squeezed his knees into Duff's flanks, urging the animal to turn so that his side was exposed to the oncoming warriors. The stallion's ears drew back and he nickered in protest at the position, for he was a trained warhorse and was used to facing battles head-on. But the angle would allow Jerome to shield the lass more with his own body and give him greater freedom with his sword arm.

"Steady," he murmured as the four riders thundered closer, but he wasn't sure if he was speaking to Duff, the lass, or himself.

"Nay, don't——" the lass began, but one of the charging brigands shouted over her.

"Unhand her, you bloody bastard!" The riders reined in, and as with the lass's arrival, their horses kicked up clumps of mud and grass as they fought for footing.

"And turn her over to the likes of ye scoundrels? Nay, I dinnae think so," Jerome replied lowly.

The apparent leader snarled in anger and lifted his drawn sword. Jerome braced his own sword for the blade's impact, but before the other man's weapon descended, a high, clear voice sliced through the valley.

"*Stop!*"

Her attacker froze for half a heartbeat. "Fear not, Lady Elaine——"

"Brett, stand down."

Lady Elaine? From the brief glimpse he'd gotten, Jerome had seen a simple-clad lass with muddy boots and wind-snarled copper hair, not an English noblewoman.

Before he could untangle that knot, another realization hit him. The outlaws knew the lass—and she knew them.

"Milady, this Scot is trying to—"

"Protect the lass from brigands," Jerome cut it, comprehension beginning to dawn. He dared to lower his sword an inch, eyeing the four men. "And I take it ye are trying to do the same."

The lass in his lap shifted, and Jerome was suddenly acutely aware of her slight, soft body in his hold.

"These are my guards," she said, looking up at him.

Thick russet lashes framed eyes as bright blue as the Highland sky on a summer day.

"And the fear I saw written so clearly on yer face a moment ago…"

She held his stare. "…Was for you. But seeing as how you tried to protect me, I gather I was wrong."

Jerome lowered his sword fully now, as did the lass's guards. "Nay, ye were right to be wary of a stranger." He couldn't help himself as he gazed down at her bonny face—he let one side of his mouth lift in a smile. "Especially a Highlander."

A fetching pink blush broke over her creamy cheeks, and Jerome nearly cursed himself for a fool. He wasn't here to dally with a wee bonny English lady. He had a mission to complete.

He cleared his throat, willing himself to tear his gaze from the lass's face. "I should have announced myself. I am Jerome Munro, and I travel with King Robert the Bruce's express permission to Trellham Keep."

She cocked her copper head at him. "Trellham? On what business?"

His assignment was no secret—in fact, quite the opposite. Like ripples over a loch's surface, word of Jerome's task had spread rapidly throughout Scotland. But this wasn't Scotland. Though the Bruce had controlled this region for several years, it was still technically England, so he shouldn't be surprised that he hadn't been anticipated.

"I've come to collect Lord Henry Beaumore's seal for the King's declaration of freedom from the English."

The lass stiffened in his hold. Jerome should have set her on her own horse by now, but instead he found himself loath to let her go. Damn it all, she was a noblewoman, despite what he'd first thought—an *English* noblewoman.

He dropped his gaze to her once more, expecting to find confusion at best or downright disgust at worst upon hearing his business. Despite the peace in the Borderlands of late, Scottish freedom was no doubt a sore subject for the English—even a noble lass who most likely knew not a single wisp about politics and war.

But to his shock, the lady's rosy lips pulled wide in a radiant smile. Involuntarily, Jerome's knees clenched around his horse in an attempt to keep from falling from the saddle at her blindingly becoming grin. The stallion sidestepped in annoyance at Jerome's movement.

She didn't seem to notice. "Henry Beaumore is my father."

Bloody hell. Jerome had already acted the rogue for dragging the lass onto his lap when he thought her in danger. Worse, he'd kept her there despite the fact that the threat had evaporated—and her, a noblewoman.

But she was the daughter of the man with whom the Bruce had allied to secure this section of the Borderlands? That meant she was the sister-in-law of Finn Sutherland, one of the members of the King's Bodyguard Corps—an elite group of warriors into which Jerome had just been admitted.

He hastily sheathed his sword and wrapped his hands around the lass's waist, lifting her out of his lap. Thankfully, her gray mare had remained next to Duff despite all the turmoil a moment before.

As he set her in the saddle, she continued, staring at him wide-eyed. "You're the one, then. The one the King sent for the Declaration of Arbroath."

So word of his mission *had* reached this corner of Northern England. More surprising, though, was that the lass knew the declaration's name. So much for his assumption that she knew naught of political affairs.

"Aye," he replied. "Yer father's seal is the last to be collected before the Bruce will send the declaration to the Pope."

Lady Elaine's face took on an awed expression that made an unwarranted knot of pride tighten in Jerome's chest. Clearing his suddenly thick throat, Jerome attempted to lighten the mood. "I'm sure the Bruce will be honored to hear of Lord Beaumore's welcoming party."

Lady Elaine flushed and she opened her mouth to speak, but Brett cut in. "Aye, and Lord Beaumore will no doubt hear of this too, milady," he said reprovingly. He cast a frown at Jerome, but then fixed a stern look on the lass.

Her blush deepened. "I-I apologize for giving everyone such a fright."

Brett's scowl remained as he and the others re-sheathed their swords. "Come, Munro. Lord Beaumore and Finn Sutherland will be eager to greet you."

As Jerome nudged his horse into motion, the guards fell into a loose circle around Lady Elaine, leaving him to ride by her side. As they crested the nearest hill, he let himself glance surreptitiously at this most unusual English lady.

She rode the dappled mare well, sitting straight in the saddle with the reins held in a relaxed grip. Her russet hair flowed in loose waves down her slim back, and her lithe, lissome form rocked with the horse's steps.

A jolt went through him as he remembered the feel of her, soft and light in his lap. Her blue gown was plain but well-cut enough to reveal the high, round swells of her breasts, the narrow swoop of her waist, and the flair of slim hips. The hem was muddy where it rose around her knee-high boots.

Not at all what he would have expected from a lord's daughter. After nearly a month spent traveling to every corner of Scotland—and a few points in Northern England as well—Jerome had thought himself immune to surprises, yet Lady Elaine was the rarest gem he'd seen in quite a while.

As they topped a second rise, he tore his gaze away from her to take in the sight of Trellham Keep.

It was more of a glorified manor house than a

stronghold. No curtain wall protected it, nor a moat or turrets. It was comprised simply of a central keep with two towers rising on either side, one on the east and one on the west. A small village of three dozen or so thatched cottages sat below the keep on the south side.

No wonder Lord Beaumore had struck up an alliance with the Bruce four years past. The keep would have fallen quickly to the kinds of sieges the Scots had laid against far more fortified castles. Jerome felt an unexpected stirring of relief at the thought of Lady Elaine being safe under Scottish protection here.

Brett lifted his hand in signal to the guards on the towers' battlements as they mounted the hill atop which Trellham sat. By the time the small party reined their horses at the base of the west tower, the keep was aflutter with activity.

Jerome swung down from Duff's back and moved instantly to Lady Elaine's mare. Without thinking, he wrapped his hands around her waist—damn, but they fit well there—and lifted her from the saddle.

"What goes on here?"

Jerome turned to find a barrel-chested Englishman with the same bright blue eyes as Lady Elaine pushing his way through the keep's double doors. His russet hair was faded with streaks of gray, but the family resemblance was undeniable.

"Lord Beaumore," Jerome began, but before he could continue, a second man joined the English lord.

Despite never having met the man, Finn Sutherland was unmistakable. He wore the blue-and-green checked Sutherland plaid around his waist and over his shoulder, setting him apart from the breeches-clad Englishmen all around. Jerome found himself dipping his head in respect to Finn. He'd heard much of the man's fierceness and loyalty to Scotland, two traits Jerome valued above all others.

Finn fixed him with dark, hard eyes, but when his gaze landed on Jerome's plaid, the tension in his shoulders relaxed slightly.

"Munro. We heard we should be expecting ye."

Jerome nodded again but kept himself rigid. Though they were practically family now that Jerome had joined the Corps, the man was still a Sutherland, and no self-respecting Munro could so easily overlook that. "Apologies for keeping ye waiting. The Bruce would like me to have already returned to Scone by now, but it's been a damned tall order."

Lord Beaumore's wrinkled face eased somewhat as well, but his gaze locked on Lady Elaine. "And what are you doing with this man, daughter?"

Lady Elaine swallowed, but before she could speak, Finn cut in. "Inside," he said brusquely. "Munro is no doubt weary from his travels, and tonight promises to be of great import."

Lord Beaumore tilted his graying head and motioned everyone into the keep.

Chapter Three

E laine twined her hands in her mud-splattered skirts as she followed her father into Trellham's great hall. Aye, she was worried for her father and Finn's reaction to hearing that she'd led her guards on a merry chase right into potential danger. It would only confirm what they already thought—that she couldn't be trusted with more than childish fripperies.

But a second rope of nerves twined with the first in her stomach. Jerome Munro's nearness sent a bolt of awareness through her that had her skin warming.

She'd been entirely mistaken about him with her first glance. Indeed, he was a dark, imposing figure. As they crossed the hall toward one of the trestle tables, she noted that his head was level with Finn's, who normally towered over everyone. And like her brother-in-law, Jerome was built for battle. His broad shoulders and muscular arms were unmistakable beneath his loose white shirt. He carried himself with taut control, the coiled power of his strong, lean frame obvious even when he was at ease, as he was now.

She had felt that power when he'd held her fast against his chest, and again when he'd lifted her down from her horse as if she were naught more than a leaf. *Gracious.* Her wayward thoughts were bringing heat into her face.

Yet he was no lawless rogue, as she'd initially feared. He was one of Robert the Bruce's elite warriors, trusted enough to take on the mission of collecting seals for the Declaration of Arbroath. Jerome's presence would make her set-down all the more embarrassing—and not just because she found her gaze tracing each hard-set line of his face and the contours of his body.

There were few things in Elaine's life that truly stirred her. Riding with Gertie was one such thing. The other was Robert the Bruce's cause for Scottish freedom.

To an outsider, it made no sense, of course. By all appearances, Elaine led the comfortable, easy life of an English lord's daughter. Yet living her whole life on the border, Elaine had seen more than most young women the true cost of warfare—and what a blessed gift peace was. She had the Bruce to thank for that.

But even more than calm and safety, what truly moved her in the core of her heart and the marrow of her bones was the Scottish fight for freedom—for freedom was what she longed for most of all.

Finn called for a servant to bring ale, bread, and cheese. But before the refreshments arrived, her father turned on her, his frown disapproving.

"Let us have it out, daughter. What have you gotten up to this time?"

"She dashed off on Gertie without waiting for an escort, milord," Brett, who'd followed them into the keep, offered.

Henry's frown deepened. "Lainey," he chided, his voice low.

To her surprise, Finn spared her only a brief scowl before turning his glower on Brett. "And why did ye let her do that?"

Finn was a hard man and had taken Trellham's guards to task when he'd arrived four years ago. Originally, the purpose of hammering the guards into shape had been for Rosamond's safety, but now that they were all family, Finn had extended that adamant overprotection to all at Trellham.

Brett faltered, shifting on his feet. "She was in the village, and we didn't see her head out from the stables."

"And?"

"And when we caught up to her, Munro here had come upon her."

Finn pinned Brett with a long look. "Ye are dismissed. Take up Samuel's rotation on the east tower. I'll address this matter with ye and the others later."

Elaine winced, knowing that Finn would likely put her guards through a grueling training session for letting her give them the slip.

"It wasn't Brett's fault," she said, the words slipping out before she could think. Under Finn's stare, she hurried on. "I should have waited for them, but I merely wanted…"

Her throat tightened and the telltale burn started behind her eyes. *Nay*. She did not want to cry—not now, not in front of Jerome, and not over her own foolishness.

She swallowed hard, digging her fingernails into her palms. "I merely wanted a moment of freedom," she choked out.

Through the tears blurring her vision, she saw her father's eyes soften, but Finn remained unmoved.

"I ken that, Lainey, but all ye've proven by dashing off is that ye havenae earned that right."

Frustration heated her face. Out of the corner of her eye, she saw Jerome cross his arms over his chest. "No harm came of the lass's flight," he offered, his voice deep and soft.

Finn shifted sharp eyes to Jerome. "Aye, no' this time. She was lucky ye werenae a foe or a less...*honorable* man."

Jerome's shoulders stiffened, but he remained silent —wisely, for this was a family matter. Still, warmth spread through Elaine at the fact that he'd spoken up for her.

Finn pinned her once more with a hard look, but she was saved from another lecture by her sister.

"You didn't tell me a guest had arrived, my love." Rosamond emerged from the stairs leading to the east tower, her golden hair and warm smile as radiant as the sun.

She was as round as the sun, too, for she was only a month or so away from delivering their second child.

When Finn's gaze landed on Rosamond, his whole demeanor softened, as it always did in her presence.

Elaine let a breath go, silently giving thanks for her sister's timing.

Finn moved swiftly to Rosamond's side, extending his arm to her. "This is Jerome Munro, sweeting. He's the man the Bruce sent regarding the Declaration of Arbroath."

Rosamond's already convivial smile brightened even more. "Ah. You are most welcome, Jerome."

Jerome bowed stiffly.

"I hope I'm not interrupting," Rosamond continued. "Rand just went down for a nap—that's our three year old, whom Finn calls the wee hellion," she said in an aside to Jerome. "I thought I'd come have a bite while I could."

Just then, the servant returned with a platter of bread, cheese, and a pitcher of ale.

"Ah, excellent timing." Rosamond moved to sit at the table the family normally dined at, but their father cleared his throat.

"My dear, we are in the middle of something."

Though she was always the perfect gentlewoman, Rosamond's sweetness masked a sharp, discerning mind. "Oh?" Her violet eyes fell on Elaine. "Something involving Lainey?"

Elaine shot her a pleading look. Rosamond seemed to instantly understand.

"Surely that can wait," Rosamond said smoothly. "Our guest would no doubt like to rest, and I'm sure there is much to discuss regarding the declaration. Mayhap we should arrange a celebration this eve?"

Elaine hurried to sit down across from Rosamond, wordlessly thanking her with her eyes. Still, as the men lowered themselves onto the table's benches, Elaine couldn't help the hot stone of shame that sank in her stomach. Leave it to her to make a mess—and leave it to her older sister to clean it up.

"Is this to be yer last stop, Munro?" Finn asked, settling beside Rosamond. His hand absently made a circle on Rosamond's back.

"Aye," Jerome replied. "The Lairds and noblemen nearest Arbroath have already affixed their seals, and a few close to Scone will do the same when I return to the Bruce's court."

Despite Elaine's embarrassment from a moment before, a flutter of pure exhilaration stole over her. This was one of the most important moments in the Bruce's cause to secure freedom for Scotland—and in a small way, she was part of it.

She'd first heard about the Declaration of Arbroath from Finn and her father. Because Finn was one of the Bruce's most trusted warriors, he'd learned of the King's plan to take a bold stroke toward freedom now that he'd secured a short-term truce with England's King Edward II.

Lord Beaumore was still technically the keeper of Trellham in the Bruce's name, though Finn had taken over much of the responsibilities as her father's health had continued to flag. Out of respect for Lord Beaumore's position, however, Finn kept him abreast of all Trellham's goings-on, as well as the Bruce's larger plans.

And knowing how interested Elaine was in the Bruce's cause, Finn and her father had indulged her by letting her sit in on their talks from time to time.

That was how, a few months past, she'd first heard of the Bruce's plan to draft a document declaring Scotland's sovereignty from England, to be delivered to the Pope himself. The Pope, who'd long refused to acknowledge Scotland's freedom, or the Bruce as its King, was apparently the Bruce's next target in the long struggle for independence.

They'd gotten word not long ago that the document had been completed at Arbroath Abbey. The King was calling on all his allies to provide their seals to be affixed to the declaration to show their support. But because Scotland's Lairds and nobles were spread far and wide across the country, the King had selected a warrior to travel to each holding, collecting the seals to be attached to the declaration.

Now that warrior, Jerome Munro, sat across from her in Trellham Keep's humble great hall.

"Ye must be relieved to be at the end of such a mission," Finn commented, filling a mug with ale and passing it to Jerome.

"It was a great honor to be chosen for it," Jerome replied seriously. "It has been a long three sennights since I departed Scone with the declaration, aye. But I dinnae take the Bruce's trust lightly."

"I understand Colin MacKay and his cousin Graeme were the ones to suggest that ye join the Bodyguard Corps," Finn said. "They seemed to think that yer loyalty to yer Munro Laird could be harnessed in service of the Bruce."

Elaine didn't miss the skeptical, sharp edge to Finn's gaze. From the tightening of Jerome's jaw, neither did he.

Of course, Finn was suspicious and slow to trust everyone—he'd even suspected Elaine's brother Niall of being a danger to Rosamond when he'd first arrived at Trellham. Yet there seemed to be more than simple wariness in the silent look that passed between Finn and Jerome.

"I have pledged my loyalty—my *life*—to both my Laird and my King," Jerome said levelly. "I am only glad the Bruce thought me worthy of the honor of his trust."

Rosamond, too, must have sensed the tension in the air, for she cleared her throat and smiled. "It must have been a privilege to see so much of Scotland's beauty on your travels," she said lightly.

His gaze flicked to Elaine, and her stomach tightened. "Aye," he said. "And some of England's as well."

"And what is the mood of the people?" Lord Beaumore asked. "How has your procession been received?"

"Verra well," Jerome answered. "The King has instructed that I publicly read the declaration in its entirety so that no' only the nobles but the people can say aye or nay to their sovereign's aims. Thus far, the country is united behind him."

"As am I," Lord Beaumore said resolutely. "The Bruce needn't ever ask for my support, but I'm honored that in sending you, Munro, he has. I'll gladly give my seal in support of his cause."

Elaine's eyes pricked with emotion. Four years past, her father had made an alliance of necessity with the Bruce. Their lands and people had been much battered in the struggle between the English and the Scots for control of the Borderlands. Yet since siding with the Bruce, peace and prosperity once again reigned at Trellham. Her father, like the rest of her family, had fully embraced the Bruce's cause, much to Elaine's pride.

"We should indeed have a celebration this eve, then," Rosamond said, smiling. "It will give the villagers a chance to hear the King's message, and serve to honor Trellham's commitment to the cause for freedom." She rose slowly, carefully balancing her round belly. "Lainey, I'm sure you'll be eager to help me with the preparations."

Though she spoke sweetly, Elaine didn't miss the pointed firmness in her sister's gaze. Elaine rose and followed Rosamond toward the kitchens. As they walked, Rosamond looped their arms and leaned close.

"I hope I was right in diverting Finn and Father back there," she said, glancing up at Elaine. Though she was nine years Elaine's senior, Rosamond's petite frame put her a hand shorter than Elaine.

"I'll explain," Elaine replied, worrying her lower lip with her teeth.

"Good," Rosamond whispered back. "And I hope you can also explain the look in Jerome Munro's eyes whenever he stole a glance at you, or the blush on your face every time he spoke, for I am most curious about that as well."

"Rosamond!" Elaine hissed, a betraying heat rising once again to her cheeks. *Gracious*. She cursed her easily-read features, but knew she couldn't hold aught back from her sister.

Letting a breath go, she began at the start.

Chapter Four

J erome had done this two dozen times in the last three sennights, but for some reason he found his stomach clenched with nerves as he descended the spiral stairs toward Trellham's great hall.

Finn had kept him busy in the keep's solar for most of the afternoon while preparations for the celebration were being made. They'd discussed the state of affairs in Scone where the Bruce was holding parliament until Lady Rosamond had entered and informed them that the villagers were gathering and a hastily prepared feast was nearly completed.

Lady Rosamond had kindly insisted that he use her and Finn's chamber to wash away his travels and change into a clean shirt. He hadn't had time to scrape away the dark bristle on his cheeks, though. But why should he care about his appearance when he ought to be focused on his assignment?

Damn it all, he knew why—it had everything to do

with the blue-eyed, copper-haired beauty who'd tugged at his thoughts all afternoon.

He cursed himself for a fool as he drew closer to the great hall. He would be leaving in a matter of hours for Scone. Aye, if the festivities dragged on, he might stay the night here at Trellham, but even still, what was the point in letting himself long for Elaine when he would likely never see her again?

He needed to focus on his mission, he told himself firmly as he descended the final steps. The Bruce had entrusted him with this gravely important task. No lass —no matter how bonny and spirited—could get in the way of that.

Despite his silent chastisement, he found himself scanning Trellham's small, modest hall for the russet-haired gem all the same.

The hall was abuzz with excitement. Several dozen simply-clad villagers were filing in through the double doors, which were thrown wide, letting the sweet, fresh spring air mingle with the smells of roasted boar and baking bread wafting from the kitchens.

The high-vaulted ceilings gave the space a lofty feel, yet the hall boasted no raised dais or other lavish adornment. Jerome had gathered from what little time he'd spent with Lord Beaumore that those at Trellham, including the noble family, did not put on airs. That explained Elaine's plain garb and free-spirited abandon when he'd first laid eyes on her.

The large wooden table he'd sat at before remained pulled away from the back wall, and Lord Beaumore was already seated, along with Lady Rosamond. Finn stood protectively by her shoulder, yet to Jerome's frustration, he didn't see Elaine anywhere.

As he crossed the hall, the villagers parted for him, murmurs rippling in his wake.

"I can begin whenever ye like," he said to Lord Beaumore when he reached the table.

Lord Beaumore nodded, pushing up from the bench. He coughed into his fist a few times, giving the hall a chance to quiet.

"Jerome Munro comes to Trellham bearing a request from King Robert the Bruce," Lord Beaumore stated. He fixed Jerome with his bright blue gaze and tilted his head.

At the cue, Jerome pulled a rolled parchment from the pouch on his belt and lifted his voice so that all those gathered could hear.

"These are the sentiments King Robert the Bruce sends to the Pope, and which he asks Lord Beaumore to co-sign." He raised the scroll and began reading. "To the most Holy Father and Lord in Christ, the Lord John, by divine providence Supreme Pontiff of the Holy Roman and Universal Church…"

Jerome had read these words many times, yet they never failed to stir him. Once the initial preambles were completed, he recited the atrocities committed by the English against the Scots, and of the Bruce's ongoing fight for independence.

Though the villagers in attendance had no doubt once thought of themselves as English, they, mayhap more than anyone, knew the cost of the former King Edward's obsession with controlling the Scots, and of the bloody struggles that had ensued. Edward II could have let his father's campaign go, yet he'd pursued it, and sacrificed the Borderlands and their people in the process.

They might not be Scots, but those gathered listened in rapt silence as Jerome continued, recounting the Bruce's commitment to freedom and his dedication to all those who had placed their trust and safety in his hands.

When he reached the section of the declaration that proclaimed that if the Bruce failed his people in their fight for sovereignty, then it was their right to replace him, whispers of surprise traveled through the crowd. It was unheard of for a monarch to place so much control in the hands of the people, yet the Bruce was committed to something far larger than his own power. He didn't just want to rule Scotland—he fought for the country's freedom above all else.

As Jerome neared the most rousing passage in the declaration, he lifted his gaze from the parchment. These words were etched on his heart and he could recite them from memory.

"...As long as but a hundred of us remain alive, never will we on any conditions be brought under English rule. It is in truth no' for glory, nor riches, nor honors that we are fighting, but for freedom—for that alone, which no honest man gives up but with life itself."

Just as in every corner of Scotland, those gathered broke into cheers of support, drowning out Jerome's voice for a long moment. He let his gaze sweep across the villagers, their earnest faces hopeful at the King's message.

When his eyes landed on the arched entryway to the east tower stairs, he froze. Elaine stood on the lowest stair, her bright gaze riveted on him. To his surprise, those vibrant eyes shimmered with unshed tears. He read in her unguarded features a swirl of emotion—awe, respect, and most of all a reverent sincerity that made something like pride tighten his chest.

From the moment the Bruce had called Jerome from Munro lands with the assignment to gather seals of support for this declaration, Jerome had been acutely aware of just how heavy a responsibility he bore—and just what an honor it was to be selected for the task.

Yet standing here in this small, modest hall some-where along the English border, a jolt of powerful emotion shot through him at Elaine's transfixed gaze. He was humbled to see so clearly what the words he spoke meant to her. And in that moment, he longed to learn more about the soulful, spirited lass who made the hall and all those in it fall away for a long heartbeat.

As the cheers died down, Jerome ended the recita-tion, reading from the scroll once more.

"This declaration was given at the monastery of Arbroath in Scotland on the sixth day of the month of April in the year of grace thirteen hundred and twenty and the fifteenth year of the reign of our King afore-said," he concluded. "Directed to our Lord the Supreme Pontiff by the community of Scotland, and endorsed by all who freely give their seal."

He lowered the scroll and turned to Lord Beaumore.

"Do ye willingly give yer seal of approval, Lord Beaumore?"

"Aye," he replied loudly, bringing on another round of cheers and stomping feet.

Lord Beaumore lowered himself to the bench once more, muffling a few more coughs with his fist while Jerome returned the scroll to his pouch and removed two strips of parchment.

"One for the Pope's copy, and one for the King's," he said, sliding them across the table to Lord Beaumore.

The older man took up a stick of red wax and held it into a nearby candle's flame, then smudged first one and then the other strip of parchment with a blob of melted wax. He clenched his right hand and pressed his signet ring into each of the cooling dollops of wax, then nodded, a pleased smile lifting his mouth behind his graying beard.

As those in the hall roared their approval once more, Jerome carefully lifted the two seals. Just as he dropped them into his pouch and secured the fastening, Elaine was suddenly at the table. Her tears were gone, replaces with a radiant smile.

"What a moment," she said, her eyes shyly darting to his before returning to her family. "And what an honor to witness it."

"We are entering a new stage of warfare," Finn replied, ever serious.

"Aye," Jerome replied. "One in which the weapons are no longer blades and pikes but ink and parchment."

Finn eyed him with guarded calculation. "From

33

what I hear of yer time serving the Munro Laird, ye've done yer share of fighting, man."

"Sometimes honor and loyalty demand it," Jerome said carefully. He'd heard rumors of just how distrustful Finn Sutherland was. The man was clearly testing Jerome, but whether it was because whispers about Jerome's past had reached him or simply because he was a Munro, Jerome couldn't be sure.

Finn tilted his head toward Jerome, but his eyes still probed. "We need men committed to honor and loyalty at the heart of the cause."

Such words seemed to be the closest thing to acceptance he'd get from the stoic, wary Highlander, so Jerome let them stand with naught more than a nod.

He felt Elaine's curious, intent gaze on him, but just as he turned to her, Lady Rosamond rose with some effort from the bench.

"Come, enough of this serious talk," she said, smiling warmly. "This is a joyous occasion—let us celebrate."

Finn smoothed his hard features and gave his wife a bow. "As my lady requests, so it shall be."

Chapter Five

◦✦◦

Jerome stalked around the perimeter of light cast by the large bonfire blazing merrily before Trellham Keep. To accommodate all the villagers and to savor the mild spring night, they'd moved the celebration outdoors.

The village boasted reasonable musical talent. Several men had taken up pipes and drums to fill the cool air with jaunty music. Trenchers piled with roasted meats and vegetables were being passed around, and frothy mugs of ale filled many a hand.

He'd visited more than two dozen Lairds and noblemen on this mission. At every grand castle and modest keep, every tower house and defensive strong-hold, he'd been met with unfettered excitement and eager celebration.

In truth, he'd grown weary of all the fanfare surrounding his assignment. People were largely the same everywhere he went—including England. Though he shared their joy for the advancement of the Bruce's cause, he couldn't help feeling rather world-weary at this final stop on his grand journey. In fact, the only thing that had stirred a deeper curiosity, a spark of life in him in the last several sennights was—

Damn it all, he was thinking of Elaine again, involuntarily scanning the crowd for her. Lady Rosamond sat with her father before the fire, Finn ever at her side, but Elaine was nowhere to be seen. She'd been wearing a becoming lavender gown in the great hall earlier. Her russet hair had been loose, adorned only by a matching lavender ribbon woven through the strands around the crown of her head.

He had so many things to ask her, to learn about her, and so little time left. Why had her eyes brimmed with tears as he'd read the declaration? What had sent her galloping like a wild banshee across the green hills that afternoon? And why—

An eruption of giggles cut into his thoughts. Through the crowd, two lasses wearing elaborately stitched gowns plowed toward him—dragging a reluctant Elaine behind them.

"It's true," one of the lasses said, halting before him and pinning him with brown eyes. "He is just as fearsome as your brother-in-law, Lainey."

A matching set of eyes joined the first to coyly assess him. "But I dare say more handsome. You didn't mention that!"

The lasses tipped their heads together and giggled again. Jerome's gaze skipped to Elaine, who was an unnatural shade of red in the flickering firelight. From what little he knew of the lass, he doubted she would speak so brazenly, even if these silly geese were her friends.

"Judith! Julia!" she hissed, averting her eyes. "How could you speak so to our guest?"

"Highlanders are a plain-talking sort, aren't they, sir?" one of the lasses, whom Jerome realized now were twins, said, taking a step closer.

The other nearly butted her sister out of the way as she, too, moved in. "Mayhap you could tell me all about the Highlands—over a dance."

Jerome noticed that the grass before the musicians had been cleared and couples were beginning to gather.

"I dinnae dance," he said bluntly.

The twins turned crestfallen gazes on him, but before they could beg him to relent, Elaine spoke. "Rosamond wished to discuss cloth for the new babe's clothes," she blurted. "If it is a girl, she won't be able to use Rand's old things."

Judith and Julia—Jerome wasn't sure which was which—brightened substantially. Clutching hands, they made their way toward Rosamond, whom Jerome suspected was unaware she was about to be set upon.

"Forgive them," Elaine breathed, her gaze fixed on the ground and the blush stubbornly lingering in her cheeks. "They are far too bold, but they mean no har—"

He caught her hand to halt her. Her head snapped up, surprise widening her eyes.

"No need," he said simply. "I should be thanking them, for they brought ye to me."

Elaine's rosy, lush lips parted on a quick exhale. The dancing light of the fire made her hair look like burnished copper and gilded her pale skin with gold.

Her pulse beat visibly at the base of her creamy throat, which was exposed by the scooping neckline of the lavender gown. Jerome had never paid much attention to women's fashion, but he liked that she wore no adornment or frippery, unlike Judith and Julia, whose gowns had been trimmed and edged with every scrap of fabric imaginable. Elaine's plain ensemble, on the other hand, allowed for her natural beauty to shine through.

"Dance with me," he murmured.

She blinked. "I thought you said you don't dance."

"Aye, well." He lifted a brow. "I lied."

He extended his arm to Elaine, and when she accepted it, her hand coming to rest on his forearm, a strange thrill ran through him. He felt as though he'd drank one cup too many of the Munros' powerful whisky, yet he'd had not a drop this eve. Still, he certainly wasn't acting himself.

He normally preferred to keep to the outskirts of these celebrations. The anonymity of being ever the stranger at a new castle or keep these last few sennights had been welcome, yet as the bearer of good news, he was often thrust into the middle of far too much attention.

It wasn't his way to stand out in a crowd—ironic, since the Bruce had tasked him with a very public assignment. Yet when all the speeches and ceremonies were over, he preferred to watch from the shadows, to keep his head down and his hands busy with ensuring his clan's—or his country's—safety.

The *last* thing he'd normally do was take a bonny lass on his arm and dance in a crowd. Yet Trellham—and Elaine—were doing strange things to him.

Mayhap it was the knowledge that he would likely never see her again. Mayhap after three long weeks of travel, he longed for the simple yet powerful pleasure of Elaine's brilliant smile and soulful eyes on him.

Whatever the case, he could think on it more tomorrow when he set out for Scone—alone. Tonight, he would give over to the pull he felt toward Elaine.

He halted them next to the rows of dancers, who wove together in a pattern he was familiar with. Yet he kept Elaine at the edge where firelight melted into shadow, selfishly not wanting to share her with the other merrymakers.

With only a foot between them, they acknowledged each other, he bowing and she curtsying. Then Jerome stepped forward and linked their elbows, turning in a slow circle.

"I've been wondering something since the moment I first laid eyes on ye," he murmured, dipping his head to her ear.

"Oh?" Her voice was thin and breathy.

"Why were ye riding like the Devil himself was on yer heels earlier today?"

She was silent for a moment as they switched elbows and rotated in the other direction.

"It was foolish of me," she said at last.

"Foolish to run from yer guards? Aye. Ye are a bonny

lass. I can see why yer brother-in-law wants ye protected."

In the dim light, he was gratified to see her blush. They parted, each turning before coming together once more, their palms raised and pressing together. Her hands looked so small and white compared to his. Aye, if he were Finn, he'd have Elaine's guard doubled—nay, tripled—so that no rogue or brigand could ever steal her away.

Either that, or he'd stay by her side himself to ensure her protection.

"Nay. Or rather, aye, that was foolish of me, but I don't just mean that," she said softly.

"What, then?" The desire to know more about the lass, to understand the soul behind those bright, beguiling eyes gnawed at him.

She let a breath go. "It only confirmed what my family already thinks—that I am a silly girl in need of constant watching."

Jerome felt his brows rise. "And ye arenae?"

Elaine lifted her chin. "I'll be nineteen in a month's time."

He had nearly ten years on her, but damn if he didn't feel older after sleeping on the ground for the last three sennights. At least tonight he'd be indoors, mayhap even on a pallet, for he'd decided from the moment Elaine had taken his arm that he would stay the night if it meant another chance to see her tomorrow morn before he departed.

"I'm sure they only act out of love for ye."

Now it was Elaine's turn to circle him. "That's just

it," she murmured as she stepped behind him. Jerome felt the hairs on his nape stir but held still, willing himself to follow the rules of the dance. "They love me, aye, but in protecting me, they've left me overly sheltered."

She rounded his shoulder and looked up at him in the flickering light. Slowly, Jerome circled her. Based on what he'd seen this afternoon in the great hall, her words made sense. Her father, though disapproving of her antics, clearly doted on her, as did her sister. Even gruff, severe Finn had only given her a few stern words.

"And riding off like a madwoman is—what? Yer attempt to live a less sheltered life?" He softened the words by keeping his voice low as he came to face her once more.

To his surprise, her face was tight with pain. But before he could apologize for speaking bluntly, she cut in.

"You are right," she whispered, dropping her gaze to the center of his chest. "Riding Gertie, slipping away from the guards—it is all a game. That little bit of excitement—it isn't real. There are no stakes. As I said, it was foolish of me."

Jerome groped for soothing words, but the truth was, he wasn't much for flowery language, nor did he know how to ease the hurt shining in her eyes.

Elaine suddenly scrubbed her palms over her damp eyelashes with a frustrated breath. "This is why they treat me like a child—because I am quick to tears. They call me a sensitive soul, as if I couldn't handle aught that exists in the wider world beyond Trellham."

Jerome closed the narrow distance between them and looped an arm around Elaine's slim waist. He lifted her off her feet and turned a slow circle. Thank God for this portion of the dance giving him an excuse to touch her, to hold her close, for he might have simply pulled her to him in that moment anyway, propriety be damned.

He continued to turn them, gradually lowering her to her feet. He relished the feel of her lithe, supple body sliding against his, her breasts drawing down his chest, her soft hands coming to his shoulders.

"I saw ye in the great hall earlier," he said, at last setting her on her feet. Her hands curled into his shirt as if they were still spinning. "The emotion in yer eyes as I read the Bruce's words was no' merely that of a sensitive soul. Ye were deeply moved. Why?"

Her lips parted, seemingly in surprise that he had noticed, and he knew he'd touched some part of that burning spirit behind her wide, innocent eyes.

"As I said before, so much of my life is naught more that games. What to wear. Which direction to ride Gertie." She met his gaze. "But not this—not the Bruce's cause. He fights for freedom, for justice, for right." A breath escaped her. "How I long to know what it feels like to be a part of something so important, so bold—something that matters."

Just as quickly as she'd revealed the fire behind her eyes, she shuttered it. She glanced over his shoulder. "No doubt that sounds foolish to the likes of you, the silly musings of a naïve girl. But I envy the sense of purpose you must have, the mantle of honor you wear in serving King, country, and cause."

Suddenly Jerome's throat tightened with a knot of shame. Of course Lady Elaine Beaumore, a sheltered English lass, didn't know of the shadow blackening his past, the shadow that still hounded him like a bedeviled wolf, ever nipping at his heels.

He jerked himself away from his dark thoughts. It was better if she didn't know. Selfishly, he longed for her to continue to think of him as a man of honor.

Yet what he wanted to do in that moment was far from honorable.

Mayhap it was weariness that made him do it. Mayhap it was the way the fire danced across Elaine's copper locks and illuminated those sky-blue eyes. Or mayhap it was the glimpse of that kindling soul she'd given him, her words about the Bruce's cause as stirring as aught in the Declaration of Arbroath.

Whatever the case, Jerome stopped thinking in that moment. Instead, he acted.

Gripping her narrow waist, he took two large steps forward, driving her out of the circle of firelight and into the shadows. Her hands tightened on his shoulders in surprise, but she let him guide her deeper into the darkness.

"Nay, that doesnae sound foolish to me. Yer family is mistaken," he said, his voice coming out low and rough. "Ye arenae a sensitive soul—ye've got fire in yer veins."

Just as she sucked in a breath, he lowered his head and met her lips with his.

Chapter Six

Elaine clung to Jerome as if he were her anchor in
a storm.

And in truth, a storm was breaking within her at the
feel of his lips against hers, his hands warm and heavy
around her waist.

When he'd pulled her onto his lap earlier that afternoon, she'd been so stunned that she had hardly noticed
more than his large, hard frame, like a living stone wall.

Now her senses flooded with every detail. The scents
of wood smoke and sweet spring air clung to him. He
was tall enough that he'd had to stoop his head low to
join their lips. And he was warm—so warm that the air
seemed to heat between them despite the cool night.

Beneath her hands, he felt solid yet rangy, the lean
strength of him coiled tight.

And his lips… Though he'd kept them in a neutral,
firm line throughout the events of the day, they were
wondrously soft now.

His fingers sank into her waist, yet he kept his mouth gentle on hers, exploring slowly. With each press of his lips, each subtle angling of his head to find yet another corner of her mouth to attend to, she felt herself begin to melt against him.

When she sighed, his tongue flicked out and touched hers. A jolt of heat and awareness shot through her at the feel of the velvety contact. He did it again, this time lingering, caressing her until her slippered toes curled against the grass.

One of his hands rose from her waist to delve into her hair. Prickles of pleasure shot through her as his fingers tightened slightly. He tipped back her head, giving himself greater access to her mouth.

So awash was she in sensation that she gladly let him take control of the kiss. She surrendered to his lips, his tongue, the firm hand in her hair even as her body rioted inside. Her heartbeat hammered wildly in her ears, her breath coming short. Liquid longing began pooling in the pit of her stomach, hot and achy. Aye, she was indeed sensitive—sensitive to Jerome's every touch.

"Lainey!"

Her sister's distant call roughly yanked Elaine from her rapidly spiraling desire. Jerome jerked back, his hands falling away and his body turning rigidly distant. Yet his dark eyes scorched her, his breath ragged.

"Lainey," Rosamond called again, nearer now. Her rounded form was silhouetted by the bonfire as she approached. "I wondered if you might help me fetch more honey for the oatcakes. Maggie has her hands full with keeping them from burning, and…"

Elaine's face blazed hot as she felt Rosamond's gaze land on them in the shadows. Though a good two feet now separated them, it must have been obvious what they'd been about.

Desperate to escape further embarrassment, Elaine bolted forward, taking Rosamond's arm. "Aye, of course."

Elaine knew she was imagining it, but she swore she could feel Jerome's gaze following her as she walked with Rosamond back to the keep. Rosamond remained silent, but when they slipped inside, instead of heading for the kitchens, she pulled Elaine into the west tower stairwell.

"What was *that*?"

"It was nau—"

"Don't lie, Lainey." Rosamond's voice took on the stern edge of an older sister, yet a smile danced in her violet eyes. "I know an interlude when I see one. I told you he's taken with you!"

Earlier that afternoon, Elaine had told Rosamond about slipping away from her guards, encountering Jerome, and the misunderstanding that had landed her in his arms. Rosamond had insisted that Jerome was undoubtedly enamored of Elaine.

Elaine had firmly told Rosamond that her romantic side was carrying her away—or that being so round with child had somehow muddled her sight, and her wits as well. But some girlish longing within her chest had fluttered at the thought of Jerome's attention.

"H-he is returning to Scone soon," she forced herself to say. "I'll likely never see him again."

She cursed the hitch in her voice as she spoke, sure it

would only prove how addlebrained and naïve she was to Rosamond. But to her surprise, her sister lifted her shoulders in a shrug.

"Then there is no harm in one stolen kiss," she said. Her eyes softened. "I know you long for excitement beyond our quiet life here at Trellham. Mayhap you can consider this an adventure."

An adventure that was over before it had begun. Elaine bit her lip to force down the emotion that rose in her throat at the thought. She felt all the more ridiculous because Rosamond, ever the warm-hearted sister, was trying to be kind. Yet Rosamond's nurturing sweetness made her feel like the family's coddled babe all over again.

"You know it's not just stolen kisses with a handsome warrior I long for," she murmured. "I want to be like Niall, and Father, and you and Finn. I want to have a purpose. I want to serve a cause that matters."

Rosamond's features grew somber. "Aye, I know," she replied quietly. "You have a big heart, Lainey, and spirit to match. We only worry that you will come to harm because of it. The world can be a cruel, dangerous place."

Elaine swallowed, dropping her gaze. She knew her family loved her, but the only thing that had ever hurt her was the knowledge that they thought her so frail.

Rosamond's mouth lifted in a sad smile. "Tonight might not have been the grand adventure you dream of. But you cannot deny that kissing a...what did you call him? A handsome warrior? You can't deny that it is nice."

Despite herself, Elaine puffed out a breath that was half-snort, half-giggle. "I beg you not to start in with your tales of stolen kisses with Finn, dear sister."

Pretending not to hear her, Rosamond took Elaine's arm once more and began strolling—waddling, more like—toward the kitchens. "Oh, aye, a particular tryst comes to mind, now that I think on the topic of handsome warriors. It was the night you and Judith and Julia had decided to wash your faces with the May Day dew to ensure everlasting beauty. Finn and I were supposed to be watching over you, but of course we were not, for we were ki—"

"Rosamond!"

Despite a sad heart, a spinning head, and lips that ached for another of Jerome's kisses, Elaine let herself laugh with her sister as they set off in search of honey.

Chapter Seven

Jerome muttered a curse as a soft rain began to fall. But it wasn't the turning weather that had him in such a foul mood this morn.

He quickened his pace as he scaled Trellham's hill, his horse in tow. Having slept on a pallet in one of the guards' quarters in the west tower last night, he'd risen at dawn and gone to the village stables to prepare Duff to depart.

He'd woken with a headache, likely from grinding his teeth all last eve. After Rosamond's interruption, he'd only seen Elaine from afar before she'd retired for the evening.

He could have saddled Duff then and ridden a few hours into the night. There was no reason to stay. But damn it all, he'd wanted the chance to see Elaine one last time before he departed.

And good thing he had, because it wasn't until this morn, when he'd awoken with a throbbing head, aching bollocks, and a sour temper, that he remembered the missive the Bruce had given him, to be delivered to Lord Beaumore.

It was an excuse to stay another moment, to enter the great hall and mayhap spot Elaine again. He should have been grateful, but instead, all he felt was foul.

Never before had he forgotten himself so completely that he might have neglected the Bruce's instructions to deliver the missive. And never before had he dragged his feet when it came to his mission. He should have been eager to return to Scone, the first half of his task complete. Instead here he was lingering in the damn Borderlands.

All because of that spirited, soulful lass that had filled his dreams and left him as achy as a green lad.

He needed to leash this cursed longing—now. No more of this moon-eyed foolishness. He was a High-lander, a Munro, and one of the King's most trusted warriors. It was time to start acting like it.

Handing Duff's reins to one of the guards standing before Trellham's double doors, he pushed his way inside. The keep had been stirring when he'd headed to the village, but now it bustled with the day's activities. Servants moved around the trestle tables and benches that had been pulled out for the morning meal.

Lord Beaumore, Lady Rosamond, Finn, and a wee lad of mayhap three summers were already seated at one of the tables. And—aye, there she was. Elaine's back was turned, but that burnished hair was unmistakable.

Jerome nodded to Lord Beaumore as he

approached. "Many thanks for the hospitality last night, milord."

"Must you leave so soon?" Lady Rosamond asked kindly, her violet eyes flicking to Elaine. "Surely you can stay and break your fast, or mayhap join Lainey on another ride."

"Rosamond," Elaine hissed softly. Jerome could feel her gaze dart to him, but he willed himself not to meet it.

"Thank ye, milady, but the Bruce awaits me in Scone, and I am already later than he would like. There is just one more matter of business before I go."

He reached into the pouch on his belt, his fingers sifting through the seals he'd collected for the King's declaration. When he brushed folded parchment, he pulled out the missive and handed it to Lord Beaumore.

"The King wished for me to deliver this to ye, milord."

Lord Beaumore's bushy gray eyebrows drew together as he broke the wax seal and unfolded the parchment. He squinted at the document, but his eyesight must have been failing, for he handed it to Finn, who scanned it quickly.

When Finn lifted his head, he wore a thoughtful frown.

"We'd best go to the solar," he said, casting his gaze around the table. "This concerns all of us."

RELUCTANTLY, Jerome followed the family up the west

tower stairs to the solar. Rand had been sent to Maggie, the cook, but Rosamond and Elaine had both fallen in behind Lord Beaumore and Finn. Jerome wasn't sure what he had to do with whatever the missive contained, but he held his tongue as the ladies and their father lowered themselves into upholstered chairs and Finn planted his feet.

"The Bruce wishes to honor the Beaumores with an extensive grant of lands," Finn said without preamble.

Lord Beaumore made a noise of surprise, which turned into a coughing fit. As he slowly regained his composure, Finn went on.

"Now that King Edward has agreed to a truce, the Bruce believes he can safely redistribute much of the lands along the border he reclaimed from the English. He wishes to reward those who have been loyal to him —including ye, Henry. Trellham's lands would more than double."

That sent Lord Beaumore into another coughing fit. Both Elaine and Rosamond gasped.

"That is...quite the honor indeed," Rosamond murmured.

"The Bruce intends for the bestowal of these lands to be a grand affair," Finn continued, glancing at the missive. "After the Declaration of Arbroath is sent on its way to the Pope, the King wishes to host a ceremony, followed by a sennight-long feast, to honor those most loyal noblemen. He means to show all of Scotland—and England and the Pope as well—that just as his people are behind him, so too does he look after them."

"And why does this involve all of us?" Elaine asked cautiously.

"The Bruce has invited the entire family to his grand fete," Finn replied. "As this is Jerome's final stop before returning to Scone, the Bruce suggests that we travel with him."

Finn's gaze shifted to Jerome, who stiffened. Damn it all. When the Bruce had given Jerome that missive three sennights past, he hadn't mentioned anything about Jerome serving as an escort to the Beaumores.

Would this mean—nay, he wouldn't let himself think of it. Spending more time with Elaine would only cloud his thoughts and distract him from his mission. And given his past, he had no room for error when it came to proving himself to the Bruce.

"We would leave…today?" Rosamond's voice was dubious as she glanced down at her rounded belly. "I'm afraid I won't be able to move very fast. In fact, I doubt traveling would be comfortable—or wise—for me."

"I'll stay with ye," Finn said immediately.

"Nay, go," Rosamond replied. "Represent the both of us. Besides, you'll only be gone a few sennights, I imagine. The babe will not come before you return."

Finn frowned, clearly unconvinced, but before he could speak, Lord Beaumore cut in. "You can represent me as well, Finn," he said, tugging on his graying beard. "Though I long to thank the Bruce in person for his generosity, I cannot pretend my health would allow it."

Jerome had noticed the Englishman's frequent coughing jags but hadn't wished to comment on them. He couldn't deny a flood of relief that he wouldn't be responsible for seeing a pregnant woman and an elderly, ailing man on the sennight-long journey to Scone. But that still left—

Elaine had been sitting quietly, her hands balled in her lap. But now she spoke.

"I wish to go."

Jerome and Finn both jerked in surprise. Finn recovered first.

"Lainey, dinnae ye think yer sister would appreciate having ye here to help with Rand?"

To Jerome's surprise, Rosamond spoke up. "She needn't be forced to remain on my account. I can look after Rand, with Maggie and the servants' help, of course."

Finn's lips compressed, but he didn't gainsay his wife.

Jerome, on the other hand, had held his tongue long enough.

"This journey will be no place for a lady," he said, willing his voice to be even.

She lifted her head, her gaze clashing with his, and for the first time since he'd met her, her sweet, soulful eyes held a stubborn glint.

"I am a strong rider," she replied. "And I am not some pampered princess. We live simply here at Trellham. I would not require—"

"Servants?" Jerome cut in. "Because ye willnae have any. Or a bed. My mission first and foremost is to deliver the seals safely to the Bruce. That means we'll avoid roads and villages. The risk of being waylaid or even merely pickpocketed by some fool who doesnae ken what I carry is too great."

Elaine swallowed. Damn it all, Jerome was being an arse. Yet he had to make her understand that this would be no merry jaunt into Scotland. Everything depended on him successfully delivering the seals—the Bruce's declaration, the cause, and mayhap even Jerome's own life.

But the truth was, he wasn't merely trying to scare her out of coming for the sake of the mission. Nay, a darker, more dangerous truth lurked in the back of his mind.

He didn't want her near him, for he feared he'd lose his head just as he had last night if she were close. How could he see his assignment done when he couldn't stop staring at her, couldn't get the scent of her, all spring air and new grass and woman, out of his mind? And aye, he couldn't forget the feel of her body against his, her mouth soft as she yielded its inner heat to him.

Damn it all.

"I know it won't be easy," Elaine said, shifting her gaze to Finn. "But I promise not to complain or slow you down."

Finn seemed to have taken Jerome's warning to heart more than Elaine had. He crossed his arms. "It could be dangerous."

"Aye, and I could fall down the stairs tomorrow as well," Elaine shot back in a surprisingly droll tone considering the way her fierce brother-in-law was scowling at her.

"Ye ken this will be different, Lainey," he replied.

Elaine opened her mouth to respond, but Rosamond spoke first.

"I think she should be allowed to go."

Now it was Rosamond's turn to face glowers from Jerome and Finn.

"We all know that Lainey wishes to see more of the world," Rosamond hurried on, turning to her father for support. "We can keep her locked away at Trellham for the rest of her life—or until she's married," she added, nodding to Lord Beaumore, "but I think it would do her good to step out of Trellham's shadow a bit before then."

Lord Beaumore considered Rosamond's words, his weathered features drawn as he tugged on his beard distractedly. At last, he turned to Elaine.

"This is what you want, my dear? To endure a sennight of hard travel just to go to the Bruce's celebration, then spend another sennight returning?"

Elaine's blue eyes grew impossibly brighter with the sheen of unshed tears. "Oh, aye," she breathed.

Lord Beaumore hesitated for a long moment, but at last, he nodded slowly. Jerome barely stifled a curse.

"Very well," Lord Beaumore said. At Elaine's exclamation of joy, he held up a hand. "But when you return, no more of these wild antics with the guards, do you hear me, Lainey? I have indulged you a great deal, for you are a dear treasure to the entire family, but you are a young lady now. It is time to find a proper husband for you."

Elaine stilled in her chair, much of her excitement

dampened by her father's words. Still, she nodded. "Aye, Father," she said.

"Come," Rosamond said, rising and taking Elaine's hand. "I'll help you pack."

Lord Beaumore shuffled out of the solar after his daughters, but as Jerome moved to follow, Finn caught his arm.

"Rosamond told me what she saw last night," he said, leveling Jerome with a hard look. "Dinnae think that just because ye have another sennight with my wee sister-in-law, ye can touch her again."

Jerome stiffened, an unexpected jolt of hot anger hitting him. "Ye've been living among the English so long that ye forget what a Highlander's honor means."

"Oh, I ken something of Munro honor," Finn replied softly.

The Sutherlands and Munros bordered each other, and though the clans had entered a wary truce of late, memories were long in the Highlands.

"And I ken something of *ye* as well," Finn went on. "They call ye the Munro Laird's hound, though I imagine few outside yer clan ken the reason why. I, however, have heard the story."

The heat of Jerome's ire turned to icy trepidation in his veins. "I am no' like my father," he murmured. "I have proven that to my Laird."

"The Bruce seems to agree, else he wouldnae have made ye a member of the Bodyguard Corps." Finn at last released Jerome's arm but kept his gaze cool and sharp on him. "Still, Elaine's happiness and wellbeing mean everything to my wife—and therefore to me as well. If ye harm her in any way—"

"Ye heard my words, didnae ye?" Jerome snapped. "I didnae try to lure her along. I warned her against coming."

Finn tilted his head in acknowledgement, yet the hardness in his eyes told Jerome he hadn't been convinced. "All the same, I'll be watching ye, Munro."

Bloody hell. What had this damned mission turned into?

Chapter Eight

O ut of the corner of her eye, Elaine saw Jerome look up at the sky, which had turned from light gray to sooty charcoal as evening approached.

"We'll stop for the night."

Elaine had to sink her teeth into her lip to keep from sighing in relief. Gertie, too, seemed more than eager to halt. Though the spirited mare was good for galloping, she'd never been made to walk an entire day.

Nor had Elaine ever ridden so long. It was yet another reminder that her life at Trellham had been limited to only the tamest activities.

Even though she nearly groaned as she eased out of the saddle, she managed to stifle the noise. They were only one day's ride from Trellham, yet it was the farthest she'd ever been from home. But how could she complain when she was on her way to meet the King of Scotland himself?

Finn and Jerome both dismounted smoothly. Without speaking, Jerome took Gertie's reins along with his big stallion's and walked the two animals to a nearby tree to begin hobbling them for the evening.

Finn had decided not to take any of Trellham's guards with them, saying he'd rather leave them at the keep to watch over Rosamond, Rand, and her father. Jerome had agreed, for they'd move faster without a large retinue.

Though Elaine felt safe enough with both her brother-in-law and Jerome, she couldn't help but notice an air of tension hanging around them as they'd traveled today. Finn seemed torn between allowing Elaine to ride between him and Jerome so that they flanked her, and wedging himself between the two of them, all the while casting Jerome narrowed looks.

For his part, Jerome had acted as though she weren't even there. His coldness after the kiss they'd shared stung, yet part of her was relieved. She wanted no mistake made—she wasn't coming along to moon after Jerome. Nay, this meant far more to her than that. Still, she couldn't help her gaze from sliding to him, sitting strong and straight in the saddle as they'd ridden throughout the cool, damp day.

Finn went about building a fire as Jerome saw to the horses. Elaine stood in the little clearing between the newly leafing trees, feeling useless.

After a silent meal of dried meat, cheese, and cold oat cakes, Finn rose from the fire.

"I'll take the first watch," he said, leveling Jerome

with a look. "Dinnae forget what I said back at the keep."

With that, he stalked off into the darkening woods. Jerome remained quiet, idly throwing sticks into the fire.

Silently cursing the mysterious strain that had stolen over the two mulish Highlanders, Elaine rose and gingerly walked to Gertie. She returned to the fire with a woolen blanket Rosamond had thoughtfully packed in her saddlebags.

Jerome didn't look up from the flickering flames, but when she settled with a muffled grunt of discomfort, he spoke.

"There isnae shame in hurting after the day of riding we had."

"Ah, so you *didn't* leave your tongue at Trellham after all."

Elaine clamped her teeth shut, but the tart response was already out. Aye, she was tired and sore, but she'd been so determined not to draw attention to either—or to let Jerome know just how much his taciturn distance smarted.

And why did she have to mention his tongue? The word reminded her of just what he'd done with that tongue in the shadows back at the keep. *Gracious*.

"Ye arenae used to such conditions," he went on, ignoring her barb, "but I did warn ye this wouldnae be pleasant."

Was his coolness, his silence, meant to be part of the unpleasantness, then? Elaine bristled at the thought that he was laying some sort of challenge for her, yet part of her longed to rise to it. All her life she'd been cosseted. This was the first real chance she'd gotten to prove herself—thanks to her sister speaking on her behalf. She wouldn't fall short now.

"I am fine," she replied evenly, notching her chin. "It is you and Finn who seem most…uncomfortable." Her curiosity at her brother-in-law's comment got the better of her. "What did he say to you at the keep?"

Jerome lifted his gaze from the fire. His chestnut eyes were unreadable as they reflected the dancing flames.

"He told me no' to touch ye again."

Her breath seemed to freeze in her lungs and stick in her throat. "What?"

Jerome's dark gaze was unwavering. "He didnae like that I kissed ye. He told me I had better no' harm ye in any way."

Elaine's thoughts scattered in a hundred different directions. Finn had threatened Jerome? Was that why Jerome had been so distant all day? And what had Finn meant, warning Jerome not to harm her?

She grasped at the first thread of reason that scuttled past. "I didn't ask to come with you because you kissed me."

Even as she spoke, she felt her cheeks burn, and it had naught to do with the fire. She'd thought that in letting her travel to Scone, her family finally saw her as a woman grown. But in truth, they imagined she was so harebrained that she'd chase after some man because of one kiss.

"I ken that," he said quickly, easing at least some of

her embarrassment. "After only a few minutes speaking with ye, I understand yer reasons for wanting to leave. All the same, Finn wishes to protect ye."

A second wave of shame hit her. She'd believed she had finally managed to make an inroad with her family, yet it seemed they would forever think of her as a girl in need of sheltering, not a woman with hopes and dreams of her own.

"To tell ye the truth, lass, I agree with Finn." Jerome dropped his gaze to the fire once more, his mouth set in a hard line. "Ye are a rare treasure. Ye shouldnae be out here in the elements, sleeping on the ground and eating cold bannocks. If it were up to me, ye'd never want for aught."

Something stirred low in her belly at his words. Yet at the same time, frustration burned through her veins.

"You think I am the same as Judith and Julia, the twins who cornered you last eve, don't you?"

"Nay, I—"

"Interested only in ribbons and lace, and flouncing about like peacocks looking for a mate."

"Elaine."

His voice held a warning, but she barreled on.

"Well, the truth is…" A lump rose in her throat. "The truth is…I *was* like them."

Surprise flickered across his hard-set features.

"When I was fourteen, there was naught in the world more important to me than Judith and Julia's opinion. And then Rosamond was kidnapped."

"What?"

"That is why the Bruce sent Finn to us—to protect Rosamond. She was taken one night from the keep, and God knows what would have happened to her if Finn hadn't rescued her."

She swallowed around the emotion clogging her throat.

"You cannot imagine how frightened I was—and Niall and our father, as well. But we realized we couldn't just be scared. We had to do something, had to become strong enough to defend against those who would harm us. Father had already thrown his support behind the Bruce to protect our people. Niall decided to join the Bruce's Bodyguard Corps, like Finn—and you. And Finn and Rosamond have all but taken over the running of Trellham in the name of the Bruce and his cause."

Jerome's dark, keen eyes searched her. "And ye feel as though ye dinnae have a place in yer family's dedication to the King."

"The lives of everyone in my family changed four years past," she replied softly. "Yet in their eyes, naught has changed for me. But in my heart, *everything* changed. I'm not the helpless, silly girl I used to be—or at least I don't want to be anymore. So don't tell me I shouldn't be here. I want naught else in the world more than this."

He assessed her for a long moment before speaking. "The Bruce should have sent *ye* to read his declaration and collect seals," he said, his low voice tinged with admiration. "Ye could stir a stone with yer spirit, lass."

A new warmth swept her as he stared at her, his jaw working for a moment.

"Ye should ken why I spoke against ye coming. It

isnae because I thought ye as harebrained as Judith and Julia. I willnae deny that I still dinnae think this is a place for a lady, but it isnae because I doubt yer conviction or yer desire to represent yer family before the Bruce."

"Then…why?"

A muscle in his cheek clenched and the only sound for a moment was the popping of the fire. "Because I thought ye'd be a distraction from my mission. Because…I wasnae sure I would be able to think of aught else with ye near."

Elaine pulled in a breath. Ever since they'd kissed, she wasn't sure she'd been thinking clearly either. Something about Jerome hypnotized her. It wasn't just his dark, handsome features or his powerful build. Some inner fire burned within him, some tangle of fierceness, loyalty, and another, shadowed emotion she couldn't put her finger on that lay just below his gruff surface.

She hadn't wanted to contemplate it. Like Jerome, she'd feared that allowing her fascination for him to rule her would mean sacrificing all she'd longed for these past few years. And he bore the same fear? The same desire?

He dragged his gaze back to the fire. "This mission is everything. I've worked so hard to prove myself, first to my Laird and now the King. I cannae fail."

Curiosity flickered through her. "Prove yourself? Why?"

A shadow dropped over his features, turning them hard and cold. "I dinnae wish to speak on it. Ye should—"

A twig snapped in the distance. Jerome moved so fast that before she could blink, he'd bolted around the fire, yanking his sword free as he went. She jerked to her feet, clutching the blanket around her shoulders and staring wide-eyed into the surrounding darkness.

Jerome wedged her between the fire and his broad back, one arm snaking behind him to rest on her hip, steadying her.

Cautiously, he pursed his lips and made an owl call, yet the cadence was just slightly altered. It would be a signal to an alert ear, yet go unnoticed by anyone who wasn't honed in on the sound.

After a long pause, an answering call echoed from the forest, in the same modified cadence Jerome had used. He let a slow breath go, but kept his sword raised and Elaine in place behind him.

"I thought I told ye no' to touch her." Finn materialized from the trees, a fiercer scowl than usual on his face.

Jerome dropped his hand and his sword in the same instant.

"Ye also said ye were on watch," he snapped.

Finn glared at him. "Aye, well, I spooked a rabbit from its hidey hole, so I imagined ye'd be wondering what the rustling was about. That is, assuming ye were paying attention to yer surroundings."

Jerome made no comment as he re-sheathed his sword.

"Why dinnae ye take a turn at watch," Finn said evenly, stepping to the fire. He cast a stern look at Elaine, which she met with her chin held steady.

As Jerome stalked off into the night, she lowered herself once more, preparing for one of Finn's lectures. He surprised her by remaining silent for a long time as he crouched on his haunches before the fire, watching the flames.

"I ken ye fancy him," he said at last.

Elaine's mouth fell open, but Finn went on.

"There are things I would tell ye about him, to warn ye to be careful, but I am no' yer father. It isnae my place."

The words she'd summoned to defend herself—she was a woman, and if she took a fancy to a man, it was nobody's business but hers—died on her tongue. What *things* did Finn know about Jerome that she didn't? Apprehension rippled through her. Did this have to do with the shadow that had fallen over Jerome's features earlier, and his comment about needing to prove himself?

"All the same, we are family, and I dinnae want to see ye hurt," Finn continued. "So I will say this. Remember that when we reach Scone in a handful of days, Jerome Munro will continue on to Avignon to deliver the King's declaration to the Pope, whereas we will return to Trellham."

Where she would be wed, as per her father's wish. Finn didn't need to speak the last bit, for the knowledge hung in the air between them.

Dread and sadness twined together in the pit of her stomach. Aye, Jerome bore secrets behind his dark façade, yet they would never be Elaine's to learn. They

only had another sennight before fate drew them apart
—forever.

That cold thought settled into her chest as she
lowered herself to the hard ground and prayed for sleep
to numb the pain.

Chapter Nine

❦

"There it is—Scone Abbey." Jerome pointed across the slow-moving waters of the River Tay toward a single spire rising above the trees in the distance.

Despite the dour air that had hung over their traveling party for the last sennight, Elaine's face broke into a wide, achingly bonny smile as she gazed at the top of the abbey.

True to her word, she hadn't complained during the journey, though he knew it must have been hard on her. They'd kept a brisk pace, stopping only for their most basic needs and sleeping on the ground every night.

She had dirt under those delicate white fingernails of hers. Her plain woolen dress was muddy around the hem. She'd wrangled her russet hair into a long, simple braid to keep it out of her way, which gave him a clear view of her features every time she winced from a long day in the saddle.

Though he hated knowing she'd been uncomfortable, he couldn't help being awestruck at her beauty, even dirty, rumpled, and travel-weary as she was.

But he'd been true to his word as well. He hadn't touched her again—not that he'd had an opportunity. Finn had insisted that Jerome take the first watch every night, ensuring that Elaine would be asleep by the time he returned to camp to trade places with Finn.

It was for the best, he reminded himself for the hundredth time. He knew the Bruce would be eager to send the declaration to the Pope with all haste once Jerome returned with the seals. Which meant he likely only had a day or two left with Elaine once they reached Scone.

He guided Duff along the western bank of the Tay, Elaine and Finn following. Ahead, a wooden bridge spanned the wide river. They'd left behind the shelter of the deeper forests earlier that day, and it was strange now to ride out in the open. Several people and even a few carts rumbled along the bridge, most heading toward the abbey.

They fell into the stream of people and crossed the bridge. As they drew closer to the abbey, the air seemed to hum with excitement and activity. The King was preparing for not one but two grand celebrations—the delivery of his declaration and the fete to honor his loyal nobles. No doubt all in the area had been hard at work getting ready for both.

As they continued on, the trees thinned, revealing a wooden palisade encircling the abbey. For several years, Scone had served as the site of the Scots' parliament, but because the Bruce had been occupied with securing the Borderlands from the English, the abbey had seen little activity.

But ever since the King had turned his attention from warfare to governance in the last few months, he'd taken up residence—as the guest of Scone's Abbot—at the palace attached to the abbey. The palisades, which had been under construction when Jerome had left for his trek across Scotland, was a hasty effort to protect the King, yet the fifteen-foot tall wooden wall, with sharpened spikes along the top, did the job well enough.

Though the makeshift gate that had been built into the palisades stood open, admitting carts of food and supplies for the King's celebrations, a guard halted Jerome as they approached.

"Ye there. What is yer business at the abbey?" the guard asked.

"I am Jerome Munro," he replied evenly, "come bearing the seals of all those who support the King."

The guard's eyes widened before he ducked into a swift bow.

"Tell the King," the guard said to one of his companions on the inside of the palisades. "Jerome Munro has returned."

Murmurs of surprise spread like wildfire around him. Several farmers and craftsmen who'd been headed into the abbey stopped and stared at him. He turned to find Elaine watching him, her vibrant eyes inquisitive.

"It seems your name is as well-traveled as you," she murmured.

Though he hadn't enjoyed the attention this mission

had garnered him until now, a swell of pride rose in his chest at the light of admiration in her eyes.

They dismounted and led their horses through the wooden gate. A stable lad hurried toward them and took their horses' reins, leaving them free to continue on toward the palace.

The abbey's single spire rose high into the overcast sky, yet other than that, the structure as a whole didn't resemble a holy house. Several buildings had been added to its base so that it sprawled wide with additional meeting rooms and chambers to accommodate not only the holy men there, but also the nobles of parliament and the King and his attendants.

Jerome approached the addition to the left of the spire, knowing it to be the great hall, which the Bruce used for not only feasts but official business as well. Several corridors splintered off from the back of the hall, one of which would lead to rooms where he, Elaine, and Finn could refresh themselves after their travels before being presented to the King.

But just as they stepped through the double doors and into the lofty, impressive space, a commotion at the back of the hall snagged Jerome's attention.

"…greet him myself," someone with a booming, commanding voice was saying as he stepped into the hall from one of the corridors. "The man has done enough to earn my thanks, I think."

Amongst the handful of servants hurrying into the hall, Jerome spotted a russet and gray head towering over the rest.

The man was unmistakable. Robert the Bruce himself approached them.

"Is that...?" Elaine breathed beside him, her gaze fixed on the approaching group. "Oh, gracious."

Her gaze skittered down to her travel-worn gown, her dirty hands, and her mud-caked boots. *"Oh, gracious,"* she repeated. "I cannot...I cannot meet the King of Scotland like this."

She swayed precariously on her feet. Without thinking, Jerome's hand shot out, clamping around her waist to steady her. At Finn's sharp look, he withdrew somewhat, but still kept a grip on her elbow to ensure she wouldn't stumble.

"I'm afraid ye dinnae have a choice," he said softly to her as the Bruce neared. He gave her elbow a squeeze. "Dinnae fear, lass. A little mud willnae shock him."

She shot him a wobbling smile, and gratitude flickered in her eyes before she turned her attention to the Bruce.

The King halted before them, a broad grin curling his red and gray beard up at the edges.

"Munro! Never have I been so glad to see such a grim face, man!"

Jerome made a quick bow but then straightened and took the Bruce's extended forearm in a firm shake. It had been a shock to learn when he'd been made a member of the Corps that the Bruce allowed such informalities among his inner circle of trusted warriors, but Jerome wasn't one to criticize his King's choices.

The Bruce turned to Finn. "I take it back, Munro. Sutherland here has ye beat for gloomy scowls."

Finn's mouth quirked as he repeated Jerome's motions, bowing but then taking the King's forearm.

"And who is this lovely lass?" The Bruce asked, shifting his dark, intelligent gaze to Elaine.

Elaine instantly dropped into a deep curtsy, remaining lowered with her head bowed.

"May I present my sister-in-law, Lady Elaine Beaumore," Finn said. "Thanks to yer generous invitation, sire, she'll represent the Beaumore family in accepting yer gift of lands."

The Bruce blinked. "How unexpected."

"Lord Beaumore's health wouldnae permit him to attend, and my lady wife is close to her time with our second bairn." Finn shrugged, his lips twitching with good humor again. "Only the wee lass was up to the task."

Jerome saw Elaine's cheeks pinken, and he spoke without thinking. "And a fine representative she'll be. Sire, ye are meeting one of yer fiercest supporters and most loyal subjects."

With her head still lowered, Elaine angled her chin and sent him a grateful look.

Damn it all, he was beginning to fear he'd do aught for another one of those wee smiles or looks.

The Bruce stepped forward and bent so that he could take Elaine's hand. She stared at the King in awed bewilderment as he helped her rise and dipped his head over her hand.

"Och, then it is I who should be bowing to ye, milady," the King said gallantly. "For I am naught without yer support—and that of yer family."

"Th-thank you, sire," Elaine mumbled.

"And pray tell," the Bruce went on, still holding Elaine's hand up. "What has made ye one of my—what did ye say, Munro? My fiercest supporters and most loyal subjects?"

Another flush stole over Elaine's face, but to Jerome's surprise, she spoke steadily.

"You've met my father, haven't you, sire?"

"Aye."

"His pledge of loyalty to you brought peace to our lands and people. And you've met my sister, and Finn, obviously."

At the Bruce's amused nod, she went on.

"They have maintained that peace by looking after Trellham Keep and by continuing to serve you. And of course you admitted my brother Niall into your Bodyguard Corps."

"I understand his training is going well in the Highlands," the Bruce replied, understanding twinkling in his dark eyes.

"As my mother passed to Heaven when I was born, and with no other siblings, that leaves only me in the family, sire. It seemed only natural to follow tradition and join your cause."

The Bruce threw back his head and laughed heartily at that. "Ye are a rare treasure, arenae ye, lass?"

Elaine ducked her head, her cheeks glowing pink and a smile curving her lips. But then she sobered and met the King's gaze once more.

"Truly, sire, I am humbled to stand before you, for you fight for the greatest gifts of all—peace, prosperity, and freedom."

The Bruce stilled, his gaze warm on Elaine. Jerome noticed her eyes shimmering with emotion, and another wave of pride hit him. Though he couldn't claim any responsibility for Elaine's noble spirit, it felt as though simply knowing her was an honor.

"Ye are the one who has humbled me, lass," the Bruce said softly, patting her hand before at last releasing it. He drew in a breath, squaring his shoulders. "I see we have much to celebrate this eve. Ye have the seals, Munro?"

Jerome nodded, his hand going to the pouch on his belt.

"Then tonight we'll feast," the King said, "though ye are only halfway done with yer mission." His keen eyes fixed on Jerome. "For tomorrow ye'll embark for the Papal court."

Chapter Ten

E laine gnawed on a fingernail as she watched the merry crowd in the Bruce's great hall. She stood in one of the many arched corridors at the back of the hall, lingering in the shadows like an over-awed child at the sights that met her.

She'd barely had time to notice the grandly appointed great hall when they'd first arrived, so stunned at the appearance of the King had she been. But now she took in the vaulted, arched ceiling, the colorful pennants and flags hanging from the wooden rafters, and the rich woven tapestries lining the walls.

Hundreds of candles, plus four roaring fires, one on each wall, illuminated the space, which was filled with finely dressed nobles. Some of the men wore breeches in the style of the Lowlands and Borderlands, but many more wore their clan plaids with pride, the array of colors adorned with silver-plated sword hilts, belts, and brooches.

And the ladies wore gowns that would have left Judith and Julia speechless—for once. Every color of silk was on display, as well as elaborate brocades with silver and gold needlework to tease the eye. Every lady seemed to sparkle, their rubies and emeralds catching in the firelight.

Elaine looked down at her own gown. She'd only had room to pack one fine dress in her saddlebags. After she'd washed and rested in the private chamber the King had provided, she'd spent the afternoon attempting to get the creases out of the sapphire silk, which she'd thought complemented her eyes nicely.

Now she saw that it was far too plain for the likes of Robert the Bruce's court—as was the rest of her. She'd left her hair down, only weaving a matching blue silk ribbon through the strands at the front. She had no jewels, no elaborate veil or headpiece as many of the other ladies did.

What was worse, because this was her finest gown, she'd have to wear it again tomorrow for the King's ceremony honoring her family and others with land.

Hadn't this been what she'd wanted? Adventure, excitement, and to be a part, however small, of the Bruce's work toward freedom and peace?

Aye, and now that it was before her, her traitorous nerves were going to get the best of her. She was a coward, she thought, her eyes burning.

Just as she turned to flee into the safe shadows of the corridor, she bumped into Finn's chest. Somehow her brother-in-law had approached behind her silently.

"Where are ye off to, Lainey?"

She ducked her head, swiping quickly at her damp eyelashes. "I-I don't know."

Finn caught her wrist, giving it a light squeeze. When she lifted her eyes to his, she saw a rare softness to his features that was normally reserved for Rand.

"Dinnae tell me ye're afraid of a few puffed-up nobles," he said, giving her a wry grin. "They arenae half so fine when ye see them in daylight. And wait until they get into their cups a wee bit. Ye'll see they are no different than Trellham's stable master, or the black-smith—or Judith and Julia."

At her weak smile, Finn frowned.

"I thought this was what ye wanted most—to be a part of something so grand."

"It was—it is," she whispered. "But mayhap you and Rosamond and Father have been right all along. Mayhap it is all too much for me." She gazed out at the chattering nobles and winced.

"Come now," Finn said firmly. "If ye could meet the King of Scotland looking like a beggar, ye can face this lot."

She shot him a glare, but his words had the intended effect. She fought a smile as she thought back on her shock and terror earlier that day, but also that she'd done her family proud by managing to find her compo-sure nevertheless.

"Thank you, Finn," she said, straightening her spine.

He extended his arm and she took it, stepping into the glowing great hall at last.

She needed every drop of courage as she felt several dozen sets of eyes shift to her, curiously assessing her from head to toe. Her nerve began to falter as she swept her gaze over the crowd—until her eyes landed on a group of men standing before the raised dais at the other end of the hall.

Jerome.

Everyone else seemed to fall away, along with her nervousness. He wore the same simple linen shirt and Munro plaid as he always did. Though his jaw was freshly shaven and his dark hair pulled back in a neat queue, his handsome, serious visage was familiar in a sea of strangers.

He stood with four other men, one wearing a red plaid, two wearing Lowlanders' breeches, and the fourth in a holy man's robes. It made for a strange assortment.

"Who are those men standing with Jerome?" she asked, glancing up at Finn.

His normal scowl deepened, no doubt because he seemed to have made it his personal mission to keep her away from Jerome.

"I dinnae ken," he replied grudgingly, "but I will introduce ye."

As they approached, Jerome's dark gaze landed on her, and he visibly stiffened.

"Did ye hear me, Munro?" one of the Lowlanders was saying. "If England breaks into a civil war, then France will—"

When the man's gaze followed Jerome's to Elaine, he cut off abruptly.

The men seemed to know Finn, for they all nodded to him. "Sutherland," they murmured. It was a reminder of just how important her brother-in-law was to the Bruce's cause.

"May I present my sister-in-law, Lady Elaine Beaumore," Finn said.

The man who'd been speaking with Jerome took Elaine's hand and dipped his blond head low over it in an elaborate bow. "Milady, it is truly an honor to meet the most bonny woman in attendance this eve."

Elaine eyed him as he straightened, still holding her hand. He was as tall as Finn and Jerome, though lankier than either of them. His refined courtly manner and practiced smile seemed more English than Scottish, yet his soft Lowland lilt said otherwise. Though she had little experience with noblemen, she instantly recognized him as a flatterer.

"This is Sir David de Brechin," Jerome commented.

"You are too kind," she said evenly, tilting her head toward de Brechin.

"Ah," he said, his sandy blond brows lifting. "An Englishwoman."

The other Lowlander dipped in a stiff bow. "A pleasure, milady." When he straightened, she noticed that his brown head was a hand shorter than Jerome's, his build compact. "Sir William de Soules, at yer service."

"And this is Bishop Kininmund," Jerome said, turning toward the holy man.

He wore snowy-white robes, over which draped a black cowl. The cowl bore an elaborately embroidered cross over his chest and shoulders in gold thread. Elaine dropped into a low curtsy as he acknowledged her with a subtle nod.

"Good God, it's hotter than the Devil's bollocks in here," the fourth man said abruptly in a broad Highland burr. Impossibly, he stood a few inches taller than Jerome, and he was even broader of shoulder beneath his linen shirt.

Elaine blinked in shock, and the bishop coughed disapprovingly.

The Highlander huffed a breath but grudgingly turned to first the bishop and then Elaine. "Beg pardon, Yer Excellency, milady. But ye must admit it is da—" He barely caught himself before cursing again. "It is mighty warm with all these bodies crammed in here."

He eyed the crowds of elegant nobles suspiciously even as Jerome introduced him.

"Kieran MacAdams," Jerome said simply, lifting a dark brow at the man.

The conversation lulled for a moment, and Jerome took the opportunity to step toward her. Her stomach did a little flip at the heat in his eyes.

"Ye look beautiful," he murmured, his low voice like a caress.

Despite the simplicity of his words, they warmed her more than a dozen of David de Brechin's flowery compliments could have.

Before she could respond, though, de Brechin cut in, ending the intimate moment. "Ye must find us an unlikely group, milady," he said with a smooth smile. "But the array before ye has a purpose, I assure ye.

These four men—" he swept a hand over his companions, "—are the members of the envoy hand-selected by the King himself to deliver the Declaration of Arbroath to the Pope."

He seemed to take Elaine's curious gaze on the group as encouragement to go on.

"Bishop Kininmund here is to be our religious representative. He will be the one to present the declaration to the Pope. And now that the Papal court has been moved to Avignon, de Soules is to be the envoy's French expert, seeing as how he owns a small holding there and had become familiar with the workings of the country."

De Soules's brown eyes flicked to de Brechin as he nodded in acknowledgement.

"Aye," Kieran inserted. "And I am to be the muscle."

Elaine didn't doubt the Highland giant's brute strength, but nor did she miss the intelligence in his light blue eyes either.

"And Munro here is the luckiest of them all, for the Bruce has entrusted him with carrying the declaration himself all the way to Avignon."

Elaine's eyes met Jerome's, and liquid warmth stirred in the pit of her stomach.

"I, however, am the unluckiest," de Brechin went on. "For I was no' selected to accompany these fine men. I will have to find something else to get up to while they are away."

Once again, de Brechin and de Soules exchanged a quick look, but no one else seemed to notice, for the King entered the great hall.

The Bruce held up a hand as those gathered

applauded and genuflected as he strode toward the raised dais.

When he reached them, he jumped nimbly onto the dais and circled around the enormous oak table that was clearly meant for important occasions like tonight.

"Ladies, Lords," the King intoned in a rich, deep voice. "Ye are witnessing one of the greatest moments in the history of our fine country this eve." When the cheers died down, the Bruce went on. "I have here a proclamation unlike any penned before, crafted at Arbroath Abbey by the most esteemed Abbot Bernard of Kilwinning and completed just a month past. In it, the Abbot has captured the essence of our noble struggle against the English, and the people's will to be free of their tyranny."

Much like the reading of the declaration Jerome had performed at Trellham, the King waxed on about Scotland's valiant fight for freedom, and his place as both the leader of that fight and the sovereign ruler of the country.

"This declaration I shall present to the Holy Father, Pope John XXII, requesting that he recognize no' only my place as the leader of our people, but our nation as sovereign and free of English rule," the Bruce continued.

He reached into the inside of his doublet and withdrew a large rectangle of parchment. As he unfolded it, several dozen seals came into view, each one dangling from its fastening on the bottom of the parchment. Jerome must have turned over all the seals he'd gathered while Elaine had been resting that afternoon so that they would already be affixed for this moment.

"Those of ye gathered today have given me yer seals to show yer support. And my trusted warrior, Jerome Munro, has spent the last month collecting even more."

Elaine felt many eyes shift to Jerome, who bowed formally to the King from where he stood below the dais.

"In all, we have gathered the support of fifty-one nobles and Lairds in every corner of Scotland," the Bruce went on. He waited until the applause died down once again. "But in truth, the work is only just begun. I have assembled an envoy that will carry my declaration to Avignon. It will be their task to see the document safely delivered, and ensure that the Pope hears Scotland's voice."

He waved at Jerome and the three others, who stepped onto the dais and knelt before the King, all except the bishop, who bowed but remained standing, as befitting his elevated status.

"I am entrusting ye with the future of our beloved homeland, men," the King said to those before him.

With a ceremonial flourish, the Bruce refolded the declaration and extended it to Jerome, who accepted it and tucked it away in the pouch at his waist, keeping his head bowed all the while.

The great hall erupted into its loudest cheers yet. "Rise!" the Bruce shouted over the applause. "And make merry tonight, for yer King is most pleased!"

As the men on the dais rose and stepped down to the

cheers of those gathered, the Bruce's gaze landed on Finn. He bent so that his voice would carry the few feet to where they stood. "Finn, a word. We have much to discuss about the state of the Borderlands."

Finn cast Elaine a frown, clearly reluctant to leave her alone, but he couldn't refuse the King's summons. He slipped his arm from hers and stepped onto the dais, leaving Elaine with David de Brechin.

Jerome's gaze locked with hers as he descended from the dais, but before he could reach her, de Brechin took her arm, holding her hand in place over his. He guided her through the crowd toward the other end of the hall.

"You must permit me to introduce ye to all these curious nobles, milady," de Brechin said as she swept her away.

Elaine glanced over her shoulder, but the crowds were swallowing Jerome, offering congratulations and well-wishes for his impending journey.

"Aye," she said reluctantly. "Very well."

As THE HOURS dragged on and the evening stretched toward night, Elaine grew weary of the sea of noble faces, the endless string of introductions, and the florid displays of manners from de Brechin. He kept her close to his side for the elaborate feast, and held her on his arm even when the King's musicians began to play.

When she was sure she'd met every single lord and lady in attendance—twice—she at last managed to pull away.

"Excuse me, milord," she said to de Brechin, "but I am in need of some air."

De Brechin cast her a knowing look, which she didn't understand, but then bowed his head. "Of course, milady."

Elaine slipped into one of the corridors, which was refreshingly cool compared to the lively, crowded great hall. But just as she leaned against the back side of the arched stone entryway, de Brechin stepped beside her.

"What are you—"

"Dinnae use yer lips for words when ye could use them to kiss me instead," he said, his tall frame cornering her against the stones.

Without waiting for a response, his mouth came down on hers, muffling her startled cry.

She managed to wrench free by shoving against his chest. "Stop," she panted. "I do not wish to kiss you."

His practiced smile faltered and for the first time, something like anger crossed his eyes. A shiver of foreboding snaked up Elaine's spine.

"Dinnae be foolish," he said, his normally smooth voice now edged with annoyance. "Ye have been toying with me all night."

"Nay, I haven't."

"And what was this wee jest about then, if no' a clear invitation to follow ye for a tryst?" he demanded, waving at the shadowed corridor.

"I never—"

"Come now," he cut in, his features turning hard. "No more games. I will take what ye have dangled before me all eve."

His hands closed around her arms, pinning them to her sides. He pressed her into the stone wall despite her struggles against him.

And when she tried to scream, he stifled the sound with a brutal kiss.

Chapter Eleven

Though the great hall was crowded and the line of nobles wishing to congratulate him seemed never-ending, Jerome couldn't help but keep one eye on Elaine all night.

That bastard de Brechin was hogging her to himself, pretending to be the gallant gentleman while keeping her pinned to his side. De Brechin wasn't the only man casting appreciative looks at Elaine, but it was de Brechin's nigh constant hand on Elaine's that had Jerome seeing red.

She was not de Brechin's to touch, God damn it. The problem was, she wasn't Jerome's either, but logic didn't penetrate the fog of frustrated longing that clouded his mind.

Besides, with Finn still locked in deep conversation with the Bruce, Jerome felt responsible for her protection. So he watched her from afar, silently cursing de

Brechin, but also himself for being fool enough to let himself care about a lass he could never have.

Until he saw de Brechin follow her like a wolf stalking a lamb as she slipped from the hall.

He'd been in the middle of a conversation with the Gordon Laird about improvements to his curtain wall. Without preamble, Jerome strode away from the man.

"What in…" Laird Gordon sputtered, but Jerome paid him no heed. The hall and everyone in it seemed to fall away and his vision narrowed on de Brechin's receding back.

He had to unceremoniously push his way through several groups of nobles, uncaring of the surprised exclamations that followed in his wake. Naught mattered except for Elaine in that moment.

When he heard her muffled cry on the other side of the arched corridor entrance, he broke into a sprint for the last few strides.

What he found sent white-hot rage into his veins even as icy fear spiked hard in his gut.

De Brechin had Elaine pinned against the wall. Kissing her. Restraining her.

Jerome's mind went blank and he let his body take over.

He ripped de Brechin away from Elaine so roughly that he sent the man careening into the opposite stone wall. Elaine, too, stumbled, for de Brechin jostled her as he went flying.

Jerome gripped her waist, propping her on her feet. In the precious moments while de Brechin struggled to regain his footing, he met her tear-filled eyes.

"Are ye all right?"

Her bottom lip, which was bruised from de Brechin's mouth, trembled, but she nodded. "A-aye."

He rounded on de Brechin then. Just as he raised his fist, preparing to smash it into the bastard's face, two of the nobles from the great hall appeared in the corridor's entryway.

"What goes on here?" one asked.

"Naught," Jerome snapped. "Return to the celebration."

As the two men retreated into the great hall, Jerome turned to de Brechin once more. The man stood panting, his eyes wide and fixed on Jerome's raised fist.

Jerome ached to drive his knuckles into de Brechin's mouth, but the nobles' interruption gave him several precious seconds to regain his wits.

Damn it all. Jerome was the King's representative now. Here he was ready to kill a man who'd been one of the lords to add his seal to the declaration. He couldn't be caught brawling on the eve of departing for his most important mission yet.

And yet nor could he let de Brechin's offense against Elaine go unanswered. He stepped forward, closing the distance between himself and de Brechin, but instead of punching the man, he caught his throat and thrust him back against the wall.

"What the bloody hell do ye think ye were doing, accosting her like that?" he demanded through clenched teeth.

"S-she has led me around by my nose all night!" de Brechin sputtered, pointing at Elaine.

"Nay, I didn't!" Elaine breathed. Though Jerome couldn't see her face, he heard the emotion clogging her voice.

He squeezed de Brechin's throat tighter. "I watched her all night," he said, leaning closer to the man. "She did no such thing. And even if she had, that doesnae give ye the right to assault her when she was clearly struggling."

"It was a misunderstanding!" de Brechin croaked, his blue eyes rounding. "A game!"

"If ye want to play games," Jerome ground out, "next time why dinnae ye pick someone yer own size to tangle with—like me."

It took all his willpower, but Jerome forced himself to release de Brechin. The man folded over, clutching his throat and coughing.

"Get out of my sight before I decide to give ye what ye deserve," Jerome snapped.

Once de Brechin had scurried back into the great hall, Jerome let himself look at Elaine.

She stood pressed against the wall, her wide eyes brimming with tears and her gaze fixed on him.

In one step he was before her, but he forced himself not to yank her to him. She had been through enough tonight without having another man grab her. Yet to his surprise, she looped her arms around his neck and pulled him into an embrace.

She buried her face in his shirt, and he could feel her warm tears dampening the linen. He simply held her for a long moment, feeling her tremble in his arms and silently cursing de Brechin with every foul word he knew.

"I was so scared," she said against his chest. "I prayed you would come. And then you did."

Something broke deep inside his chest in that moment. Yet it wasn't a shattering, but rather a cracking wide open to accommodate the flood of warmth swelling in his heart.

"Come," he murmured. "I'll see ye safely to yer chamber."

She nodded, her arms slipping slowly from around his neck. She dashed away the lingering tears with her palms, bravely straightening her back.

Jerome fell in behind her as she headed down the corridor. He glanced over his shoulder into the great hall to ensure that de Brechin hadn't caused a scene. The celebration continued and his and Elaine's absence seemed to have gone unnoticed. At least he hadn't endangered his mission by nearly throttling de Brechin within an inch of his life. Yet thoughts of his assignment left him surprisingly cold compared to having Elaine in his arms.

After winding their way through the corridor for several moments, Elaine halted before a door.

"I'll tell Finn ye've retired for the night," Jerome said, clasping his hands behind his back to stop himself from touching her again. "Bar the door when ye are inside and dinnae open it for anyone."

He willed himself to keep his voice firm and emotion-less. Aye, this was how it had to be. He would leave tomorrow for France, and he would likely never see her again. Whatever he'd briefly felt—an attraction, a fascination, a longing for more—was over now. His mission came first. He couldn't afford even the slightest error or hesitation, else the shadow from his past, the shadow cast by his father's actions, would catch up to him at last.

Yet when his gaze landed on Elaine, who stood in the dimly lit corridor looking up at him, his iron grasp on control began to slip.

"Don't go," she said, her blue eyes tracing his features. Jerome's skin prickled as if she'd caressed him. "Don't leave me alone with the memory of de Brechin's kiss."

He gritted his teeth. "If I stay, I'll do something that we'll both regret."

"I will never regret spending every moment I can with you," she breathed, dropping her gaze. A blush rose from her neck to her creamy cheeks.

Jerome exhaled, raking a hand through his hair. "I depart on the morrow for Avignon. And when ye return to Trellham, yer father wishes to see ye wed—no doubt to some border lord or other."

She flinched as if the reminder hurt her. Damn it all, it hurt him too. But it was true.

"Then at least give me something to remember you by." She met his gaze once more, and he saw that spark of determination in her eyes. "Leave me with a memory to replace what de Brechin did."

"Ye dinnae ken what ye are asking for," he ground out. Bloody hell, if he kissed her now, he feared he wouldn't be able to stop, wouldn't be able to accept the fact that they could never become more.

"I'm not a child," she replied. "I know what I want. I want you to kiss me."

His control snapped then. His hands found her waist and he pulled her to him. Just before his mouth claimed hers, though, he froze.

"This is what ye want?" he rasped.

Her warm breath fanned his lips, her scent invading his senses.

"Aye."

He closed the distance between them, his lips meeting hers with a hunger like none other he'd experienced.

Their first kiss had been slow, gentle. He'd savored every corner of her lips, and then the heated depths of her mouth, thinking to draw out the sweet contact.

Now he was like a man dying of thirst, and Elaine was a cool drink for his parched soul.

And this would be his last taste of her.

He delved his tongue into her mouth, no longer able to hold back. When he met the velvet heat of her tongue, fire shot through his veins—straight to his manhood.

Distantly, he felt her fingers clutch the front of his shirt, holding him close. She leaned into him, her breasts pressing into his chest.

He had the wild urge to push her against the door and grind his hips into hers, showing her just what she did to him. Yet she was an innocent, some last shred of sanity reminded him. Besides, the invisible threat that kept drawing them together would be snapped come morning.

That thought wasn't enough to make him stop kissing her, though. He was a greedy bastard, and selfish too, yet like her, he wanted to remember this long after they parted.

One hand slid from her trim waist to her narrow ribcage, gliding along the blue silk of her gown. He dragged his thumb along the underside of her breast, the tantalizing softness sending a new ache into his cock.

He could feel her heart hammering wildly, her breath coming short as he traced just under her breast once again. Heaven help him, he was barely touching her and yet she seemed to nigh crackle with desire.

They would have been good together, he thought distantly. Judging from her fierce reaction to even his lightest touch, and his own rock-hard cock beneath his kilt at a mere kiss, they would have likely set the bed linens aflame with the heat that burned between them. But they'd never know. They only had this moment.

At last he lifted his hand and cupped her fully. They both sucked in a breath at the same moment, their mouths stilling for a heartbeat before they lost themselves in the kiss once more. Her nipple was already taut and pebbled against the silk. God, how he longed to strip her dress away and lick each breast until she writhed against him and cried out his name.

When he slid his callused palm along her peaked nipple, she made a noise deep in her throat that was nearly his undoing. She arched, giving herself over to him. He rewarded her by circling her nipple with his thumb. Her breaths grew ragged and her fingers were like talons against his chest, but he gave her no quarter, teasing her breast even as he claimed her mouth.

A peal of distant laughter drifted down the corridor from the great hall. He jerked back, breaking their kiss with a muttered curse. Elaine gazed up at him, her blue eyes glazed with passion and her lips parted and red from his attentions.

"Christ," he breathed, withdrawing his hands from her. "I shouldnae have let it go that far."

"I wanted you to," she said. That bonny blush was back in her cheeks again, but she held his gaze. "I asked you to give me something to remember, and you did."

A sudden realization hit Jerome like a punch to the chest. "I dinnae ken what the King has planned for our sendoff tomorrow morning, but I doubt we'll get another moment alone together." He swallowed, his jaw tightening. "We had better say our farewells now."

She pulled in a breath, her eyes flickering with pain, but then she nodded.

"I wish we'd had more time," she said softly. "You seem to carry a weight in your heart that I long to understand." She swallowed, her lovely eyes shimmering with emotion. "But I do know one thing—you are a good man, Jerome Munro, a man of honor. I am grateful to have met you."

Fourteen years past, when his father had nearly destroyed the clan and Jerome along with it, Jerome had hardened his heart, thinking to ward off dangerous weakness. Never in all those long years had he come close to opening up to someone, to allowing his heart to soften—until Elaine.

He swiped away a tear as it rolled down her cheek.

"I am glad to have met ye too, lass. Remember something for me—no matter what anyone else thinks, ye are brave. Ye have a fire in ye. Let it burn bright."

She gave him a wobbly smile, the tears running freely down her cheeks now.

"Good luck with your mission."

Jerome stepped back and gave her a stiff bow. How he ached to pull her into his arms once more, to forget what tomorrow would bring, even only for another moment. But it would only make things harder come morning. The longer he remained near Elaine, the more in danger he was of destroying everything he'd worked for these past fourteen years.

So he walked away. He felt her gaze on his back but willed himself not to turn around. He listened for the sound of her door opening and closing, and then the reassuring thunk of the bar falling into place.

He let a breath go, but inside his chest compressed painfully.

She was safe. And she was gone from his life.

Chapter Twelve

E laine woke with puffy eyes and a throbbing headache. She'd cried herself to sleep in the wee hours of the morning, but her numb oblivion hadn't lasted long. She'd dreamt of Jerome, his rich brown eyes turning liquid with desire, his mouth on hers, kissing away all her pain and sadness.

But when morning light streamed into her chamber, the dream had fled and she'd awoken to the cold reality that whatever they'd shared was over.

What a fool she was. How she'd longed for adventure, to experience the world beyond Trellham's quiet walls. And hadn't she found adventure in coming to Robert the Bruce's court? Hadn't she experienced more of desire and pleasure and heart-wrenching longing in less than a fortnight with Jerome than she ever had before?

Aye, she'd wanted this, dreamed of the grand escapades she'd lead if only she'd been allowed. Well, she'd gotten what she wished for, and all she was left with was an empty, broken heart.

How could she go back to her old life now? How could she go back to being the coddled, sheltered girl her family saw her as when she'd felt like a woman grown in Jerome's arms? Everything about her life seemed drab and colorless in the harsh light of morning. She hadn't even participated in the Bruce's celebration honoring her family yet, but already she knew that her adventure was over—now that Jerome was gone.

She dragged herself from bed and dressed in a simple green woolen gown, unsure what the day would hold. When she opened her door, she found Finn leaning against the corridor wall, waiting for her.

"There ye are," he said, eyeing her. "Are ye well?"

"Aye, just…tired."

"Well, the King has organized a sendoff party for his envoy. We'll miss it if we dinnae hurry."

Elaine barely managed to bite back a moan. Saying goodbye to Jerome last night had been hard enough. Seeing him one last time—and having to pretend that her heart wasn't breaking—would be far harder.

She followed Finn through the great hall and into the dreary, overcast day. The grounds between the abbey and the wooden palisades were swarming with people and horses. Finn hadn't been exaggerating when he'd spoken of a party. She recognized several of the nobles from the night before, most of whom were already mounted.

At Finn's whistle, a stable lad approached with their

horses. As they mounted, Elaine spotted the King and his envoy—including Jerome.

She ripped her gaze away, but not before she saw the dark shadows under his eyes and the bristle on his jaw. He sat atop his enormous stallion, his face set in a grim frown.

The King urged his horse into motion, and soon the entire crowd was streaming through the opening in the palisades.

"Where are we going?" Elaine asked.

"East along the river, until it is deep and wide enough for sea-faring vessels," Finn replied. "We are to see the men onto their ship bound for France."

Elaine sank her teeth into her lip but held her tongue as the entourage trotted eastward.

The hour-long journey stretched painfully. Normally Elaine loved any opportunity to ride Gertie, but now she felt as though she were headed to a funeral.

In the distance, several tall masts rose above the trees lining the river. The King urged the party into a gallop for the last stretch, and before Elaine realized it, they'd all reined in at the riverbank.

Sitting placidly in the middle of the now much wider river were a half dozen ships, one of which was far larger than the rest. No doubt the smaller ships had business of their own if the river was used to connect the region surrounding Scone with the open waters of the North Sea, yet the massive ship, flying the Bruce's pennants along with the Scottish flag, could only have one purpose.

In numb silence, Elaine dismounted along with the

others. Distantly, she heard the King's voice booming out over those gathered. He was saying something about the beginning of a new era for Scotland, the dawning of a more complete and sovereign freedom, but Elaine couldn't concentrate on the words, for her gaze was fixed on Jerome.

She'd given up her effort to keep her eyes from him. Nay, instead, she would look her fill—and look her last. His jaw was set hard, a curling lock of dark hair falling against his forehead. He and the rest of the envoy—the bishop, the giant Highlander named Kieran, and William de Soules—stood on the riverbank as the Bruce continued speaking.

A small rowboat darted through the anchored ships and pulled toward the wooden docks built along the bank. When it reached the envoy, the Bruce concluded his speech to enthusiastic cheers from those gathered. Then the four men stepped into the boat and they were rowed alongside the largest ship.

When they bumped into the ship's wooden hull, a rope ladder dropped and each man scaled it, Jerome going last.

The four stood on the ship's deck as the anchor was raised and the sails unfurled. Finally, the enormous ship began to move, slowly drifting downriver, where Elaine could see the waters widen in the distance into the North Sea.

She blinked away sudden tears, unwilling to let them blur her last glimpse of Jerome. He stood rooted in place on the deck, his dark gaze cutting across the distance —to her.

She remained frozen for a long time, watching Jerome grow smaller and smaller as the ship carried him away, until at last she realized Finn had been speaking to her.

"...sure to be another grand celebration this eve," he was saying as he mounted his horse. "Elaine? Lainey? Arenae ye coming?"

She looked up to find his sharp, assessing gaze on her. "I ken ye are sad, lass, but in time..." He faltered, apparently at a loss when it came to comforting a heart-sick girl.

Aye, her heart ached, but Elaine forced herself to draw a deep breath. If she didn't want people treating her like a fragile piece of glass, ready to shatter at any moment, then she couldn't act like one. She would let herself feel the pain in her own time, but right now she couldn't simply fall apart. Not when she'd fought so hard to be seen as a strong, capable woman and not a child.

She discreetly dragged her sleeve over her damp eyelashes and mounted Gertie smoothly. As she fell in with the King's procession once more, she willed herself to remain facing forward—despite the pull of her heart toward Jerome.

DESPITE HER DETERMINATION TO set aside her self-indulgent sadness, Elaine couldn't help but find the evening rather dour.

Tonight, she and the other families most loyal to the Bruce were to be honored, yet as she donned her blue silk dress—the same one she'd worn last night—and entered the great hall, the festive atmosphere seemed hollow. The same nobles milled about chattering and preening in anticipation of the Bruce's arrival. The same snippets of conversation drifted to her—of castle improvements and the latest brocades and what might be done with all the new lands they were to receive.

When she'd dreamed of aiding the Bruce's cause, even in a small way, she'd imagined urgent communications, delicate negotiations, or even life-or-death circumstances in which she would rise to the occasion, doing her part to help in the fight for freedom.

Surely she should be grateful that she was at the King's court for a feast rather than on some battlefield or in enemy territory. Still, the sense that she was meant for something greater stirred in the pit of her stomach once more.

It was a silly thought, for she had no special skills or abilities, no talent for fighting or healing or spying. All she knew was she was capable of more than discussing the latest fashions with fellow noblewomen.

If she were honest, she would admit that at least half of her glum mood was because all the spark, the light, the energy seemed to have disappeared from Scone Abbey with Jerome's departure. But nay, she would not dwell on that, else she forget to savor what little excitement remained for her at Scone.

As usual, Finn sat with the Bruce on the raised dais, no doubt speaking of far more fascinating and imperative matters than the nobles milling around the hall. But it was not Elaine's place to insert herself into military or political concerns, so she skirted along the walls, trying not to draw attention to herself as she observed the others.

She sidled her way to the back of the hall where the row of corridors leading to the rest of the attached chambers lay. Just as she was about to pass the first of the arched passageways, she faltered.

A voice drifted from the shadows in the corridor beyond—a voice she would never forget.

David de Brechin.

She hadn't noticed him in the Bruce's farewell entourage that morning, but she knew he was still a guest of the King. After all, he was clearly a close companion of William de Soules. Besides, de Brechin had been one of the nobles to add his seal to the Declaration of Arbroath, though she hadn't heard his name mentioned among those receiving more land this eve.

Elaine hadn't wanted to make his unwelcome kiss known. Although it had been no lighthearted game, as he'd first pretended to Jerome, the fact that she hadn't seen him all day led her to believe that Jerome's warning to stay away from her had sunk in.

Still, she wanted naught to do with him, and certainly didn't want to run into him in the same corridor where he'd cornered her last eve.

She turned to make a hasty retreat to the other side of the hall, but then his words reached her and she froze.

"...but the Munro lapdog may prove a hindrance."

His voice was so low that Elaine could barely pick it

out, yet some instinct made her certain—he was speaking of Jerome.

Someone else must have been in the shadows with de Brechin, for she heard a second male voice, but she couldn't make out his words.

"Nay, we'll wait for word from de Soules," de Brechin replied firmly. "He'll handle Munro and the others."

Handle? Elaine's heart leapt to her throat. What could that mean—other than the terrifyingly obvious?

She forced herself to focus. De Brechin had mentioned de Soules—that could be none other than William de Soules, who'd just departed with Jerome and the others bound for Avignon. She racked her memory of their meeting the night before. De Soules was accompanying the envoy because he had French connections, but what did that have to do with *handling* the others?

On silent, slippered feet, she crept closer to the corridor passageway, straining to hear over the hammering of blood in her ears.

"…now that the plan has been put into motion," de Brechin was saying. "The Bruce willnae realize until it's too late to stop us."

The other man murmured some response, and then she heard them bid farewell. In a panic, she stepped away from the corridor's entrance, her gaze darting around for somewhere to hide. As footfalls echoed closer in the corridor, she dashed to the nearest hanging tapestry, pretending to study it intently.

Behind her, she heard de Brechin step into the great

hall. She held her breath, praying he didn't notice her. The noise from those gathered in the hall swallowed the sound of his boots on the stones, and she couldn't be sure if he'd continued on or was approaching from behind.

Time stretched, but when his hand didn't close on her arm and spin her around, she dared a peek over her shoulder. De Brechin was casually making his way through the hall, nodding to a few lords and ladies as he passed. He smoothed back his sandy blond hair, that practiced smile fixed on his face.

She watched him until he reached the front of the hall and casually slipped through the double doors. When he was at last out of sight, she rushed to the raised dais.

Both Finn and the Bruce lifted their heads at her approach, the Bruce wearing a curious expression and Finn his usual scowl.

"Sire, Finn, I-I must speak with you," she breathed. Her mind raced like a runaway horse with all she'd heard, but one thing was clear—Finn and the Bruce needed to know.

Finn's frown deepened as he looked at her. "Something is wrong."

The Bruce's light expression slipped. "Come, lass. Let us speak somewhere private."

Resuming a relaxed air, the Bruce stepped down from the dais, Finn and Elaine in his wake. Elaine hardly noticed where they were headed as they crossed the hall to the bows and curtsies of those gathered. They slipped into one of the corridors and wound their way to a small but well-appointed chamber she could only assume was for the King's private meetings.

Once the door was closed behind them, the Bruce motioned to one of the plush upholstered chairs, but Elaine shook her head, too filled with anxiety to sit.

"What is it, Lainey?" Finn demanded without preamble. His balled fists revealed his own sudden nerves.

"I-I just heard something," Elaine began, trying to organize her swirling thoughts. "In one of the corridors. David de Brechin was speaking to another man—I'm not sure who—about…"

She hesitated, racking her mind for some indication that she was wrong, that she'd been terribly mistaken about what she'd heard, but none came. At last, she finished.

"…About treason."

Chapter Thirteen

"What?" the Bruce said sharply. All his courtly manners, all his refined polish fell away, and Elaine saw for the first time a warrior-King standing before her.

She drew in a deep breath and carefully recited every word she'd overheard. As she spoke, both the Bruce and Finn's faces darkened. When she concluded, Finn muttered a curse.

"The other man," he said, fixing Elaine with a piercing look. "Who was he?"

"I don't know."

"What did he sound like?"

She thought for a moment. "He was Scottish, but not a Highlander. His brogue was softer, like a Lowlander."

Finn cursed again, swiping a hand over his face. Clearly his thoughts now raced as swiftly as Elaine's.

"De Soules and de Brechin are in on something,

along with another man," Finn said slowly, as if he were arranging all the pieces aloud.

"*At least* one other man," the Bruce interjected.

Finn nodded absently. "The most likely explanation is that they intend to thwart the delivery of the declaration—that would explain de Brechin's comment about Jerome and the others."

At that, Elaine's stomach clenched with fear, but she shoved it aside. She had to keep her wits about her if she was to be any help.

"Agreed," the Bruce said tightly. "But why in the bloody hell would they do that? What do they stand to gain?"

"Oh, I plan on asking de Brechin," Finn replied, his voice low and foreboding.

"He slipped out of the great hall," Elaine said. "I should have tried to stop him, to delay him long enough to—"

"Nay, lass." The Bruce spared her a glance, his eyes flashing with surprising softness before turning hard again. "De Brechin left with my permission. He wasnae among those being honored this eve with land grants, so I gave him leave to depart whenever he wished."

The Bruce clucked his tongue and his gaze dropped to the floor for a moment. "Mayhap the fact that I passed him over for more lands has something to do with whatever he's scheming."

"We can determine his motives later," Finn replied. "Right now we need to catch him first."

"But what of his confidant—the man he was speaking

to?" the Bruce asked. "He could still be somewhere in the palace." His mouth drew into a hard line behind his gray and russet beard. "He could be anyone, anywhere."

An ominous silence fell over the little chamber, which Elaine broke at last. "And what of William de Soules?" What she truly longed to ask was what of Jerome. Fear for his safety clawed at her like a barely caged animal.

Finn's gaze landed on her, and he must have been able to read the storm of emotions on her face. "I hate to say it, but I believe we have to trust that Munro and the others can take care of themselves for the time being."

Elaine sucked in a breath, but Finn went on. "If I had another man I could trust here—a member of the Bodyguard Corps—I would send him after the envoy's ship, but as it is, de Brechin must be our priority. He is near enough still that I might be able to hunt him down in a matter of a few days, and he will be able to tell us exactly what de Soules and whoever else they are working with has planned."

The Bruce nodded slowly. "We dinnae ken how deep or far this scheme goes," he added, fixing them each with a look. "Therefore it must stay between the three of us. If word gets out that someone is working against my peace efforts, who kens what other rodents will come out of the woodwork when an opportunity to thwart me presents itself."

"Aye, and if they find out that ye were the one to discover their plot, ye will be in danger, Lainey." Finn tried to soften his voice, but the words still hit her like a blow.

Elaine bobbed her head in assent, swallowing hard.

"I'll ride after de Brechin—quietly," Finn went on. "And when I catch him, I vow I'll have answers out of him. The moment I have aught of use, I'll return to Scone. I dinnae like leaving ye, Lainey, nor ye, Robert, especially no' with the possibility of snakes in the rushes, but de Brechin is our best chance of foiling this scheme, whatever it may be."

"I had better return to the feast," the Bruce said grimly. "I cannae raise suspicions with my absence."

Finn turned to her. "Go to yer chamber for the rest of the night, Lainey. In fact, stay in there until I return. Claim ye have some illness or other. We cannae risk ye coming to harm."

She nodded again, her throat too tight to speak.

With a swift bow, Finn slipped out of the chamber. The Bruce followed, plastering a serene, regal look onto his face as he went. Elaine watched them head back toward the great hall for a moment before turning down the corridor and following its winding path to her chamber.

Inside, she took a few gulping breaths, willing her terrified tears down.

Jerome was in danger.

More than that, the King's entire mission for Scottish freedom might be at risk.

And she was supposed to sit on her hands behind her barred chamber door until—what? Finn returned?

Or one of de Brechin's confidants realized she'd heard too much and came to silence her?

The events of the evening spun wildly through her mind. De Brechin calling Jerome "the Munro lapdog." An image of William de Soules "handling" Jerome and stealing the declaration from his pouch.

Then Finn's words drifted through the storm. *If I had another man I could trust here—a member of the Bodyguard Corps—I would send him after the envoy's ship.*

None of the other members of the Bruce's Corps were in Scone. Aye, Finn was right, de Brechin was an easier target. But that didn't mean someone shouldn't warn Jerome and the others that they—and their mission—were in danger.

A mad idea began to take shape in the corner of Elaine's mind. It would either be the most foolish thing she'd ever done, or the bravest. She wasn't sure which, yet she could not dwell on it now.

She hastily threw a cloak over her gown and fastened the tie at her neck. She kicked off her delicate slippers and jammed her feet into her riding boots, but there was no time to do aught else. Every minute she wasted, Jerome's ship drew farther away—with de Soules plotting something onboard.

She held her breath as she opened her chamber door, but the corridor outside was empty. She glided along the passageways, angling not toward the great hall but to the attached abbey. Vespers had already been recited, so when she slipped into the abbey, she found it quiet and dim. Head ducked, she hurried through the nave until she reached the door leading outside.

Cool, damp night air hit her, and she sucked in a breath to calm her thoughts. She'd need a horse, though not Gertie, for she prized the mare too much to abandon her. And she'd need a way to slip by the guards along the palisades.

One thing at a time, she reminded herself as she crossed to the stables. She found a sleepy lad barely managing to stay propped upright against the stable doors. With a few quick words about needing to look in on an ailing relative in a nearby village, Elaine was handed the reins of a sturdy-looking mare. When she reached the guards at the palisade gates, she repeated the lie, adding that she'd been trained as a midwife and her dearest cousin needed her skills.

In moments, she was through the palisades and riding into the night. Though the terrain was dark, all she had to do was follow the river eastward until she saw the masts once more.

She pushed the mare far harder than they'd ridden that morning, and soon she could make out the dark slashes of the masts against the blue-black sky. As she approached, the glow of torchlight further illuminated the near bank.

Several men milled about, loading crates of unspun wool into a rowboat, apparently to be transported to one of the ships anchored nearby.

As she reined in the mare, the men stilled and straightened, peering at her curiously.

For the first time since she'd hatched this mad plan, her courage faltered. But she couldn't fail now, not when so much depended upon her.

She pulled herself up in the saddle, willing her voice to be loud and steady. "Are any of these ships bound for France?"

Several of the men blinked at her, but at last one of them stepped forward.

"Aye, lassie," the man said, cocking his snow-white head at her. He watched her with one pale blue eye. The other was covered by a black patch of cloth. "That'n there is." He poked his chin, which was covered in a white beard to match his hair, at one of the ships. "She's mine," he went on in his thick brogue. "Call 'er the Bonny Berta, I do."

"When will you depart?"

"Just as soon as all this 'ere wool be loaded," he replied, nodding to the last few crates that remained on the bank.

"Then I'd like to buy passage."

A few of the men scoffed, but the apparent captain only lifted his bushy white brows. "Is that so? And how do ye plan to pay for that, lassie?"

Elaine looked down at the mare. "I'll sell you my horse." She silently prayed for forgiveness, for she'd in effect stolen one of the Bruce's horses, but she vowed to repay him in full when—not if—she returned.

The captain cocked his head again, assessing the mare. "Aye, well, a fine animal." He hesitated a long moment, idly tugging on his beard. At last, he spoke. "Verra well, lassie."

As she dismounted, he called to one of the younger lads on the banks.

"Davy, take the horse just over yon rise to Errol," he

said, waving to the north. "If ye fetch a fair price, I'll let ye keep a coin for yer trouble until I'm back for the next load of cargo."

Davy nodded and turned to Elaine, ducking his head as he held out his hand for the reins.

When she passed him the reins and turned to the captain, she knew there was no going back now.

"I-I assume you can assure my *safe* passage, Captain…" she said, locking her knees to keep them from trembling.

"MacDougal," he replied, surprising her by giving her a little bow. "Captain Padraig MacDougal, lassie, and aye, ye'll be more'n safe on Bonny Berta, I promise ye." He narrowed his good eye on her, lifting one brow. "But I cannae make promises once we reach Calais. Are ye sure ye wish to make the journey? Davy can return yer horse, no harm done."

"Nay," she breathed, "I am sure."

"And what could compel a bonny wee thing like ye to ride out in the dark of night to buy yer way to France on a cargo ship?"

Elaine lifted her chin. "I have my reasons." Lying didn't come naturally to her. Since she would be spending several days aboard Captain MacDougal's ship, any falsehood she told might easily come unraveled with time.

The captain chuckled. "Verra well, lassie, keep yer secrets." The last of the crates had been positioned in the rowboat and the men hopped in. MacDougal waved to her. "Come on then. Dinnae dally."

Steeling her spine, Elaine stepped to the bank. As

she eyed the rocking boat dubiously, the captain's gnarled hands closed around her waist and hoisted her into the air. She landed with a squeak atop one of the open crates, the wool inside cushioning her ungraceful embarkation.

A few of the men chuckled, but then the captain stepped aboard and gave them a sharp eye. "Hold yer whist," he snapped. "Else ye'll answer to me."

The men instantly fell silent, and a surge of gratitude rose in Elaine's throat. At least for the next few days, she'd be safe.

"How long will it take to reach Calais?" she asked as they rowed across the inky river to MacDougal's ship.

He scratched his beard. "Five days, mayhap four if we catch a favorable wind."

When the rowboat nudged the ship's hull, the men leapt into action, some climbing the lowered ladder up to the deck, others securing ropes around the crates to be hauled aboard. At the captain's urging, Elaine gingery picked her way up the ladder and onto the ship's deck. MacDougal followed, bellowing orders to raise the anchor and unfurl the sails as soon as his boots hit the planks.

She dragged in a bracing lungful of air as the ship began gliding down the river. She could already smell the tang of salt from the North Sea. The first step in this mad plan was complete.

Now she could only pray that she reached France—and Jerome—in time.

Chapter Fourteen

Jerome nearly spit, but he'd already done that a dozen times today.

That morning, the sun had broken through the fog hanging over the sea and revealed the verdant shores of France. They'd approached Calais with the wind at their backs as they entered the harbor. But instead of docking directly before the fortified, walled city, they'd followed the curving harbor as it skirted around the city's western edge.

That had taken an extra hour, but the captain assured them that it would save them the hassle of entering the city. But of course when they'd disembarked, they'd needed horses, so Kieran had been sent through the fortified gates to procure mounts.

When Kieran returned with four strong steeds, Jerome had thought them away at last, but then William de Soules had informed them that they had to wait for the arrival of the King of France himself.

Apparently the King wished to provide them a personal escort from Calais to his court in Paris. According to de Soules, King Philip was feuding with England's King Edward II. Edward refused to pay homage and acknowledge Philip, so the French King had decided to make a show of supporting Scotland's pursuit of independence from England.

King Philip insisted on publicly making it known—to his people, to the Scots, but most importantly to the English—that Robert the Bruce's envoy was being permitted to travel across his lands all the way to the Papal court in Avignon with his blessing.

Which meant Jerome was stuck waiting on a King.

Of course, the day was fair, the sun shining, and the May air far more balmy than it had been in Scotland. Jerome had nowhere else to be, his only task to deliver the Bruce's declaration safely—which Philip's presence would ensure.

Then why was he in such a bloody foul mood?

Damn it all, of course he knew.

Elaine.

Thoughts of her had plagued him as they'd crossed the North Sea. She'd been like a breath of fresh air. She was so full of life, wearing her heart on her sleeve.

Before he'd met her, he'd treated life like a never-ending string of tasks. Complete each mission handed to him. Prove his loyalty. Outrun his family legacy.

That had been all. Though he believed in the justness of the Bruce's cause for freedom and had gladly lent whatever abilities or strengths he had when the Bruce had requested his service, he hadn't realized until he'd met Elaine that he'd turned his life into one long slog devoid of joy or pleasure.

But all that had changed from the moment he'd laid eyes on her. Jerome was not a fanciful man. He didn't read poetry or wax over emotions like a bard. He'd even scoffed at tales of infatuation and love. There was no room in his life for such softness. He'd spent every day of the last fourteen years attempting to prove that he wasn't like his father—wasn't a traitor.

Until now. Somehow in the last fortnight, Elaine had ferreted her way into his mind, distracting him from what he'd thought was most important. Even when she wasn't near, his longing for her lingered like a sweet perfume that hung in the air and filled his every breath.

If he were honest, that scared him. Terrified him, in fact. He was not some lovesick lad. He was a warrior, a Munro. Wanting Elaine, and letting that desire distract him, threatened to undo everything he'd worked for these past fourteen years.

He could have let himself believe that he would see her again once this mission was complete. The Bruce might send him to the Borderlands again, or mayhap she would find herself in Scotland once more.

But such hopes were foolish, and only made this damned persistent desire worse. She was to be wed when she returned to Trellham Keep. He clenched his fists at the thought. It had taken five days to reach Calais. She and Finn had likely already begun the journey back to Trellham. That meant she was five days closer to belonging to someone else—and five days farther away from him.

Letting a frustrated breath go, he spun on his heels, casting his gaze from where they stood on a small grassy rise down to the harbor below. The waters sparkled dazzlingly, catching the bright sun. Their ship still sat in the harbor, one amongst dozens of others. The harbor bustled with activity—cargo being loaded and unloaded, vessels being resupplied, and the constant coming and going of ships.

A smaller, squat cargo ship caught his eye as it sailed into the harbor's sheltered waters. It flew the Scottish flag—not unusual, for the wool trade between the two countries was strong, but something else drew his attention.

A splash of copper glinted like a coin from the top deck. He squinted. The figure was clad in a brown wool cloak, but beneath it, he saw a flash of blue. A gown. The figure was a woman.

Nay… It couldn't be…

Without thinking, he snatched the reins of one of the waiting horses Kieran had procured and swung into the saddle.

"Munro! What are ye about?" Kieran called behind him, but Jerome had already spurred the horse and was barreling down the slope toward the harbor.

Distantly, he heard the other men shouting after him as well, followed by the pounding of their horses' hooves, but he paid them no mind. His gaze remained locked on the woman.

As he drew near the docks, a gangplank was lowered from the ship. The woman actually hugged a white-haired, stocky man standing next to her, then picked her way carefully down the gangplank to the docks.

Just as he dragged his horse to a stop and flung himself from its back, she stepped onto the dock and lifted her head. Their gazes locked.

"Elaine—what in…?"

Her blue eyes rounded. "Jerome! I wasn't sure how I'd find you—and yet here you are. You've saved me a great deal of trouble."

"Here *ye* are." He closed the distance between them, his hands closing around her arms. Aye, she was real, and she was here.

And her presence threatened the entire mission.

Like a fanned flame, his shock blazed into anger. "What the bloody hell are ye doing here?" he snapped. "This is no place for a gentle-bred lass."

Desperation filled her eyes. "I-I need to speak with you—it is a matter of grave import."

"What could possibly be so urgent that ye sailed to France to find me? Dinnae tell me ye came alone, Elaine."

She nodded distractedly. "Aye, but that isn't—"

Jerome cursed. "Finn is going to have my head— that is, if the Bruce doesnae take it for endangering this mission."

"That is just it," she interjected. "I came because—"

"Munro! What the bloody hell is going on?"

Jerome turned to find Kieran, de Soules, and the bishop all reining in their horses next to his.

Elaine stiffened in his hold, her mouth still open with the words she hadn't yet spoken.

"I—"

She faltered, her gaze fixing on the others for a long moment before she returned it to him. For the briefest moment, pain flashed in her sky-blue eyes. Then she took a deep breath, squaring her shoulders.

"I had to come—because I am in love with you."

ELAINE'S PRIDE withered and died as she blurted the words.

She'd had five long days aboard Captain MacDougal's ship to plan what she would do when she arrived in Calais—buy a horse, ask after such an unusual group of men, and pray that she managed to catch up to them before they reached Avignon—but not once had she considered the fact that she might not have a moment alone with Jerome to explain why she was there.

When she'd met William de Soules's eyes over Jerome's shoulder, she knew she needed to lie—and well enough to fool them all until she could speak with Jerome in private. But what reason could she give to convince these men that she'd followed them all the way from Scotland alone?

It struck her like a blinding flash of lightning. All her life, she'd hated being thought of as a silly girl, interested only in ribbons and flower chains and other such frippery. At last, the assumptions about her would prove useful.

But it meant casting her pride aside—and trampling it into the ground.

"I'm in love with you," she repeated for good measure.

Jerome went stock-still. His lips, which were normally set in a hard line, parted, and a breath slipped past them.

"What?"

She had done it now. She might as well make a complete fool of herself to seal the lie.

"I-I've loved you from the first," she said, letting the words pour from her. "I didn't let myself hope, but then when you kissed me the night before you departed, I knew I could not live without you."

A low whistle sounded behind Jerome, likely from Kieran. She tumbled onward, though.

"I had to find you, to tell you that you have my heart and always will." Embarrassed tears rose in her eyes, but she didn't blink them away, hoping they would be mistaken for the lovesick blubbering of a foolish girl.

The only problem was, the words caused a painful tightness in her chest that wasn't solely attributable to the humiliation swamping her. She didn't have time to consider that, however, for she heard Captain MacDougal chuckle lowly behind her on the gangplank.

"Och, I kenned it must have been some heart-thievin' laddie," he said with another cackle. "What else could drive a bonny lassie to such lengths?"

Jerome at last ripped his stunned gaze from her and fixed MacDougal with a glare. "Ye'll take her back to Scotland immediately."

To Elaine's shock, hurt at his brusque dismissal sank

like a rock in her stomach. But why should it? She wasn't truly in love with him—it was all just a ruse.

The captain grunted, and she turned to find him shooting daggers at Jerome with his one good eye. "Dinnae be a fool, laddie," he said. "When a lassie as rare as this'n gives ye her heart, ye dinnae toss it aside so quickly."

Her chest warmed at MacDougal's defense of her. Though she'd been terrified of him at first, he reminded her of her father in some ways—or mayhap a disgruntled, one-eyed uncle. Still, his protectiveness was only making matters worse at the moment.

Jerome continued to glare at MacDougal. "I ken she's a treasure, man, but she doesnae belong here."

"Och, what is the holdup, Munro?" Kieran barked.

Jerome shot him a look over his shoulder before facing the captain again. "I'll pay ye double whatever she gave ye to see her safely back to Scotland—now."

Captain MacDougal shrugged. "My crew will be unloadin' my cargo for at least an hour, and loadin' 'er back up again for another'n. I suppose ye can wait and give the lassie a wee bit o' gratitude for all she's done for ye—" at that he shot Elaine a wink "—or send the poor thing off on one o' these other ships." He waved at the harbor. "But then again, those other captains may no' be quite so kindly as Captain MacDougal."

Jerome muttered a string of curses under his breath that rivaled anything Elaine had heard aboard the Bonny Berta. He met her gaze, but his dark eyes were shuttered and hard.

"Ye can stay *only* until MacDougal's ship sets sail again," he said. "Then ye'll go back to Scotland."

"Jerome," she said, dropping her voice. She held his gaze, silently willing him to understand—or at least give her a chance to explain in private.

Just then, a faint noise drifted from the gentle green hills above the harbor.

"Bloody hell," Kieran muttered.

The noise came again—it was tinny and high, like a horn.

"That would be King Philip's bugler announcing his approach," de Soules said, his brown eyes fixing on Jerome.

"*Shite.*"

Chapter Fifteen

Jerome clamped his teeth down on another string of oaths. He moved in front of Elaine as if he were defending her, which was idiotic, for King Philip wasn't attacking. Yet he couldn't order his thoughts enough to do aught but act on instinct to protect her.

"What is the King of France doing here?" she hissed behind him.

"He is to escort us to his palace in Paris."

He heard her pull in a breath. Aye, it had been a surprise to him as well—but not as great a surprise as seeing Elaine step foot on French soil.

Or proclaim that she loved him.

For one breathtaking moment, his heart had soared out of his chest and toward the blazing sun.

Curse him for a fool. If she truly did love him, it wouldn't change aught. His mission awaited, and he couldn't let anything—or anyone—get in the way of that.

Yet something in her eyes had given him pause. The shadow crossing their vivid blue depths had sent the hairs on his neck lifting. Could she be lying? If that was the case, then what the bloody hell was she doing here?

"We need to talk," she murmured as if reading his thoughts.

"Aye—later."

Just then, the blue and gold banners for King Philip peeked above the top of the grassy hillside. They flapped in the mild breeze blowing in from the harbor as they drew nearer.

The ground rumbled with the approaching procession, which must have been as big as an army.

A dozen mounted, armored guards crested the rise, then began streaming down toward the docks, more falling in behind them. One of the guards in the front eyed them and approached.

De Soules gave a bow. "We come in the name of King Robert the Bruce of Scotland bearing a message for the Pope."

"Ah, you are the ones," the guard replied in accented English, his gaze flicking over each of them.

"We are honored that His Majesty King Philip V has so graciously agreed to allow us safe passage across his fair lands," de Soules continued in a loud, formal voice. "And we are further humbled by the privilege of his escort to ensure that—"

"Are they here?" someone asked from the top of the rise, cutting de Soules off. "Have they arrived already?"

"*Oui, Majesté*," the guard replied.

Just then, a horse and rider so bedecked with gold

and jewels that Jerome had to squint to make them out in the bright sun crested the hilltop and rode toward them. The horse's saddle and bridle were encrusted with sapphires and gold filigree. The man himself wore an ermine-trimmed blue velvet cloak and a gold crown atop his head.

The dozens of guards shifted around the rider like a cloud, staying close but moving amorphously to accommodate his advance.

Instinctively, Jerome dropped into a low bow. This could be none other than the King himself. Elaine, too, dipped into a deep curtsy.

"Welcome to France, *mes amis*," the King said. "Arise and let me look each of you in the eyes."

De Soules was the first to respond. He straightened halfway, keeping his head tilted in respect. "Majesty, I am Sir William de Soules, at yer service."

"Ah, *oui*, you are the one with lands here in the north, is that correct?"

"Aye, Majesty. And these men are my companions, each hand-selected by King Robert the Bruce for this most significant task. Bishop Kininmund." De Soules motioned to the bishop, who inclined his head to the King. "Kieran MacAdams." Typical of the Highlander, Kieran nodded in respect but didn't genuflect as deeply as he would have for the Bruce. "And Jerome Munro."

Jerome, too, nodded, though it was closer to a bow that Kieran's had been.

He looked up to find King Philip's curious, intelligent brown eyes fixed on him—or rather, fixed on Elaine, who was still lowered in her curtsy.

"And who is this lovely *mademoiselle*?"

"This," de Soules replied, his voice tightening. "Is Lady Elaine Beaumore."

The King's light brown eyebrows winged in surprise. "And she is part of your King's envoy as well?"

"Nay, Majesty, she only just arrived."

King Philip's penetrating gaze shifted to Elaine again. "Oh? And what business does she have in France?"

Just as Jerome opened his mouth to fumble for an answer, Captain MacDougal interrupted from the gangplank. "Beggin' yer pardon, Majesty, but I just delivered yon lassie from Scotland. She came all this way for that Munro laddie. Stole her heart, he has."

Before Jerome could refute the meddling captain's words, the King's eyes lit up.

"Truly? That is most bold of you, *mademoiselle*."

"A-aye, Majesty," Elaine nigh croaked behind him.

"Rise, Lady Elaine."

Elaine obeyed, stepping to Jerome's side.

"Munro, what response have you made to the lovely lady?"

Jerome cleared his throat, but the blasted captain spoke first again.

"He's sendin' her back, Majesty! Wants me to take her away as soon as possible."

"Oh, *mais non*, Munro," the King chided, his eyes dancing with amusement. "The lady must come with us to Paris."

Propriety be damned. "Nay, Majesty," Jerome cut in. "She cannae—"

The King continued as if Jerome hadn't spoken.

"She shall be my personal guest. I intend to dazzle you with the beauty of the French countryside, Lady Elaine. And when we reach the palace, my darling wife and her ladies-in-waiting will undoubtedly fawn over that lovely hair and comely form. No doubt they will polish you up and parade you about court until Munro here is sick with jealousy."

He waggled his eyebrows at her, and out of the corner of his eye, Jerome saw a blush climbing into her face.

"Thank you, Majesty," she replied.

"Yer Majesty, I must insist that—"

The King waved him away as if he were naught more than a fly. "You Scotsmen are far too dour," he commented. "You are in France now. As my honored guests, I insist that you enjoy your time here."

The matter settled to his liking, the King reined his horse around. "Let us be off, then. If it were just us, it would take three days to reach Paris, but with the caravan of wagons we are sure to move slower."

Caravan of wagons? Jerome nearly cursed but managed to bite it back. He turned to Captain MacDougal and leveled the gnarled old bear with a hard look.

"Though ye have already been most obliging with yer...*help*," he said tightly, "I would request one last favor." Jerome withdrew a scrap of parchment and a stub of charcoal from the pouch on his belt. He scrawled a quick note that Elaine was safe in France and under his protection.

"See that when ye return to Scone this is delivered to Finn Sutherland and no other," he said, folding the note and placing a coin on top of it. He extended it to MacDougal. "Understood?"

"Aye," the captain replied, giving Jerome a wide smile that revealed more than a few missing teeth. He was loath to trust the man with such an important task, but then again, MacDougal had seen Elaine safely across the North Sea. Besides, Jerome had no other choice.

Jerome turned to find King Philip and his guards ascending the hill over Calais once more. The other three members of the Bruce's envoy were mounting their horses reluctantly and casting glances at Elaine. The bishop, in particular, wore a sour look, as he had for much of the sea crossing.

Jerome took Elaine's arm and guided her to his horse. Once he'd swung into the saddle, he pulled her up in front of him, settling her across his lap. Despite his anger and confusion, aching heat jumped in his veins to have her so near.

"I can explain," she murmured as he spurred his horse after the others.

"Oh aye," he ground out. "Ye will."

Chapter Sixteen

A s they crested the ridge, Elaine sucked in a breath. She'd thought their retinue large with nearly two score of the King of France's guards encircling their little party. But now she saw that their traveling caravan was far larger.

On the other side of the hill sat at least a dozen wagons along with another score of armored guards.

Now that she thought of it, the enormous retinue made sense. If a King were to travel—especially a King like Philip, who clearly favored luxuries fit for his station —he would need tents, furniture, food, clothes, and servants in tow.

"You said the King wished to provide a personal escort to Paris," she murmured, tilting her head up to Jerome's. "Why?"

He glanced down at her, a muscle ticking in his bristle-covered jaw. Slowly, he let a breath go. "I gather he wishes to make a show of his support for the Bruce's message to the Pope. Things have gone sour between him and England's King Edward. So he's decided that the enemy of his enemy is his friend—the Bruce, in this case."

She shifted her gaze to the wagons. "Aye, he certainly isn't making a secret of this."

"I believe he wishes to make it understood far and wide that we Scots are traveling across his lands with his express permission to Avignon."

All the King's fanfare and spectacle might make it difficult for her to steal a moment alone with Jerome to tell him what she'd learned in Scone. Still, she should be grateful that the King had arrived when he had, for she might have found herself on the Bonny Berta bound for Scotland once more.

"I cannae deny that I am glad to see ye again," Jerome murmured, cutting into her thoughts. "But ye dinnae belong here, Elaine. Though King Philip may try to make this seem like a merry picnic, this mission is actually dangerous. We are safe among his guards, but after we reach the palace, they willnae continue to escort us to Avignon. And though France is considered a friend of Scotland, the Bruce has enemies everywhere."

Elaine had to bite her tongue to prevent blurting just how well she understood that now. Apparently the Bruce had enemies in his own palace, for gracious' sake.

Instead, all she said was, "I know," keeping her voice barely above a whisper. She sensed his sharp, dark eyes on her and glanced up to find him searching her features.

"Something is wrong. I sensed it before by the docks, but now I'm sure. What is it, Elaine?"

Her gaze darted to de Soules, who rode ahead with the other men. "I can't say—not yet, anyway."

Jerome's arm, which was looped around her back to allow him to hold the reins, stiffened.

"At least tell me this," he said, his voice so low and deep that it reverberated through her where her shoulder pressed into his chest. "Are ye in danger?"

Something fluttered deep in her belly at his protectiveness, but she set it aside. There were far more serious matters to focus on for now.

"Mayhap," she said carefully. "But it isn't me you should worry about."

He worked his jaw for a long moment, his brows lowered and his eyes burning with frustration—and concern. He opened his mouth to speak, but just then the King called for the wagons to be mobilized and set his horse at a brisk walk toward the rolling hills to the south.

"Later," he murmured close to her ear.

THEY TRAVELED SLOWLY across the verdant landscape, so much more lush and fecund than anything Elaine had seen in Northern England or Scotland. The day was warm and sunny, and soon she shed her cloak, which Jerome tucked away in his saddlebags.

Without the thick layer of wool between them, she was all the more aware of his solid strength behind her

—and the fact that he still radiated taut frustration. She could only hope that once he learned the truth, he would forgive her for appearing so unexpectedly—and lying about her feelings for him.

They crossed vast farmlands and skirted villages of varying sizes. Occasionally, they drew near enough to one of the little towns to draw a crown of curious onlookers. With the King riding proudly at the front of their procession, glittering in the sunlight like a jewel, the French townspeople were understandably awed and thrilled at their passing.

When at last the sun dipped toward the horizon, the King called for a halt so that their camp could be erected. As Jerome helped Elaine dismount, servants jumped down from the wagons and began unloading their supplies. They made surprisingly fast work setting up an enormous circular tent made of blue- and yellow-dyed canvas for the King. Several other, much smaller tents were assembled for the Bruce's men, the guards, and the servants themselves.

It was dusky twilight by the time the camp was arranged. As one of the servants lit a fire, the King approached the Bruce's men, who'd been standing aside to allow the servants to work.

"I hope you will forgive me, *mes amis*," he said, adjusting his ermine-trimmed cloak around his shoulders. "I find I am weary after the day's travels and wish to retire to my tent. I hope you will not judge French hospitality too harshly just yet, for I plan to show you all of France's luxuries when we exchange these rustic conditions for the palace."

Elaine hid her tired smile by dipping into a curtsy of acknowledgement. King Philip's tent hardly seemed rustic, but he was royalty after all, and had been born into extravagance. Still, she was surprised to see him up close and out of his saddle, for he was far younger and more physically commanding on his own two feet that she would have expected the French King to be.

He looked of an age with Jerome, and of a height with him as well. She'd heard him called Philip the Tall by her father before, and the epithet proved true. Though he still wore his crown, rich cloak, and a ceremonial jewel-encrusted sword belted to his waist, he didn't appear foppish or arrogant for all the opulence. Instead, his keen, dancing brown eyes spoke of intelligence and good humor.

"Of course, Majesty," de Soules answered with a bow. "We are most honored."

"Come, I will show you your accommodations." The King motioned the bishop toward one of the tents, followed by Kieran and de Soules.

"And for you, my lovebirds," the King said, his gaze settling on Jerome and Elaine. He gestured toward a tent no different from the first three, except that it sat at the very edge of their little camp, slightly apart from the others.

"The comforts will be limited, unfortunately," King Philip said as he walked them to the tent. "But then again, I imagine you two will be so occupied with other more...*pressing* matters that you will hardly notice." He chuckled, holding back the tent flap.

Elaine peered inside. A wooden folding table sat on

one side of the small space, a pitcher and basin placed atop it. On the other side sat a cot. A single cot. A *narrow* cot.

Elaine tried to cover an unladylike choking sound with a cough. "You are…most kind, Majesty."

The King's eyes twinkled with mirth. "I instructed the servants to give you a little extra space as well. I have heard you English ladies can be shy."

Before Elaine could choke again, Jerome gave the King a formal bow. "Thank ye, Majesty. This is most appreciated."

"I'll send someone with food," the King commented as he strode toward his own enormous tent. "But I'll instruct them not to disturb you. *Bonne nuit, mes amis.*"

Cheeks blazing, Elaine ducked into the tent. Jerome followed, dropping the tent flap behind him. Without the blue glow of twilight coming through the tent's opening, they were cast into darkness.

With a muttered curse, Jerome fumbled for something, then she saw a spark from the striking of his flint stones. He lit a candle she hadn't noticed beside the pitcher and basin, then turned to her.

"What the hell are ye doing here?" he demanded unceremoniously.

She drew in a deep breath. "The day you left for France, I overheard David de Brechin say something…disturbing."

Jerome's dark eyes flared. "Did he speak against ye? Or try to attack ye agai—"

"Nay," Elaine cut in hastily. "Nothing like that." She swallowed. "Something far worse. He spoke William de

Soules's name in connection with some plot against the Bruce."

"What?" he snapped.

"He called you 'the Munro lapdog' and said you might hinder them, but that de Soules would 'handle' you and the others."

Jerome's hands clenched at his sides. "What else?"

"De Soules is supposed to send word to de Brechin and the man he spoke with—and possibly others. De Brechin said that once the plan had been put into motion, the Bruce wouldn't realize until it was too late to stop them."

"Bloody hell," Jerome hissed. He began pacing in the small space, forcing Elaine to step back or be bowled over. She bumped into the edge of the cot and sat down.

"What of the other man?" Jerome asked, not looking at her.

"I don't know, but he was likely a Lowlander."

"Did de Brechin see ye?"

"Nay, I don't think so. He left the great hall after that, and he didn't cast me a look as he departed."

Jerome halted, facing her. "And then ye simply— what? Threw yerself on the nearest ship and came after me?"

She knew he was overwhelmed by what she'd just told him, but the blunt words still stung. She straightened to her feet once more. "Nay, I am not so foolish as that, despite what you might think of me. I told Finn and the King."

He started pacing again. "Good. And what did they say?"

"Finn believes de Brechin is the key. He went after him that night with the intent of capturing him and forcing him to reveal their plans. For all I know he's already dragged de Brechin back to Scone."

"And the Bruce?"

"He wishes to keep this quiet. If anyone linked to de Brechin—including de Soules—suspects we are on to them, the others, however many there are, might disappear into the woodwork once more."

Jerome grunting, swiping a hand over his face as he continued to pace.

"Both the King and Finn believe this must have something to do with the delivery of the declaration," she went on. "As do I. Which is why I came. Finn said that if he'd had another man he could trust, he would have sent him to warn you, but as there was not, he would focus on de Brechin."

"Does he ken ye're here?"

Elaine hesitated. "Nay." Jerome rounded on her, but before he could admonish her, she hurried on. "But de Soules is clearly part of some scheme against the King. I heard de Brechin say so myself. I couldn't simply sit in my chamber with the door barred, twiddling my thumbs and hoping the mission—and you—would be fine. I needed to warn you."

When Jerome remained silent, his restless steps growing faster, Elaine hitched her chin.

"I would have told you all this straightaway, but de Soules was right behind you at the docks. I had to think of some way to explain my presence that wouldn't rouse his suspicion."

Jerome faltered mid-step, his gaze sharp on her. "Then what ye said—that ye loved me—" He cleared his throat. "It was a lie to cover yer true purpose."

Heat climbed into her face and a knot of conflicting emotion tightened her throat. Frustration. Indignation. And something dangerously close to regret.

"Aye," she replied. "And apparently it worked, because everyone, even the King of France, believed it. Even *you* believed I was foolish enough to have done something so rash. I saw it in your eyes when I spoke the words."

He ripped his gaze away, turning his back to her so that she couldn't again read his features.

"You can think me idiotic if you wish, but I did what needed to be done," she said, fighting back a surge of embarrassment.

He fell silent for a long moment, his shoulders stiff and his broad back like a wall separating them. "Nay," he replied at last. "No' idiotic, lass." Slowly, he faced her. His features were tight and guarded, but he kept his voice soft. "Brave? Aye. Rash and mad? Aye, a wee bit of each. But no' idiotic."

Elaine released a breath she hadn't realized she'd been holding.

"There'll be hell to pay when this is all over," he muttered. "But that cannae be our concern now. What are we to do about de Soules?"

Elaine blinked. "You are asking me?"

He leveled her with a stern look. "Well, ye're here, arenae ye? This is both of our problem now."

"I-I'm not sure," she admitted. She'd been so

focused on reaching Jerome and telling him what she'd overheard that she hadn't thought beyond that.

"I cannae figure why de Soules and de Brechin would want to thwart the delivery of the declaration," he said, "but it does seem the most logical explanation."

"Has he done aught to raise your suspicion so far?"

"Nay," he said, raking his hand through his hair. "The declaration has been secure with me this whole time, and de Soules hasnae once tried to take it."

Elaine thought for another moment, but when naught came to her, she sighed. "Whatever his plan, something is afoot. I agree with the Bruce that this must be kept quiet."

Jerome nodded. "Aye. We'll need to be cautious, but we must watch his every move."

"Isn't there more we should do?" she asked. "If he means to steal the declaration or harm you in any way—"

"Dinnae fash, lass. I can take care of myself. It's more important to try to uncover whatever he is about. There are at least three men—Scotsmen, no less—involved in this scheme. Who kens how many more there might be."

"Then we simply…wait?" The five days it had taken to reach France had felt like an eternity, her stomach in knots and her mind running wild with fears that she would be too late. And now all they could do was wait?

"And watch," Jerome said. "If we act rashly, any others working with de Brechin and de Soules could take to the wind, and we'll never ken just how deep this plot—whatever it may be—runs."

"Then we are to carry on as if I am truly here because..."

The words died in Elaine's throat. Their gazes locked, and she swallowed involuntarily.

"Aye, we'll pretend we are lovers."

Lovers. That was different than pretending to be in love. Elaine didn't have experience in either, yet in her mind, being in love meant writing verses to each other, picking flowers and holding hands. Being *lovers*, on the other hand, meant...what they'd done outside her chamber back in Scone. And more.

Her skin prickled with awareness. The tent was so small that for both of them to stand as they were, they had to be nearly touching. And then there was the problem of the cot.

"Ye neednae look so horrified," Jerome said evenly. "It is only pretend."

Elaine cursed her easily read features, yet for once, they hadn't betrayed her true thoughts. She wasn't horrified. Nay, instead, she felt a pang of longing. Her face heated with embarrassment—for her wayward thoughts, and for the seed of curiosity at just what such *pretend* would entail. "A-aye, of course."

"Ye can take the cot. I'll sleep on the floor."

She nodded mutely.

This was going to be a long night—and a long journey to Avignon.

Chapter Seventeen

J erome stared up at the canvas ceiling, his eyes bleary from lack of sleep. The interior of the tent was already starting to lighten with the morning sun's rays, yet he'd only caught a few winks of sleep all night.

He'd slept near Elaine before. Though Finn had tried to watch the two of them like a hawk when they'd been traveling to Scone, he couldn't prevent them from both needing to sleep. Yet even then, Finn had always been nearby, and Jerome hadn't been close enough to hear Elaine's soft, steady breaths or smell the delicate, womanly fragrance of her skin and hair.

Last night, they'd found a tray of bread, cheese, meat, and the season's first strawberries, along with a jug of wine, outside their tent. After washing their faces and hands in the basin, they'd taken the simple meal together, she sitting on the cot and he standing.

Jerome had turned away to give her a moment to

unlace her silk gown and drape it over the little folding table, for it was her only one. He'd heard the rustling of fabric and then her hurried steps to the cot, all the while imagining what she looked like standing in naught but a chemise—and within arm's reach of him.

When she was settled with the coverlet pulled up to her chin, he'd turned back around and stretched himself alongside the cot on the ground. And then lain awake damn near the whole night listening to Elaine breathing.

He huffed a sigh, sitting up. He wasn't likely to sleep anymore now that the sun had broken the horizon, so he might as well rise.

He pushed to his feet from his makeshift bed. Elaine had insisted that he sleep on her cloak, despite the fact that he had spent many a night with naught to separate him from the ground but his plaid. No wonder he hadn't been able to sleep—her scent had nigh enveloped him all night.

With a barely suppressed curse, he let his extra length of plaid fall in a pile with her cloak, then hoisted his shirt over his head and went to the basin. He needed to clear his head, and naught was more likely to help with that than cold water. Besides, he hadn't properly washed since disembarking the ship.

He began scrubbing himself using what was left of the water in the pitcher and a linen cloth one of the servants had left. Today was a new day. The shock of seeing Elaine in France had retreated, and now only the grim reality that his mission was in danger remained. Aye, they would have to maintain the ruse of being in love, but that shouldn't be—

Behind him, he heard a little gasp. He spun to find Elaine sitting upright in the cot, her hair like a copper halo around her head and her creamy shoulders peeking out from the coverlet.

Her bright blue eyes were fixed on him, her berry lips open in shock.

"What are you doing?" Her gaze roved over his bare chest with a hunger that sent blood rushing straight to his cock.

"I needed more of a wash," he replied, his voice coming out harsh because of the sudden tightness in his throat.

"Oh. Of course. I—that is…" Absently, she pushed aside a lock of russet hair from her face. The coverlet slid away to pool around her waist, and it was Jerome's turn to stare.

Her skin was nearly as pale as her white chemise. Her collarbone cut a delicate ridge across her chest, and below, he could see her breasts rising and falling with unnatural speed against the linen.

The material was thin enough that he could just make out the pinkish shadows of her nipples.

He swallowed hard. "I'll just…" He lifted the washing cloth but couldn't manage to turn back around to the basin. Instead, he simply stood there like a fool, letting her look her fill and gazing his own as well.

Distantly, he registered the sound of footsteps approaching their tent, but he assumed it was a servant —until he heard a casually commanding voice just on the other side of the canvas.

"And how are my lovebirds this morning?" King

Philip's tone was filled with merriment. "I hope I will not find you indisposed."

Elaine's eyes widened. At last Jerome snapped out of his daze. His gaze fell to the ground beside the cot. Elaine's cloak, plus his plaid and discarded shirt, made for quite the cozy-looking nest—and if the King saw it, their ruse would be up.

He did the only thing he could think of. In two swift steps, he was to the cot. He kicked his makeshift bedding asunder even as he dove under the coverlet with Elaine.

"What—"

He stopped her next word with a kiss just as the King pulled back the tent flap and bright sunlight poured inside.

When he heard the King chuckle, Jerome knew he'd seen enough to convince him that he'd walked in on a tryst. He broke off the kiss, his gaze snagging on Elaine's rounded eyes and softly parted lips before he managed to look at the King.

"Forgive me for interrupting," he said with another chuckle. "Ah, *jeune amour*. You remind me of what it was like to court my Queen. Always stealing away, enjoying each other wherever we could."

He waved at the now disheveled pile of clothes that had a moment before been Jerome's bed. "And always in a hurry, *non*? I am sorry that I have caused you to rush over that which should be given all the time in the world, *mes amis*, but we must be off if we wish to reach Paris in another three days."

Jerome barely managed to stifle a curse. He'd been so caught up in thoughts of Elaine that he hadn't even heard the stirrings beyond their tent walls. Through the open flap, he saw that the other tents were being disassembled and the wagons loaded.

"Aye, of course, Majesty," Jerome replied gruffly.

With another chuckle, the King dropped the tent flap and left them alone.

In bed. Half-naked.

Belatedly, Jerome realized that in his haste to convince the King of their ruse, he'd pulled Elaine flush against him. One hand lingered on her hip while the other was buried in her cascading copper locks.

Her chemise was like a whisper between them, providing little barrier between their skin. He could feel the heat of her, the softness of her breasts against his chest.

"Forgive me," he murmured, yet he couldn't seem to pull away. "My only thought was to maintain our cover story."

She didn't draw back or push his hands off her. Instead, she continued to gaze at him, her eyes roaming over his bare shoulders, his jawline, and at last his lips. "Of course," she replied absently. "You did what you had to."

Damn it all. He couldn't take the look in her eyes anymore—a look of hunger, of longing. Of desire.

The kiss he'd stolen a moment before hadn't been enough, only a brushing of lips to satisfy King Philip. The memory of it left him burning. Some unthinking, instinctual part of him howled for more.

Unbidden, he lowered his head, his lips coming within a hair's breadth of Elaine's. But he wouldn't catch her by surprise again. He wanted her to know exactly what he was about and wanted her to long for it just as badly as he did.

She made a frustrated sound in the back of her throat, her breath fanning his lips in a maddening tease.

He could take no more. He closed the distance between them with a ravenous kiss. Though he attempted to leash his desire, his control snapped the moment their lips touched. When she moaned, he immediately claimed her mouth, his tongue delving and tangling with hers.

His cock grew painfully hard beneath his kilt as their voracious kiss continued. To his surprised pleasure, she met him stroke for stroke despite her innocence. She clung to him as if he were her anchor in a storm, her arms looped around his neck and her fingers buried in his hair.

Lost in the building heat, he rolled on top of her, pushing her down into the cot. Even as he propped himself on his elbows, taking some of his weight to avoid crushing her, she arched up into him, silently demanding that their bodies' contact not be broken.

Her breasts brushed his chest, the pearled nipples dragging a burning path over his skin. He lifted a hand to one breast, but instead of slowly teasing her as he had before, he cupped her fully, swallowing her gasp of pleasure with his kiss.

He thumbed her beaded nipple, feeling her jolt beneath him. Heaven help him, Elaine's pleasure was like the finest Munro whisky—heady, powerful, and intoxicating. Like a drunkard, he couldn't get enough.

He longed to draw out her ecstasy. He would lave each breast with torturous thoroughness, then move between her legs until she was trembling and begging for all of him.

Bloody hell. He rocked his hips against her, needing more contact, needing her to feel the hard length of his desire. She responded on instinct, lifting one knee so that he settled between her legs. He could feel the heat of her womanhood even through her chemise and his thick wool plaid.

A nigh-blinding urge to rip off his kilt and her thin chemise stole over him. He felt himself teetering on the edge of sanity, a heartbeat away from doing something irrevocable.

The realization of just how close he was coming to spreading her legs wider and driving into her, consequences be damned, was like a splash of cold water. He jerked back, breaking their kiss, and hissed a curse as if he'd been burned.

"What are you doing?" she mumbled, her voice thick with passion.

"I'm stopping," he said on a ragged breath, "before I do something we'll both regret."

Hurt flashed through her eyes as he threw back the coverlet and rose from the bed. Cursing the tremble in his legs and his throbbing cock, he snatched up his discarded shirt and yanked it over his head.

"Was that part of the ruse as well?" she asked behind him. He turned to find her propped on one elbow, looking thoroughly ravished. Her hair was a riot of russet waves, her lips swollen and glistening from their kiss. Her rapid breaths pushed her breasts against the thin chemise, which hung somewhat askew from her shoulders.

"Bloody hell, Elaine," he rasped. "I dinnae ken. Something powerful burns between us, but that doesnae mean—"

"Then why would we both regret where we were headed?"

He cursed again, raking his hair away from his forehead. "Ye dinnae understand of what ye speak. Ye dinnae ken the consequences of what we were about."

That damned hurt look flickered in her vibrant eyes again, and it was like a knife to his chest.

"I may be innocent, but I am not a child, nor an idiot. I…" She swallowed hard, her cheeks flushing. "I want you."

He let a long breath go. Good God, what was she doing to him? "Ye ken I want ye, too," he replied at last, keeping his voice low. "But there are far greater things at stake than our desire. We must remain focused on the mission—and the threat from de Soules."

She sat up, pulling the coverlet over her chest. "Aye, but you'll forgive me for being confused as to where you draw the line between the task of pretending to desire me and your true feelings."

She was right, damn it. There was naught he could say, for he'd agreed to this ruse, yet he'd also initiated that blazing kiss.

And the shameful truth was, when she'd first proclaimed her love, he'd wanted it to be real. Some irrational part of him didn't *want* it to be a ruse at all.

But while their desire was genuine, her feelings weren't —she'd admitted it had been a lie.

He should be glad, for it made matters simpler, but instead his chest ached and his thoughts swirled in confusion. So all he said was, "Dress yerself. We cannae keep the King waiting."

He knew even before he saw her eyes fill with frustrated tears that he was being an arse. She was not some cheap whore to be tumbled and then kicked out of bed. Nay, she was a lady, and what was more, a soulful, spirited, deeply feeling woman.

But she was not his, regardless of the ruse they had to maintain or the undeniable heat that crackled between them.

As he threw the extra length of his plaid over his shoulder and gathered her cloak from the ground, Jerome silently cursed himself up and down. Bloody hell, what had he gotten himself into?

Chapter Eighteen

Though the day was warm and pleasant again, and the landscape verdant and bursting with spring's plentitude, Elaine let it wash over her without enjoying the beauty all around. Her mind was too occupied with chewing on the conversation she'd had with Jerome to pay attention to her surroundings.

His strong, lean body in the saddle behind her was a constant reminder of the longing he'd awoken that morning. But the scorching desire he'd kindled had ended in a blunt assertion that whatever lay between them came second to the task of delivering the Bruce's declaration safely into the hands of the Pope.

Aye, of course it did, but to ferret out whatever William de Soules was about, they had to pretend to be lovers. Yet where was the line between pretend and the truth? She feared the longer this ruse went on, the greater the danger that whatever line lay between the two would be so blurred that she would no longer be able to tell fantasy from reality, hope from truth.

And she didn't think her heart could take such ambiguity. What a tangle they were in.

By the time they halted for the evening, her head ached and her back was stiff from trying not to lean against Jerome's solid chest. He dismounted and lifted her from the saddle. When she looked up at his face, he seemed to be in as foul a mood as she. His brows were lowered into a stern line, as were his lips. The chestnut depths of his eyes were clouded with frustration.

He turned away to see to their horse, so she stood by herself, feeling useless as the servants rapidly erected their camp, the guards set up a perimeter, and the others in the envoy hobbled their animals for the night.

All except William de Soules.

Elaine had watched him as they rode, but he hadn't done aught to indicate he was part of some nefarious scheme against the Bruce. He'd simply kept pace with the others, only speaking to lavish gratitude and respect upon King Philip for his hospitality and aid.

But now as Jerome, Kieran, and the bishop walked their horses to a nearby copse of birch trees, de Soules lingered behind, then peeled away. He guided his horse to the right so that the King's tent, which the servants had just hoisted, blocked Jerome and the others' view of him, then mounted and rode west into the dusky twilight.

Elaine's pulse leapt. Of course, he could simply be seeking some privacy to relieve his bladder or bowels, but why wouldn't he just walk several paces away behind one of the other clumps of birches instead of mounting his horse and riding into the drawing night?

"Jerome!" Elaine hissed, keeping her voice low as he and Kieran returned from hobbling their horses. The bishop had already headed toward his tent, complaining of soreness after two long days of riding.

Kieran shot Jerome a knowing look. "Yer lady isnae easily satisfied, Munro. I though ye were a Highlander, man."

Jerome glared at Kieran, who only barked a laugh and dropped away to see about the evening meal.

"What's wrong?" Jerome asked softly when he reached her. His eyes were unreadable in the falling darkness.

"It's de Soules," she breathed, nodding in the direction he'd gone. "I thought he was hobbling his horse with the rest of you, but then he rode off."

Jerome instantly stiffened, his hand dropping to the pouch on his belt. But the Bruce's declaration must have still been there, for he relaxed a hair's breadth. His eyes scanned the camp, then followed her gaze. "Did he do aught else?"

"Nay, but he made a point of going around the King's tent so as not to draw your attention," she replied. "Then he headed west."

"Mayhap his lands lie that way," he said, though suspicion laced the words.

"Mayhap, but why wouldn't he simply tell someone —anyone—that he was going to check on his estate?"

Jerome let a breath go. "Ye're right, but I cannae go after him now—no' in the dark, with no trail to follow.

If he comes upon me tracking him, he'll ken we are aware that something is afoot."

"What will we do, then?"

"We'll wait," he replied. "I'll make sure I see him return, and mayhap I can ask him a few questions without rousing his suspicion."

She nodded, but unease coiled in her stomach. Never had doing naught felt so daunting.

KING PHILIP WAS in higher spirits that night, so he invited all of them to dine with him in his grand tent. Elaine couldn't help staring. Impossibly, the French King's traveling accommodations were finer and more luxurious than much of what she'd seen at the Bruce's court in Scone.

Dozens of lit candelabras cast a warm glow over the tent's interior, and woven rugs covered the ground. A flap at the back separated the King's bed from the main space, which was filled with a long wooden table that was actually a series of segments fitted together. A dozen chairs upholstered in red velvet circled the table. And atop the table sat gold and silver platters and trays loaded with food.

The food itself was simple, for the traveling cook could only do so much without a proper kitchen. Still, the meats, cheeses, breads, fruits, and roasted vegetables seemed like a veritable feast to Elaine after eating hard tack and salted jerky on the Bonny Berta. What was more, the servants kept their crystalline goblets full with rich French wine, under the King's proud surveillance.

When the meal was completed, King Philip insisted that they all take their chairs outside. He'd ordered that a large fire be built so that they might linger together before retiring for the evening.

How surreal her life had become, Elaine mused as she leaned forward in her chair to extend her hands toward the warm flames. Only a sennight ago, she had met the King of Scotland, and now she was seated across the fire from the King of France.

Jerome had carefully placed himself at her side. Despite the air of cool detachment that had hung over them all day, they still needed to maintain appearances before the others.

The King arranged his blue velvet cloak around his shoulders as he eased back in his ornately carved chair. His dark eyes danced with the firelight as he gazed at Elaine and Jerome.

"I hope my interruption this morn did not lead to a lovers' spat, *mes amis*," he said casually. "You two have seemed prickly all day."

Elaine pressed her lips together against an unladylike curse. So much for maintaining their ruse. The King had clearly picked up on the tension between her and Jerome. At least he assumed it was a lovers' quarrel rather than a crack in their farcical relationship.

Kieran snorted, casting them a rueful look.

"I ken one remedy for such a tiff. Munro, why dinnae ye take yer lass back to yer tent and—"

"Shut yer mouth, MacAdams," Jerome snapped. His

dark gaze flashed to Elaine, and she understood the bind he was in. He longed to escape to their tent to avoid further scrutiny from the King and Kieran, but to catch de Soules returning from wherever he'd slipped off to, he needed to linger out here.

"I wish to stay by the fire," she said airily, casting Jerome a faux-haughty glance. Though it meant more humiliation, it was better to let the others think they were squabbling.

Kieran snorted again and the King chuckled.

"I am so glad you have accompanied us, Lady Elaine," King Philip said. "This journey would have been far duller without you, as I'm sure Munro here will agree."

At Jerome's flat look, the King held up his hands, a broad smile on his face. "Peace, man. Though I tend to agree with MacAdams about how to soothe the sting of a lovers' quarrel—" a wicked, mirthful glint lit his eyes at that "—I am wise enough to know it is not another man's place—even a King's—to interfere in matters of the heart."

King Philip sighed, settling deeper into his chair. "In truth, I must thank you, for you have provided much diversion and entertainment on the journey thus far. Your presence has been a welcome distraction from the burdens of a King. I have only just secured a tentative peace with Flanders, and now the Pope wishes for me to launch a new crusade in the Holy Land. And Edward II refuses to play his part."

"I didn't realize Kings had to pay homage to each other," Elaine said, grateful for the shift in conversation.

King Philip waved a hand. "When it comes to matters of money, land, and power, things grow complicated quickly. Edward is not only King of England, but also holds the title of Duke of Guyenne here in France. As such, he is my subject, and beholden to pay homage to me. Yet he refuses."

"What will you do, Majesty?" Elaine asked tentatively. The King had been relaxed and forthcoming with them all evening, yet it seemed outlandish to question a sovereign thus.

To her relief, he lifted his ermine-covered shoulders in a casual shrug. "I admire the leeway and power King Robert gives his nobles," he said, nodding to Jerome. "The declaration you carry proves how much he values their free and willing support."

"Indeed, Majesty," Jerome replied.

The King's eyes turned sharp. "Though I respect the Bruce's approach, I am not inclined to follow suit. I wish to bring Edward to heel, yet unlike King Robert, I cannot simply declare war with him for misbehaving." His teeth flashed in the firelight. "But I *can* punish Edward by aiding Scotland's freedom efforts."

"The enemy of our enemy can make a fine friend," Kieran said.

The King chuckled. "I appreciate you Scots' plain speaking—and your King's blunt actions. In fact, I aim to be bolder, like him." He spread his arms wide. "That is one reason why I decided to escort you to Paris. I am getting a small taste of what it was like for him in his army camp, am I not?"

Kieran barked a laugh. "I wouldnae exactly call this

an army camp, but then again, I dinnae ken how many rulers sit gabbing around a fire with glorified messengers."

Elaine stiffened at Kieran's brusque reply, but true to his word, King Philip only seemed amused by the High-lander's bluntness.

But then the King turned his intelligent gaze on her, and her pulse leapt.

"And what of you, Lady Elaine? You speak as if the Bruce is your King as well, yet your English accent is unmistakable. Will you not take up King Edward's defense?"

"Nay, Majesty," she replied. "For Edward is no longer my King. He ceded the Borderlands, where I grew up, to the Bruce several years ago—and blessedly so, for now we know peace and prosperity, where once we only knew war and destruction."

King Philip nodded thoughtfully. "And so the Bruce has won over not only your lands, but your loyalty as well."

"Aye, Majesty. And if there were a place in the Bruce's cause for an English lady like me with no special gifts or talents, only deep devotion and abiding belief in the fight for freedom, I would gladly give not only my loyalty but my life to Scotland."

The King dipped his head to her. "I applaud you, *mademoiselle*. Such conviction for a young woman. And now I am doubly envious of the Bruce, for he is not only bold and battle-tested, but he has won the devotion of both his nobles and fair English ladies alike!"

Kieran grunted in amusement, and even Jerome's

mouth quirked. The King leaned back in his chair once more, clearly pleased.

"Most diverting company, indeed," he said, smiling. "Sir William will be sore he missed such an agreeable evening."

Nerves spiked in Elaine's stomach. Her gaze darted to Jerome. He gave her a look that wordlessly told her to play along with him.

"I dinnae doubt he will regret his departure," Jerome said casually. "But when I saw him ride off headed west, I assumed he wished to see to his estate. An unfortunate but necessary interruption from a fine evening."

The King's brows drew together. "I am afraid you are showing your ignorance of French geography, *mon ami*. It is true, we are in Picardy, which is where Sir William owns land, but his holding is a day's ride east of here, not west."

Elaine clamped her lips shut to prevent from gasping. The King had just confirmed what they'd both suspected. William de Soules was clearly up to something tonight.

"Ah, my mistake," Jerome said, his voice low and soft.

Kieran was frowning across the fire at Jerome. "I had assumed de Soules had merely retired to his tent like Bishop Kininmund," he commented. "Ye didnae tell me ye saw him ride away."

Jerome lifted one shoulder in an indifferent shrug. "As I said, I assumed he was visiting his lands. Mayhap he sought some...*other* diversion."

Elaine didn't miss the implication in Jerome's words, nor his subtle attempt to redirect Kieran's attention.

The King chortled. "There are certainly plenty of pleasures to indulge here in France. I hope he is enjoying his time here."

Elaine would have expected Kieran to bark a laugh at the King's ribald insinuation, yet the Highlander still stared at Jerome with a scrutinizing frown on his face. Rising worry tightened her throat. As far as she knew, Kieran had no part in whatever de Brechin and de Soules planned, yet she couldn't be entirely sure. And even if he were innocent of their schemes, it was best not to raise his suspicions regarding what she and Jerome were about.

She had to act fast to disrupt this conversation.

"I am beginning to understand that the French value pleasure in all areas of life," she interjected. "Food, wine, good conversation…"

The King turned to her, his gaze flicking meaning-fully to Jerome. "And of course most importantly in a lover's arms."

Elaine repressed a curse. Still, speaking of her fabricated love affair with Jerome was a safer topic than de Soules. She lowered her eyes demurely. "Of course, Majesty, but a lady doesn't speak of such things. Tell me, will I find conversation at your court in Paris so scandalous?"

King Philip's eyes glittered with merriment. "Oh, indeed, *mademoiselle*. I dare say you will be shocked by our *joie de vivre*."

The King began regaling them with tales of life at

the French court. Though some of the stories made her face heat with modest shock, it seemed that de Soules's whereabouts were forgotten for the evening.

When the fire burned low, the King stood and stretched. "You will experience the wonders of life at court soon enough, *mes amis*," he said. "But not unless we ride swiftly tomorrow and the next day—which means it is time to say *bonsoir*."

As he shuffled back toward his tent, Kieran rose slowly. "I suppose I will be off, as well," he said, though Elaine didn't miss the searching look he cast once more at Jerome. Kieran lingered for a moment, but then stepped into the surrounding darkness toward his tent.

When they were alone at last, she turned to meet Jerome's serious gaze.

"How much longer must we wait for de Soules?" she whispered.

"As long as it takes. But ye should get some rest."

She blinked. "I am as much a part of this as you are."

"Aye," he replied, sounding tired. "But we neednae both stay up all night. Ye are a strong rider, but I can tell that ye are saddle-weary."

In truth, she wasn't so much achy from riding as she was from trying to hold herself apart from Jerome in the saddle. The way her bottom bounced in his lap and her legs dangled over his powerful, plaid-covered thighs atop his horse was downright mind-addling. Her back and shoulders were a ball of tension from such close proximity to him.

"Aye, well…" She was saved from having to form a

reply by the sound of an approaching rider. At the very edges of the light cast from the dying fire, she spotted de Soules dismounting and guiding his horse to where the others were hobbled.

Jerome must have followed her gaze, for he rose suddenly.

"Dinnae fight me on this, Elaine," he said tightly. "Go back to the tent. I'll speak with de Soules."

She rose and reluctantly turned toward their tent, which the King had again placed farther away from the others. Before she moved off, however, she caught his arm.

He froze, and she could feel the coiling strength in the taut muscles of his forearm.

"Be careful," she breathed.

He gave her a nod, but then to her surprise, he dipped his head and brushed his lips against hers. Before she knew what had happened, he'd slipped away into the darkness toward de Soules, leaving her to pick her way back to their tent, her mind swirling with renewed confusion and his soft kiss burning her lips.

Chapter Nineteen

Jerome tried to push all thoughts of Elaine out of his head as he strode toward de Soules. Damn it all, why had he kissed her? There had been no one to see it, no excuse to pretend to be lovers. Yet her slightest touch left him dunderheaded, so he'd acted on instinct.

He had to stop mooning over her and come up with a way to approach de Soules without raising his suspicions—and fast. Just as de Soules turned to him, squinting through the dark, an idea came to him.

He slowed his steps, dragging his feet through the grass and letting his body sway.

"De Soules?" he said, slurring his speech. "Is that ye, man?"

"Munro," de Soules replied coolly, the tension in his shoulders visibly relaxing. "What are ye still doing up?"

"Needed to piss," Jerome said, stumbling to a halt

before de Soules. "My God, man, ye missed a hell of a night. King Philip invited us to dine in his tent, and let me tell ye, he was more than generous with that wine of his."

A slow smirk pulled at de Soules's mouth.

Good. Jerome had the man right where he wanted him—thinking Jerome was drunk, inattentive, and unaware of what de Soules was about.

"Aye, these French treat their wine like ye Highlanders treat yer whisky," he said. "They take great pride in its strength." He began to sidestep around Jerome, but Jerome pretended to stumble and catch himself on de Soules's shoulder.

"I'll tell ye this much," Jerome went on, swaying slightly. "I've never kenned a Highlander to be so generous with his whisky as King Philip was with his wine. Every time I looked, my goblet had magically refilled itself. Ye should have been here, man."

Though he kept his body loose and his words thick, Jerome sharpened his gaze on de Soules. Even in the low light, he could see de Soules considering his next words carefully.

"Aye, well," he began slowly. "What with my estate in this area, I felt bound to check on things."

Jerome grunted in understanding. "Of course, ye must see to yer responsibilities." He cocked his head as if remembering something. "But I thought the King mentioned that we wouldnae be close enough to yer lands to allow ye a visit."

Beneath his hand, which still rested on de Soules's

shoulder, he felt the man stiffen. The silence stretched for a heartbeat, then two.

"It seems ye caught me, Munro," de Soules said at last.

Jerome's blood turned to ice. Somehow, he willed himself to maintain his drunken act. His sword was still strapped to his belt—next to the Bruce's declaration. If he had to, he could draw his blade like lightning, but not unless de Soules made the first move.

"Ye are right, I didnae go to my estate," de Soules continued, his voice even.

"Nay?" Jerome replied, feigning confusion. "Where were ye, then?"

"Come, Munro," de Soules coaxed, "what do ye think? I went looking for a whore."

Jerome turned his sharp exhale into a chuckle. "Oh, aye? Ye couldnae simply wait to reach the French court, where I'm sure a chamber maid or widowed noble-woman would gladly lift her skirts?"

De Soules chuckled tightly. "Ah, I think ye forget that the rest of us dinnae have a bonny lass bouncing in our laps all day—and warming our cots all night. Ye cannae fault me for wanting a wee bit of pleasure, too."

Red rage crashed over him at the comparison de Soules was drawing between Elaine and the whore he claimed to have sought that night, but Jerome tamped it down. He needed to keep his wits about him if he were to draw aught of use from de Soules.

He forced himself to make a sound of amusement. "Aye, well, ye have me there. Still, ye missed a most enjoyable evening. While ye were wiling away yer night in Amiens with some whore, we were dining with the King of France himself!"

Though King Philip had chided Jerome for his lack of knowledge about French geography, he knew enough to be certain the town of Amiens lay roughly east of where they were camped—the opposite direction Elaine had seen de Soules headed.

Jerome's past had made him careful. Aye, he was quick to anger when he believed those to whom he'd pledged his fidelity were threatened—and even quicker when his loyalty came into question. Yet his father's actions had taught him to be wary of jumping to conclusions—and declaring others guilty by association.

He believed what Elaine had overheard, that de Soules was involved in some plot to countermand the Bruce's efforts. But it was possible that de Soules truly had simply slipped away to visit a whore, which would put them no closer to learning what he schemed. Jerome wanted de Soules himself to prove his guilt. So he laid a careful trap, waiting for de Soules to lie again.

Just as Jerome suspected, de Soules took his bait without blinking an eye.

"Mayhap ye wouldnae be dallying with that English chit if ye kenned what these French whores are capable of," he said.

Jerome ignored the fury that once again roared in his veins. De Soules hadn't refuted his comment about riding to Amiens. It was enough to set off the warning bells in Jerome's head.

Yet confirmation that de Soules schemed something wasn't enough. The man had yet to make a move against Jerome, either to steal the Bruce's declaration or ensure that Jerome wouldn't get in his way if he did. Damn it all, he needed more information.

But it seemed he wouldn't get it tonight. De Soules moved away, and Jerome couldn't halt him again without drawing suspicion.

"Speaking of yer English chit," de Soules said, stepping around Jerome. "Ye'd better piss quick and be back to her, else she may go looking in MacAdams's tent for another Highlander to scratch the itch, eh Munro?"

Despite the burning rage clawing up Jerome's throat, he forced himself to chuckle and stumble off into the copse of birches. He hummed a tune as he pretended to relieve his bladder, all the while listening to de Soules retreat to the camp and enter his tent with a soft rustle of canvas.

When he was sure de Soules wasn't coming back out, Jerome quickly rifled through the man's saddlebags, for he'd hobbled his horse but left his saddle on the ground nearby—likely because of Jerome's distraction.

Naught of interest lay inside, however. With a soft curse, Jerome strode back to his and Elaine's tent. He doubted she had done as he'd ordered and gone to sleep already, but he was glad, for repeating to her what de Soules had said would help him think through the man's words and consider their implications. Elaine was smart and observant. Mayhap she would notice something he hadn't.

The thought surprised him. He hadn't placed his faith in anyone since his father's betrayal of their Laird fourteen years past. Yet in the space of little over a fortnight, Elaine had managed to earn his trust.

Aye, just as she'd said, she was as much a part of this mess as he was. They were in it together now.

Chapter Twenty

Elaine stifled yet another yawn despite the midday sun shining brightly overhead.

When she'd returned to the tent last night, it had already been late. But she hadn't been able to sleep knowing Jerome was speaking with de Soules, and then when he returned, she'd listened eagerly as he'd recounted their conversation.

Even once Jerome had settled himself on the ground next to the cot and she'd pulled the coverlet over herself, sleep had eluded her. Like Jerome, she was frustrated not to have learned more about de Soules's motives or aims, yet though she'd tumbled his words over and over in her mind, no answers had presented themselves.

"Rest against me."

She started mid-yawn when Jerome's gruff, low voice rumbled through her. They swayed together with his horse's steps, she perched across his lap and he with both arms encircling her so that he could hold the reins.

She had already given up yesterday's effort to put even a hair's breadth of space between them. Today, she was too tired to care.

And besides, the tension that had crackled in the air around them yesterday had apparently fizzled away now that they were both so focused on unraveling de Soules's scheme. She hadn't forgotten the fact that he'd rebuffed her, yet his suggestion now to lean against him and take some rest seemed a peace offering of sorts.

Gratefully, she eased back against his chest, her head fitting beneath his chin and her shoulder tucking under his arm.

"Ye'll run yerself ragged if ye arenae careful." The words were spoken so low that she felt more than heard them where her ear pressed against the base of his throat.

"I can't help it," she murmured. "I can't stop thinking about what de Soules could be about. If he wants to steal the Bruce's declaration, why hasn't he made a move yet?"

"I dinnae ken," he replied. "Mayhap he plans to wait until we are closer to Avignon. Or mayhap he doesnae wish to steal it at all and is scheming something else."

"And why did he slip off last night?" she continued, casting her gaze on de Soules's back. He rode Kieran and the bishop behind the King. Though the guards rode on either side of Jerome's horse, there was no chance she could be overheard, what with the rumble of the wagons behind them.

"Might he have been meeting with another conspirator? And if so, who?"

She felt Jerome shake his head slightly. "Good questions, all, lass, but we simply dinnae ken enough to answer them. I ken ye dinnae like it, but all we can do is continue to wait and stay alert."

But her tired mind could not drop the matter, so she went back over the words she'd overheard in Scone. Though no new insights miraculously came, one tidbit niggled at her.

"De Brechin called you the Munro lapdog. What does that mean?"

He stiffened, and she drew back her head to look at him. She found his jaw clenched and a muscle jumping behind the dark stubble on his cheek. He stared forward, his eyes hard and flat.

"'Lapdog' isnae new, though they usually call me the Munro hound—behind my back, of course."

Ire rolled off him just as surely as his heat and masculine scent did. This was clearly a delicate subject, but Elaine couldn't help her curiosity. Considering all they'd shared in the last fortnight—intimacies she'd never experienced with another man—she knew little of Jerome's life outside this mission for the Bruce, and even less about his past.

"Why?" she asked tentatively.

He remained silent so long that she thought he would refuse to answer. But when she settled her head against his chest once more, he spoke.

"I am known to be loyal to my Laird—to the point of being rabid, some say."

"Oh?" she murmured. "And why is that such a bad thing?"

"It isnae—no' in most circumstances, anyway. My reputation for fiercely protecting my Laird is why the Bruce brought me into his Bodyguard Corps. And why I was selected for this mission. He and my Laird decided —rightly—that my loyalty could be harnessed for the larger cause."

"I still don't understand," she said carefully. "Hound, lapdog—the epithets clearly bother you, but why?"

He let a slow breath go. "Because most who throw around such descriptions dinnae ken why I am this way."

Elaine waited, listening to the steady thrum of Jerome's pulse beneath her ear. Though tension still radiated from him, his heart beat true. Yet without having to ask, she knew they now skirted a topic which had wounded that strong, noble heart long ago.

She had seen his features harden and a shadow cross his chestnut eyes enough times to know that some unhealed hurt lived deep inside him. He compensated for it with unbending dedication and unquestionable loyalty, yet the wound was still there.

"Tell me," she breathed.

He shifted, and she feared he meant to pull away, but instead he simply lowered his nose to her hair and inhaled deeply.

"Like ye, I grew up surrounded by war and strife," he said at last, his breath stirring the locks at the crown of her head. "But in the Highlands, we were no' only fighting the English, but also each other. When the Bruce crowned himself King in 1306, it divided the country—and many a clan."

She felt her brows furrow. "I didn't realize all of Scotland didn't immediately fall behind the Bruce."

"It nearly tore us apart. Many Scots had supported King John Balliol, the Bruce's predecessor, despite the fact that he'd practically been selected by King Edward I and was little more than England's puppet. But there is a certain security in kenning who yer master is. Freedom is far harder—and more dangerous."

"And some Scots wished for Balliol over the Bruce?"

"Och, nay, Balliol was deposed back in 1296. Of course, this was all well before yer time, and nearly before mine as well, so I am no' surprised ye dinnae ken about all the tangled knots in Scotland's history, but we Scots tend to have long memories—and hold grudges."

A smile curled her lips. "But I want to know. Scotland is my adoptive country now."

He chuckled softly. "I'll give ye the short version for now. Before Balliol, King Alexander III was Scotland's King. When he died, there wasnae a clear line of succession, and several rivals competed for the crown—including the Bruce. But Edward I hand-selected Balliol kenning he would be easily controlled, making Scotland more a vassal state under English control than a sovereign country in its own right. We called Balliol Toom Tabard—'empty coat,' for he was naught more than Edward's puppet."

"Then how was he deposed?"

"Scotland's nobles and lairds rose up against Balliol

and established a council of twelve men to lead the country instead. But of course Edward didnae like that, so he launched the first of his wars against us. With his puppet King Balliol abdicated and held in the Tower of London, Edward sought to make himself King of Scotland—and bring us to our knees as his subjects. But as I'm sure ye ken by now, Scots dinnae like being told what to do. So we rose up. William Wallace was one of the first to show us that we could fight for our freedom—and mayhap even win."

"I've heard tales of him," Elaine interjected.

"Aye, he was the stuff of legends, but even he eventually fell to the English. Still, we fought on, despite no' having a King of our own—until the Bruce crowned himself and began mounting a true effort for freedom."

"And some didn't like that."

"A few Scots remained loyal to Balliol even after he was removed, for they saw rule by the English as a better alternative to the messy, complicated prospect of true independence. Though Balliol wasnae an option anymore, those who'd stood behind him tried to argue their own claim to the Scottish throne. John the Red Comyn was one such claimant, and a Balliol sympathizer. But just before the Bruce took the crown, he killed Comyn."

"What?" How had Elaine never heard stories of *that*?

Jerome sighed. "No one truly kens what happened, for they were alone in a church together. They were meeting to discuss the Red Comyn's support of the Bruce's impending reign, but apparently Comyn reneged on his word and withdrew his support. Things escalated, they fought, and Comyn ended up dead. The Pope excommunicated the Bruce for killing before the altar. That's one of the many reasons why the Bruce's petition to the Pope now to acknowledge Scotland's sovereignty and the Bruce's claim as King is so important," he said, his hand unconsciously dropping to the pouch where the declaration lay.

Elaine chewed on all this information for a long moment.

How little she truly knew about the intricate and chaotic machinations of war, politics, and power, she realized. For so long, she'd idolized the Bruce's cause, thinking it pure in its quest for freedom. But now she saw that such simplicity was childish and naïve.

Of course there had been strife and struggle along the way. It didn't change her belief in the rightness of the Bruce's efforts, but rather cast a new light under which to examine herself. Things were so much more complicated than she had ever thought when she'd dreamed of joining the cause. Yet if she wished to leave such naïveté behind, she had to be willing to see all the shades of gray in the world.

When the silence stretched, a question rose to her lips. "And...and what does this have to do with you? Certainly you were too young when all this happened to have played a part in it."

She felt Jerome's throat bob with a hard swallow. "Aye, I was only fourteen when the Bruce killed Comyn and crowned himself King. But as I said, many clans were nearly ripped asunder disputing whether to support the Bruce or the Comyns and others who declared that they had a claim to the throne. Many felt that the Bruce's acts against the Red Comyn were enough to warrant his death."

"And the Munros were one such divided clan?"

Jerome gave a curt nod. "Our Laird, Donald Munro, decided to throw his support behind the Bruce. It was our first real chance at freedom, and though the Bruce had made mistakes, Laird Munro believed the man to be an honorable, worthy King. But my father, Owen, argued that the clan should back the Comyns, who, like Balliol, would have acquiesced to English control. My father and the Laird fought—to the point that my father challenged Donald for leadership of the clan."

Elaine pulled in a breath. "And was he successful?"

"Nay." The word was spoken through gritted teeth. "Owen failed. The clan remained loyal to Donald, and my father was banished from Munro lands."

"Were…were you banished as well?"

"My mother, older brother, and I were permitted to stay—on the condition that we couldnae have further contact with my father. For a few months, it seemed the matter was resolved. We tried to rebuild our lives, to live peacefully amongst the clan. But Owen wouldnae let the matter go."

Jerome drew in a deep breath, as if steeling himself for what he was about to say. Elaine stiffened, waiting.

"Owen snuck back to Munro lands one day while the Laird and his young son, George, were out on a hunt. Owen kidnapped George and slipped away. He sent Laird Munro a missive with his demands—namely, that George wouldnae be released until Donald dropped his support for the Bruce and pledged the clan to the Comyns' claim."

"Did your Laird acquiesce?"

"Nay," Jerome said, his voice as sharp and flat as a blade. "Laird Munro understood he had to put what was best for his clan over all else—even his family. But he launched a search party for Owen and George. They hunted them down across half the bloody Highlands, but at last they found my father and the lad. Yet even cornered and outnumbered, my father still wouldnae yield. There was a scuffle and—"

His deep voice caught in his throat. He swallowed again before going on.

"And the lad was killed. My father was taken alive to face his crimes before the Laird. Owen couldnae deny what he'd done, of course—to the very end, he believed he was doing what was best for our clan, even in killing the Laird's son. George had only been eight summers old."

Sickness roiled in Elaine's stomach even as tears burned her eyes. "And...and what of your father?"

"He was given a traitor's death, which he deserved, but that wasnae all. My brother, Tavish, had apparently been in contact with Owen. Tavish had been the one to tell my father that the Laird and his son would be out on a hunt. The clan demanded that Tavish pay for the loss of the Laird's son as well. So Tavish was hanged."

"Oh, God." Elaine's heart shattered for Jerome. Tears streamed down her cheeks unchecked. "To lose your father and your brother..."

"The clan wanted my head as well." Jerome's voice

EMMA PRINCE

was emotionless, as if he were speaking of someone else, someone from another time whose pains and losses were not his own.

"Why? What could you have possibly done to deserve punishment?"

"Many thought I might have been a part of my father's schemes and aided him, as Tavish had," Jerome replied flatly. "Tavish was eighteen, a man grown in the eyes of the clan. And he'd knowingly helped my father even after Owen had been banished. I hadnae kenned what Owen and Tavish were about, but I was fourteen—still a lad in many ways, but in the Highlands, I was considered old enough to be held accountable for my family's actions."

Jerome's chest rose and fell with a deep breath, and when he spoke again, the frost in his voice began to thaw. "But Laird Munro defended me. He believed in my innocence and refused to adhere to the clan's calls to punish me. I dinnae ken how much of that was because he was still grieving the loss of his own son, but he took me under his wing, put his faith in me. And when my mother died less than a year later—some said out of grief for losing both her husband and her eldest son— the Laird became my only family."

Elaine lifted her head from Jerome's chest so that she could meet his eyes. She finally understood the pain that lurked in their dark depths.

"That is why you are so loyal to your Laird," she said, her voice thick and low with emotion. "He saved you."

The corners of Jerome's mouth tightened ever so

slightly. "Aye, I pledged my life to serve him—and the Bruce, for my loyalty to clan and country are cut from the same cloth. But it is more than that. I willnae give anyone reason to question my allegiance again. I am the son of a traitor and a murderer. I cannae change that, but I damn well intend to ensure that I can never be accused of the same."

She rested her hand over his heart. "But how could anyone blame you for the sins of your father?"

"As I said, we Scots have long memories—and cling to our grudges. Even the slightest slipup, a hesitation or wee error could destroy all that I've worked for these past fourteen years."

Realization struck her like a blow to the gut. "That is why this mission is so important to you—because you are treating it as some sort of test, and if you fail in any way, you think you'll be branded a traitor."

Her words must have struck a nerve, for his eyes flashed with frustration. "Everything is a test. My whole bloody life is a test to prove that I am no' like my father, and one misstep would be my ruination."

"The Bruce chose you for this assignment because he already trusts you," she countered.

"Aye, and Laird Munro trusted my father—until he betrayed him. Dinnae ye see, Elaine? The past is never over and done with. It hounds me at every moment, waiting to drag me back into its jaws."

Another realization came on the heels of the first. "And that is why you rebuffed me the other night. You will not let yourself feel aught for me because you are afraid…afraid I'll distract you or cause you to fail somehow, is that it?"

The words brought a wave of emotion rising in her throat, but they had to be said. For the terrible truth was, Elaine had begun to fall in love with Jerome—and not for show, not for the sake of fooling the others or catching de Soules in his scheme.

It was as delicate as the first budding flowers of spring, yet the feeling was undeniable. He was honorable and protective, brave and noble of heart. And his touch, his gaze, even his mere presence stirred something deep in her very soul.

But was she dooming herself to a shattered heart by falling for a man who refused to care for her in return?

He met her gaze, his eyes hard as stone. "Aye," he said. "That is the bald truth—there isnae room in my life for ye, and there never will be."

She sucked in a pained breath, but he went on, his words like a knife to her chest.

"My dedication to clan and country will always come first, for naught will ever be more important to me than proving my loyalty."

"And this?" she breathed. "What are we, then?"

His eyes flickered with some unreadable emotion before he shuttered them once more. "We had a dalliance at Trellham and Scone. It cannae be more than that."

Some part of her screamed that he was lying, that she knew he'd felt the same spark when they kissed, the same ache when they were apart. Yet she was already in danger of losing her heart. She could not risk more.

She ripped her gaze away from his, silently cursing herself. She'd been so determined to prove herself as well, to show that she wasn't some silly chit only good for coddling. And then she'd gone and fallen for the first man she'd ever kissed, a man who was so haunted by his past that he could not see what was right in front of him.

"I-I understand now," she willed herself to say past the tightness in her throat.

Just as she lifted a hand to swipe at the tears dampening her face, King Philip dropped back and reined his horse alongside theirs.

"Come now," the King chided, a gentle frown on his face. "No more tears, my lovebirds. I do not know what has you quarrelling again, but there is no better remedy than to kiss and make up. You are in France—let yourselves love and be happy."

Dread sank like a stone in her stomach as she dared a glance at Jerome. His jaw was set firmly and his eyes were filled with pained determination. Of course, for this mission he would be willing to kiss her—but naught more. And hadn't she been the one to bind them in this ruse with her foolish declaration of love?

She gave him the barest nod, silently telling him that she would play along—even as a fresh swell of hurt rose in her chest.

He dipped his head until his lips met hers in an achingly tender kiss.

Chapter Twenty-One

Her lips tasted of salty tears. That thought cut through the roaring inside Jerome's head as he kissed Elaine.

Bloody hell, he was making a damn fine mess of things.

He had told her everything. His father. Tavish. George. Laird Munro. Of course, plenty of people in his clan knew what had happened fourteen years past. Word had even spread to a few of their neighbors in the Highlands. Owen Munro's name was synonymous with traitor. And many knew of his one surviving son, the lad who'd grown into a fiercely loyal man determined to prove everyone wrong.

But Jerome had never willingly told anyone what had happened, and why he remained so haunted by his father's legacy. Yet Elaine had been so warm in his arms, and he'd longed to draw her closer, to let her see all the way into his heart.

And it had terrified him. Aye, big-hearted and deeply feeling that she was, she'd understood his pain all too well—he'd seen it in those vibrant, tear-filled blue eyes. Yet she had also been too discerning, too quick to draw the correct conclusion: that he could never outrun the shadow of his past. Which meant despite what he felt for her, she would always come second to his need to prove himself.

It wasn't fair to her. She deserved so much better than that—better than *him*.

Yet some selfish, aching part of him was only too glad for another excuse to be kissing her again. Only for the mission, he told himself. Only to uncover what de Soules plotted.

But in the deepest, darkest corners of his heart, he knew the truth. It was so much more than that with Elaine, curse him to hell.

Like a man dying of thirst, he drank her in, angling his mouth over hers. Unbidden, one of his hands slipped from the reins to cradle the back of her head, his fingers burrowing in her copper tresses. She softened against him, surrendering to the kiss, losing herself in it just as surely as he did.

Whatever burned between them, it wasn't controlled by logic. Nor did thoughts of his duty to King and country cool his longing for her. Even as he fought to build a wall around his heart, to keep her at arm's length for the sake of his mission—and his sanity—he feared it was too late. The stones were already crumbling. His heart was already lost.

King Philip's amused chuckle shattered the moment,

saving him from the dark longing dragging him down-ward. He dropped his hand from Elaine's hair and lifted his mouth, willing his eyes to remain detached as he gazed down at her.

She, however, couldn't mask the storm of emotion playing out on her features. Her guileless eyes met his, and he could clearly see the pain and confusion he'd caused there.

"There, see now?" the King said with a smile. "You make things more complicated than they need to be, *mes amis*. A kiss accomplishes more than a thousand words spoken in frustration."

"Aye, Majesty," Jerome replied, forcing his mouth into a grin.

"Let us stop for a repast and refreshments," the King called to the rest of the party.

The others reined in and dismounted. Jerome care-fully guided his horse to the outskirts of the group to give himself another moment alone with Elaine. He swung from the saddle and helped her down after him.

"Elaine," he began, keeping his voice low. "I hope ye understand that—"

"Munro." Kieran was suddenly at their side, his thick arms crossed over his chest. The man's mouth was turned down and his eyes were narrowed on him.

"What?" Jerome snapped at the giant Highlander.

"I heard ye last night. Talking with de Soules."

Jerome's frustration instantly evaporated, to be replaced with icy trepidation. He felt Elaine stiffen next to him, and he silently prayed she could guard her features.

"Aye, I went to take a piss and came upon him returning to camp." He kept his voice casual, but his gaze sharpened on Kieran.

"I heard ye slurring yer words as if ye were drunk, but when I left ye a moment before by the fire, ye were clear-eyed and had yer wits about ye."

Thus far, Jerome had felt an easy affinity with Kieran. Like him, the man was a Highlander and a warrior. But Kieran's towering height and heavily muscled frame had given Jerome the impression that he wasn't a man of particularly sharp wits or keen observation.

From the look in Kieran's pale blue eyes, Jerome had made a grave error with that assumption.

"Aye, well, I—" Jerome began, but Kieran cut him off.

"Ye arenae telling me something, Munro." His gaze flicked to Elaine. "What are the two of ye about?"

"Naught," Elaine blurted. Jerome barely stifled a curse.

"Oh aye?"

Though Kieran remained rooted in place, Jerome instinctively took a half-step in front of Elaine, shielding her from Kieran's scrutiny with his body.

"Strange," Kieran went on, his voice deceptively easy. "Because I've seen ye casting stares at William de Soules's back for the last two days, and I didnae miss the look that passed between the two of ye last night when the King mentioned de Soules's estate. Then ye pretend to be drunk and try to find out where he was all night."

Sharp apprehension stabbed Jerome's gut. His

instincts told him he could trust Kieran, but if he was wrong, he risked destroying his chance to thwart whatever de Brechin and de Soules plotted. He met Kieran's hard stare, wordlessly urging the man to abandon this line of interrogation.

"I dinnae claim to be a particularly clever man," Kieran continued. "After all, I was only meant to be the muscle on this mission. But ye'd be surprised how much a thickheaded brute can notice when no one is paying him any mind."

Now Kieran dropped all pretense of mildness. His features hardened into a fierce glare.

"But ken this, Munro. If ye do aught—any wee thing—to endanger this mission, ye will regret it. I dinnae ken what ye are about, but I willnae let this go."

Despite the taut antagonism thickening the air, Jerome took strange comfort in Kieran's reaction to the prospect of a threat to the mission. It meant his instincts had been right—Kieran was a man of honor. Yet Jerome couldn't risk getting him involved, for the fewer who knew that some underhanded scheme was afoot, the safer.

"Forget what ye think ye saw and heard," Jerome said, his voice a low warning. "Dinnae entangle yerself in a simple lovers' quarrel—for that is all this is."

Kieran's nostrils flared in frustration. His sharp gaze flicked between Jerome and Elaine once more.

"I'll be watching ye," he said darkly before turning and stomping off toward the rest of their party.

As he left, Elaine let out a slow breath. "He doesn't seem to suspect the truth—yet."

"Aye," Jerome replied. "But I fear it is only a matter of time."

And though it had been a relief to realize that Kieran was just as determined to protect their mission as Jerome was, the last thing they needed was to draw the Highlander's attention.

Which meant they hadn't been careful enough. If Kieran had sensed something was off, it was only a matter of time before de Soules would realize it too.

And when that happened, all could be lost.

Chapter Twenty-Two

Their final day of the journey to Paris passed smoothly—at least on the outside. But on the inside, Elaine fought to tamp down the tempest of emotion that swirled through her.

She had always felt her emotions deeply. Of course, everyone knew she was quick to tears. It was embarrassing to exhibit her feelings so easily for all to see. But it was more than just sadness she displayed readily. Whether it was a blush, a grin, a frown, or tears, her family often said she was like an open book.

Because her father, Rosamond, and Niall had always accepted that she wore her heart on her sleeve, she'd never had to learn to guard her thoughts and feelings. Now she wished she had so that she could match Jerome's stony exterior.

He'd given naught away after they'd kissed to appease King Philip. At least now she understood the shadows she'd seen lurking behind his eyes and why he was determined to push her away even though he couldn't deny the connection between them.

But unless she wanted to make an even greater fool of herself, she had to set aside her feelings for the time being and remain focused on their mission. It was what he had done. She might not be as well-practiced as Jerome, but she refused to collapse into a puddle of her own tears like some overindulged child.

To her surprise, she found comfort in her resolution not to fall apart—and strength. Though it was difficult to share a tent with Jerome for another night, and embarrassing to have to perch on his lap as they rode, all the while pretending to be addlebrained with lovesickness, it was also a relief not to feel controlled by her emotions. As he'd said, there were more important matters at hand than their feelings for each other.

Blessedly, their surroundings provided another distraction as well. By midday on the fourth day of their journey, they'd reached the outskirts of Paris. In the distance, Elaine could see a massive stone wall encircling the city, but apparently its population had grown beyond the capacity of the wall, for they rode between huts and even a few clusters of shops.

The guards were forced to tighten their ranks around the King and the Bruce's envoy as they approached the wall. Even before they reached its towering stone face, they'd drawn the attention of the townspeople, who streamed from their huts and trailed after the King's procession, waving and cheering.

King Philip reached into a pouch dangling from his

jewel-encrusted belt and began tossing coins to the townspeople, much to their excitement.

When they halted in the shadow of the wall, the inlaid wooden gates creaked open. One of the guards must have sent word ahead, for buglers heralded the King's arrival from the wall's battlements, and even more guards were waiting on the other side of the gates.

As they continued on into the heart of the city, Elaine felt her jaw slacken as she took in the sights. She understood now why the city walls could not contain everyone. Inside the walls, the streets were a tangle of cobbled pathways, some wide, but most narrow and winding between dense clusters of buildings. Most of the buildings were three or four storeys tall, with the upper levels overhanding the lower so that the streets seemed dim and even narrower.

At the sound of the bugles, townspeople began streaming toward them, shouting greetings and well-wishes to their King. The already cramped streets were now filled with people and animals alike, for it seemed they'd interrupted several shepherds and farmers on their way to market with their pigs, cattle, sheep, and cartloads of goods.

She was grateful to be seated on Jerome's lap in that moment, for though she considered herself an accomplished rider, she didn't envy his task of keeping the horse calm and guiding it behind the King through the throng of people and animals.

Seemingly unperturbed by all the chaos, King Philip reined his horse next to theirs.

"What do you think of my fine city so far, *mademoiselle*?" he shouted over the noise.

"It is...nigh incomprehensible, Majesty," Elaine replied.

The King grinned. "Your eyes are as round as the moon, Lady Elaine."

"I-I must admit that I have never been in a true city before, Majesty," she said. "Towns and villages, aye, but I have never seen aught like this."

Indeed, the scale of everything was staggering. The cramped streets and looming buildings cut off her sightlines, but as they continued their procession, she realized the city simply continued on and on like that. There must have been tens of thousands of people living within the walls—mayhap even hundreds of thousands.

"What a treasure to have your company, *mademoiselle*," the King said, watching her face with pride and enjoyment. "You give me the opportunity to see my grand city through your fresh eyes. I will greatly enjoy showing you the palace when we arrive."

Elaine nodded, unable to stop staring at her surroundings. As they made their way deeper into the heart of the city, they crossed through another, much less imposing wall that must have once denoted the boundaries of the city when it had been smaller. She noticed that the buildings grew nicer and the people greeting them more finely dressed.

"There is no other place in the world like Paris," the King commented. "For all the world is contained within it. There are so many segments of the city that you can see nearly every walk of life in one place. Do you see the Seine just there?"

He pointed off to the right, and she caught sight of a glittering waterway slicing through the city. "Aye."

"The river divides the city in two. This half represents commerce—merchants, workers, sellers, marketplaces, and the like. You saw the farmers on the outskirts of the wall," he said. "And the poorer workers just inside. Now we are entering the wealthier merchants' quarter. The western bank, on the other hand, is a place of learning. It is where our universities and chapels are built, and where our scholars, scribes, and learned men live."

As they drew closer to the river, the King continued with his exposition. "The eastern side of the river is better for docks and ports as well, so our merchant ships can sail all the way to Flanders and south to Orléans."

Elaine nodded, but her gaze was fixed on a large island in the middle of the river that forced the waters to fork. Another stone wall circled the island. Above it rose several buildings—a square tower keep, a spired chapel, and a massive double-towered cathedral.

"Ah, I see you have noticed the *Île de la Cité*, the Island of Paris. My ancestor, King Philip II, built the fortress just there, called the Louvre." The King gestured up the bank of the river toward a massive stone structure, squat and fierce-looking. "He meant for it to protect France's Kings against English attack, but alas, it was more stronghold than palace. So my father, Philip IV, transformed the island before you into a palace fit for a King."

Their horses mounted an arching stone bridge leading from the east bank onto the island.

"It is my pleasure to welcome you to the *Palais de la Cité*, the Royal Palace," the King said proudly.

As they crossed through the island-palace's walls, Elaine looked left, toward the enormous cathedral. She caught a glimpse of its double-towered façade and the sparkling, multi-colored stained glass filling its vaulted windows.

"That is Notre-Dame," the King said, following her gaze. "Just as I said, Paris is a collection of segments, many parts to make a whole. The island is divided in two. To the south is the seat of God. Our bishops live and do God's work there. And the northern half of the island is the seat of government." He swept a hand to the right, at the massive palace, with multiple towers connected by lower buildings. "This is my domain, where I rule surrounded by my people and with God at my side."

"Commerce, learning, government, and the Church," Jerome commented behind Elaine. "All the cornerstones of civilization, wedged side by side in one city."

The King beamed. "*C'est exactement*, Munro. You will not find a finer city in all the world."

"If ye dinnae mind, Majesty," Bishop Kininmund said, bringing his horse to a halt as the others began turning toward the palace. "I am most eager to pay a visit to Notre-Dame, and to speak with yer other bishops."

"Of course," the King replied, giving the bishop a respectful tilt of the head.

The bishop peeled off from the group while the others dismounted. Their arrival hadn't gone unnoticed, for servants streamed forward, taking their horses and beginning to unload the supply wagons that had trailed their procession.

"Come," King Philip urged. "You will have plenty of time to rest and refresh yourselves, but since you are my esteemed guests, allow me to show you a bit of the palace first."

There was no saying no to a King, so despite how grimy and rumpled she felt from traveling, Elaine fell in behind the others.

Chapter Twenty-Three

As the King showed them ceremonial halls with stone pillars and vaulted ceilings, a personal chapel, a walled garden and orchard, and even a private dock on the river so that he could sail directly to the Louvre fortress or one of his other residences farther away, Elaine's head began to spin with all the opulence and luxury.

The palace was like a sumptuous sanctuary in the middle of the chaotic city. Everywhere she looked, she found polished marble, shining gold embellishments, rich tapestries, delicate stained glass, and soaring arched ceilings.

Elaine couldn't have conjured such magnificence even in her wildest dreams. It made her dizzy with its lavishness. How far she'd come from humble Trellham Keep. Though the beauty and riches surrounding her took her breath away, she couldn't ever imagine being truly comfortable living an ordinary life in the midst of such opulence.

Their tour concluded in one of the ceremonial great halls they'd seen earlier. Apparently, the hall was attached to the large square tower, which the King called a *donjon*, that Elaine had seen from the outside earlier.

"Thank you for indulging me," the King said to Elaine. "I can see you are tired, but it gave me pleasure to see the city and palace through your eyes. But now I must play the part of host." He called to a servant at the other end of the hall, who darted toward the spiral stairs which Elaine assumed led to the tower.

In a matter of moments, a flaxen-haired woman dressed in a rich midnight blue silk gown descended from the stairs and glided toward them. As the woman drew nearer, Elaine felt her eyes widen.

She was stunningly beautiful. She wore the sheerest imaginable veil affixed to the crown of her head, but its purpose seemed less for modesty and more to give a glimpse at her blonde tresses, which were piled atop her head in an elaborate system of plaits and curls. Her delicate features remained perfectly smooth even as her dark blue eyes took in the sight of them.

No doubt Elaine looked more than a little bedraggled. She'd weaved her hair into a simple braid for their travels. Her dress, while silk, was badly wrinkled and stained from so many days of riding, and her mud-caked boots appeared to be leaving tracks on the marble floors.

Still, the woman, who looked to be a few years older than Elaine, had refined enough manners not to stare.

Instead, she dipped her head and lowered herself into a curtsy before all of them.

"*Majesté*," she said.

"This is Lady Vivienne, one of my Queen's ladies-in-waiting," the King said with a tilt of his head toward the woman. "Lady Vivienne, these are my honored guests, come all the way from Scotland bearing a communication for the Pope. I wish for them to be made comfortable and happy during their stay at court."

Lady Vivienne rose from her curtsy, her lips curving in a demure smile. "Of course, *Majesté*."

"Kieran MacAdams," the King said, gesturing toward the Highlander. Elaine glanced at him to find his features blank yet his gaze riveted on Lady Vivienne.

"Milady," Kieran said gruffly, sketching the faintest bow without breaking his stare.

"Sir William de Soules."

De Soules made a far more elaborate genuflection. "A pleasure, *mademoiselle*. We are most grateful for your hospitality."

Elaine glanced at Lady Vivienne to see if she would be impressed by de Soules's overdone deference. To her surprise, however, the woman's smile vanished and her large blue eyes grew tight.

"*Oui*," she said vaguely, a thin crease appearing between her perfectly arched brows.

Unease twisted in Elaine's stomach. The lady-in-waiting was clearly accomplished in manners and etiquette. What had caused her to slip when she'd looked upon de Soules?

"And the lovebirds of our party, Jerome Munro and Lady Elaine Beaumore."

Elaine attempted to hide her blush at the King's introduction with a quick duck of her head, but when she lifted it again, she found Lady Vivienne's gaze on her.

"It must have been trying to travel with so many men, Lady Elaine," she said, her voice surprisingly kind. "I assure you that you will find your time here far more comfortable."

"Thank you," Elaine breathed gratefully.

"If you will allow me, I'll show you to your chambers so that you can rest and refresh yourselves." Without waiting, Lady Vivienne turned and began gliding toward the stairs at the back of the hall, her silk skirts rustling softly.

As the four of them fell in behind her, the King called, "Enjoy yourselves, *mes amis*. I will see you on the morrow, for I think I shall retire for the evening. My Queen will wish to welcome me home." His chuckle echoed through the hall even as they mounted the stairs.

At the first landing, Lady Vivienne motioned to a closed door. "Sir William." Elaine didn't miss the tension of her voice. She shot a glance at Jerome, who was also frowning slightly as he watched de Soules bow and slip into the chamber.

They continued higher up the tower, halting at another landing.

"*Monsieur* MacAdams."

"Just Kieran," the Highlander replied, his frown a contrast to the way his gaze latched onto Lady Vivienne.

She tilted her head demurely, then turned away, not waiting for Kieran to see himself in or Elaine and Jerome to follow.

"I hope the King did not give you too hard a time," she commented over her shoulder as she climbed the stairs. "He wishes for everyone to be as in love as he is with the Queen."

Jerome grunted softly. "We noticed."

"He will want you to be comfortable here," Lady Vivienne continued, politely ignoring Jerome's comment. "I hope you find your chamber suitable." She stopped before another door and pushed it open, then stepped aside so that Elaine and Jerome could move in.

Elaine's breath caught in her throat as she took in the chamber. An enormous bed was pushed against the back wall, its posters elaborately carved and hung with heavy burgundy velvet drapes. Despite the bed's size, it only took up a fraction of the space.

A matching oak armoire, dressing table, and chair were carved with the same delicate detail as the posters. There was another table opposite the armoire, this one with writing supplies laid out on it. Tapestries lined the walls, except for one section where a huge hearth was set into the stone, a fire laid and ready to be lit.

The chamber was undeniably luxurious—and clearly meant for a couple. Would Jerome insist on sleeping on the floor beside the bed? Would he turn his back as she changed out of her travel-worn clothes?

"I'll have the servants bring you a bath and a tray of food," Lady Vivienne said. "Once they've finished, you needn't worry about being disturbed for the rest of the evening."

Jerome abruptly moved to the door. "I think I'll go make sure my saddlebags are brought up."

Lady Vivienne drew back her chin in surprise. "The servants will ensure——"

"I'd rather see to it myself," he cut in.

Elaine felt her face heat. After being forced in such close quarters for the last four days—and having to maintain the ruse of their love—no doubt he wished to escape. His thin excuse to fetch his saddlebags made it all too clear that he'd grown weary of playing along.

She cursed the burn of embarrassment rising in her throat and behind her eyes, but she reminded herself not to be foolish.

With a quick nod to Lady Vivienne, Jerome slipped out of the chamber. Lady Vivienne stood frozen for a moment before her courtly manners took over once more. As if Jerome's abrupt departure had been perfectly normal, she moved to the door and called to a servant for food and a bath to be brought up.

Though Elaine assumed the woman had other tasks to see to—she was a lady-in-waiting, after all, not a servant or chamber maid herself—Lady Vivienne lingered, mayhap sensing Elaine's embarrassment at the way Jerome had fled.

As a large wooden tub was rolled in and positioned in the center of the room, Lady Vivienne attempted conversation.

"I hope you will not consider me presumptuous,

Lady Elaine, but I have a gown of green and gold that I think would complement your coloring nicely."

Servants began filing in with buckets of steaming water, and another lit the fire in the hearth. A sudden surge of gratitude hit Elaine like a punch to the gut. She let herself indulge in the simple pleasure of chatting with Lady Vivienne about gowns, the latest fashions for hair, and the Queen's preference for minimal head-dresses.

She'd been so quick to flee Judith and Julia, with their incessant talk of ribbons and fabrics, and had been all too eager to abandon her life at Trellham for the adventure and excitement of the Bruce's court.

Yet now that she was embroiled in a plot against the Bruce, visiting French court under false pretenses, and fighting with all her might against the tangle of emotions she felt for Jerome, she realized she'd too readily discounted all that she'd had before. Aye, it had been a quiet life, but one filled with family, friends, and a comfortable home.

She wasn't sure how she'd ever go back now that she'd seen and done so much. All the same, she felt thankful for this brief respite from the madness of the last few days. And grateful to Lady Vivienne for her companionship. They continued to chat until the tub was full and several soaps, fragrant oils, and drying linens were set beside it. Someone had also placed a tray of food on the desk.

"Allow me to help you out of your gown," Lady Vivienne said.

Elaine turned to let the woman work on her laces.

Though Lady Vivienne clearly possessed polished court etiquette, she couldn't quite suppress a sound of dismay as she peeled away Elaine's much abused gown and chemise.

"I'll just…see that these are taken care of," she said, gathering both garments up.

Elaine scampered to the tub, too shy of her nakedness to feel embarrassed about the state of her travel-worn clothes. She eased into the hot water with a shiver of pleasure.

"Thank you, Lady Vivienne—for everything."

Elaine sank deeper with a sigh. The bath was already heavenly, and she hadn't even sampled the finely milled soaps and scented oils yet. She tipped her head back on the wooden rim, feeling the aches and tensions of the last sennight melt away.

But the sound of Lady Vivienne discreetly opening the chamber door to depart brought her back to reality. Nay, she couldn't simply drift off and pretend that naught was going on.

"Lady Vivienne, wait," Elaine blurted.

"What is it?" the lady-in-waiting said, stepping inside once more.

It was only a faint suspicion, but her instincts told her that there was something significant in the way Lady Vivienne had reacted to being introduced to de Soules.

Elaine drew a breath, taking a moment to choose her words. "You have been most accommodating, Lady Vivienne, and I'm sure you have other duties to attend to besides looking after me. It is just…I couldn't help noticing that you seemed…surprised to see Sir William."

Lady Vivienne closed the chamber door, her blue eyes falling to the floor. "*Oui*. But I know little of Scottish politics. I do not wish to cause unnecessary discord because of my ignorance."

Cold trepidation shot through Elaine. She lifted her head from the tub's rim and plastered a smile on her face that she hoped was disarming. "As you must have noticed, I'm English, not Scottish. I don't concern myself overmuch with politics either, so I'm sure you could never offend me. I was simply...curious about your reaction."

Lady Vivienne walked slowly to the dressing table and set down Elaine's gown and chemise. Her gaze flicked to the door before cautiously returning to Elaine. "You are here on King Robert the Bruce's business, are you not?"

"Aye," Elaine replied, willing her voice to remain light even as foreboding knotted her stomach.

"It is just..." Lady Vivienne swallowed. "I have seen William de Soules before."

"Oh?" Elaine's heart hammered in her ears. "Here in Paris?"

"*Non*. I am from the Picardy region, and I occasionally return home to look in on my father."

Elaine's apprehension abruptly drained away. *Of course.* She had become so suspicious and tightly wound of late that she saw intrigue everywhere—even when it amounted to naught.

"Ah. Sir William owns land in Picardy, does he not?" she asked.

"*Oui*, but…" Lady Vivienne faltered again. "As I said, it is not my place."

Confusion swirled through Elaine once more. It was widely known that de Soules held an estate in Picardy— the Bruce had selected him for his knowledge of France, after all—yet Lady Vivienne's discomfort was palpable. What did she know? And why was she so afraid to say it?

It was time to drop her pretenses of casual interest. Elaine fixed the lady-in-waiting with a steady gaze. "Tell me."

Lady Vivienne clasped her hands before her, hesitating for a long moment. "I know where Sir William's lands are, but that is not where I saw him," she said at last. "I…I saw him paying a visit to…to Château de Hélicourt."

Elaine blinked. Curse her lack of knowledge of French estates! "Forgive me, but I do not know where that is."

Lady Vivienne exhaled slowly. "Sir William's lands lie to the east of Amiens. Château de Hélicourt is an estate in the west."

Amiens. That was the town Jerome had used to test de Soules when he'd claimed to have sought a whore on the second night of their journey. De Soules hadn't refuted Jerome's assertion, despite the fact that he'd ridden in the opposite direction of Amiens—to the west.

"And…" Elaine had to swallow. "And who owns Château de Hélicourt?"

Lady Vivienne reluctantly met Elaine's gaze. "It is owned by the Balliol family."

Elaine sat up so fast that water sloshed over the rim

of the tub. She saw Lady Vivienne's lips part with a gasp, but she couldn't hear the noise over the roaring of her own blood.

Balliol. The deposed King of Scotland who'd reigned before the Bruce. De Soules was visiting his estate.

Elaine's mind flew in several directions at once as she tried to sift through all the implications of this news. She glanced up to find Lady Vivienne staring at her, her beautiful face a mask of worry.

"You were right to tell me," Elaine said. "You did naught wrong."

From the crease in her brow, Lady Vivienne was not convinced, but Elaine couldn't worry about that now.

"I would ask that this stays between us," she went on.

Lady Vivienne nodded reluctantly. "*Oui.* As I said, I do not wish to cause discord."

Elaine snatched up one of the fragrant, creamy bars of soap. Her hopes for a long, luxurious bath were dashed, but she would settle for a rushed scrub knowing what she now did.

"May I ask one last favor of you?" she said, working the soap into a hurried lather.

"*Oui*, what is it?"

"Find Jerome and tell him to come to our chamber with all haste."

Chapter Twenty-Four

Jerome paced the length of the palace's long, well-kept stables, uncaring that he kicked straw as he went.

The grooms had insisted that, as a guest of the King, Jerome needn't bother himself with manual labor, and that his horse would be well looked after. But Jerome hadn't truly come to the stables to shovel shite or even fetch his saddlebags, as he'd told Lady Vivienne.

Coward that he was, he had been attempting to escape. Escape the luxurious chamber, the sight of the wide, decadent bed—and most of all, Elaine.

His control was slipping, damn it all. If he wasn't careful, he'd forget everything he'd worked for, everything that hung in the balance, and lose himself in those vivid blue eyes.

It had been torture these last few days, riding all day with her in his lap and sleeping within arm's reach of her every night—damned delicious torture.

But as they'd ridden into the palace that afternoon, a thought had occurred to Jerome. King Philip would remain here in Paris while the rest of the envoy continued on to Avignon. Which meant that he and Elaine needn't carry on the ruse of their love any longer.

There would be no more reason for Elaine to continue on with them—or even to remain in France. Jerome would have to concoct a way to safely ensure her return to Scone, but every time he thought of sending her away, his mind rebelled.

He told himself it was only because he knew Finn would have his bollocks, followed by his head, if Elaine came to any harm on her way back to Scotland. Whom could Jerome trust other than himself to see her safely home?

But the truth was, it wasn't just an overblown sense of protectiveness that threatened his plans. He didn't *want* to send her away. He didn't *want* to do the right thing, keep his focus on his mission, and put Elaine behind him.

That realization had sent a cold sweat beading on his brow. When his father had turned traitor and nearly destroyed not only Jerome's family but the entire clan, Jerome had sworn never to let aught come before his duty—to his Laird, clan, King, and country. And in the fourteen years since, he hadn't.

Only a few short months after his father's death, Jerome's mother had passed from a failure of the heart. Most in the clan said that the shock of losing both her husband and her eldest son had been too much for her. Ever since then, Jerome had no family other than the clan, no one to come between him and his pledge of loyalty.

And though he had dallied with a few lasses on occasion, he'd never fallen in love, never allowed himself to care, for caring would make him beholden to something other than his duty. Caring could cloud a man's mind and make him throw everything away. Just as his father had done.

The solution was clear. It was time to send Elaine away, to do what he should have done from the start. He would be forever grateful that she uncovered de Soules's plot, but there was no longer any excuse to keep her near—other than his dangerous desire for her. It was for her own protection. And his.

He pivoted at the far end of the stables, determined to end their charade and send her to safety, but the sight at the opposite end had his next step faltering.

Lady Vivienne stood in the stable doorway looking as out of place as a painted doll in the midst of a rubbish heap. Her gaze swept the stalls until it landed on him, and she hesitantly stepped forward.

He strode toward her, halting her progress in the middle.

"What?" he snapped, uncaring that his churlish tone was beyond rude.

Lady Vivienne was at least a head shorter than Jerome, yet at his brusque question she lifted her chin in such a way that she appeared to be staring down at him.

"Lady Elaine requests your presence, *monsieur*," she replied, every inch the proper French lady of court.

Jerome frowned. Had Elaine come to the same

conclusion he had—that their ruse was no longer neces-sary, and it was time she step back from this dangerous situation? Unlikely, knowing her. Well, whatever matter had her sending for him, he would say his piece and put an end to their charade.

"Verra well," he said, sketching the faintest bow and sidestepping Lady Vivienne to avoid any more of her superior looks. But to his surprise, the last glimpse he caught of her face revealed worry more than refined arrogance.

Something was brewing. Elaine had better be well when he reached their chamber, else the King of France himself would answer for aught that happened to her. Jerome stormed out of the stables and toward the sprawling palace like a bull building up speed to charge.

Ignoring guards, servants, and even a few clusters of finely dressed nobles, he plowed through the courtyard and into the great hall toward the stairs leading to his and Elaine's chamber.

When he reached their door, he didn't bother knock-ing. Instead, he barreled in, unsure of what he'd find inside.

He hadn't given himself time to consider what Lady Vivienne's fleeting look of concern could mean, but his mind had conjured vague images of Elaine feeling ill, or worse, de Soules confronting her.

The last thing he'd imagined was to see every sleek, white inch of her stepping from the tub, glistening and bare as a water nymph.

Her head snapped around, her wide blue eyes fixing on him. A wordless gasp rushed past her parted lips as she fumbled to snatch up one of the drying cloths laid nearby.

Like a witless barbarian, Jerome stood frozen, his gaze greedily drinking in the sight of her. Even once she'd covered herself, he remained rooted, the gears of his mind locked motionless as his animal body surged with lust.

"What in…" He swallowed, attempting to clear the thickness from his throat. "What are ye doing, lass?"

"Bathing," she replied in a strangled voice. "Obviously."

"And ye sent Lady Vivienne to fetch me so that I could—what? Watch ye?" Damn him if that didn't sound dangerously alluring. But some sliver of his rational mind that wasn't shrouded in a blinding fog of lust knew Elaine wouldn't attempt so bold a seduction.

"Nay!" she squeaked, confirming his suspicions.

"What then?"

"I…I didn't expect you to arrive so soon." She clutched the length of linen around her middle in a white-knuckled grasp, but it still left her creamy shoulders bare. Her russet locks curled damply there, making her skin look even paler. A flush crept over the tops of her breasts, which rose and fell rapidly just beneath the linen, to her neck and cheeks.

"Aye, well, I have something that needs saying." To steel himself, he crossed his arms over his chest, but his resolve faltered when her gaze slid over him, lingering on his body like a caress. Bloody hell.

Elaine shook her head slightly as if to clear it. "Whatever it is, it can wait. I learned something of grave import and sent Lady Vivienne with all haste to find you."

Some sane part of his brain began to function at last. "What is it?"

Her gaze darted behind him, where he realized the door still stood open. He moved to close it, dropping the bolt as well. "Ye should dress," he commended over his shoulder, at last thinking clearly—or as clear as could be expected with Elaine standing nearly naked behind him.

She didn't respond, but he heard her bare feet padding softly toward the armoire. Its doors creaked open and the rustle of fabric filled the chamber for a moment.

"You can turn around."

When he turned, he found her not dressed in a gown, but rather a delicate chemise with a dressing robe firmly secured over it. He supposed distantly that it had been too much to hope that the armoire would have contained a sensible gown to Elaine's measurements, especially considering this chamber was clearly not meant for sensible activities.

"Now, what did ye learn that was so urgent ye couldnae wait to finish yer bath before summoning me?" he demanded, stalking closer.

She drew in a deep breath. "William de Soules is meeting with Balliol."

Jerome jerked to a halt mid-step. "John Balliol is dead."

Elaine shook her head. "Very well, but de Soules has been visiting Château de Hélicourt, which is owned by the Balliol family. Lady Vivienne has seen him."

The breath rushed from Jerome's lungs as if he'd received a blow. "Edward Balliol, John's son, lives there." Without realizing it, he'd caught the rim of the tub. He clutched the wet wood as his thoughts spun wildly. "Of course. I should have realized it sooner. The Balliols havenae been a consideration for more than a decade, but I should have thought of the fact that John was exiled to France and raised Edward here. If I had been thinking clearly—"

"It doesn't matter now," Elaine cut in. "All that matters is that we know de Soules is working with Balliol. I only wish I knew what that meant."

Jerome glanced up to find her features taut with worry. Though she'd recognized the importance of this new revelation, Elaine wasn't familiar enough with the nature of Scottish politics to understand just how dire things truly were.

He straightened, his voice grim. "It means de Soules isnae trying to steal the Declaration of Arbroath, as we assumed," he said. "He's trying to dethrone Robert the Bruce—and put Edward Balliol in his place."

Chapter Twenty-Five

Elaine pulled in a hard breath. "How can you be so sure?"

Jerome's dark eyes moved restlessly over the ground between them, unseeing in thought. "What other reason would de Soules have to speak with Balliol?" he asked. "And to do so in secret, supposedly while on an assignment for the Bruce?"

"But how can you be sure that Edward Balliol even wants the throne?"

Jerome lifted his head and met her gaze. "John Balliol went quietly enough once England's King Edward turned on him. But some in Scotland will never let go of the idea of ousting the Bruce in favor of an English-sympathizing King. My father is proof of that."

Cold apprehension slithered up her spine, and she pulled her dressing robe closer. Everyone always said that Scots were a stubborn lot unwilling to forgive or forget, but Elaine always took it as a lighthearted jest.

Would some in Scotland truly dethrone their own King in favor of a Balliol even after all this time?

"Unlike his father, Edward Balliol is a grasping man, from what I've heard," Jerome went on. "John was content to take the throne, then cede it and flee to France, but Edward has lived under the shame of his father's failings nigh all his life. We have to assume he is part of de Soules's plan."

It was a shocking yet sound deduction from all Elaine knew. "And de Soules is using this mission as an excuse to be in France. To cover the need to meet with Balliol."

Jerome held her with a grim look. "Aye. And as far as we know, Balliol hasnae turned him away."

Mindlessly, Elaine walked to the large bed and sank down on its edge. "Gracious," she breathed.

"It explains why de Soules hasnae made any move against me or the declaration," Jerome continued. "If he'd truly wanted to destroy it or prevent it from being delivered, he could have stabbed me in the back, or at least attempted to trick me out of it. But the declaration doesnae matter. If aught, it provides a welcome distraction, for while we've all been focused on its safe delivery, he's been working on his true scheme."

"Then...then what do we do?" Elaine asked. Her head spun with the implications of this revelation. When she'd daydreamed about helping the Bruce's cause and leading a life of excitement, never had she imagined being thrown in the midst of an attempt to overthrow the King.

When Jerome didn't answer right away, she looked up to find him watching her, his eyes unreadable.

"*We* arenae going to do aught. Ye need to return to Scotland. I'll handle this."

She bolted up from the bed. "What?"

He closed in on her, encircling her arms with his hands. But though his eyes remained hard, his voice came out surprisingly low and soft.

"Elaine. Ye cannae remain in the middle of this danger. Besides, there isnae a reason anymore to keep pretending we are lovers."

Pretending. The word slid through her ribs and straight into her heart like a dagger. But she couldn't lose her wits to emotion now. Not when so much was at stake.

"You make it sound as though I am naught but a burden, an innocent to protect."

His mouth tightened. "Ye *are* innocent, and ye'd damn well better believe I'll protect ye."

"But you seem to be forgetting that I was the one to alert you to de Soules's scheme," she countered. "I am part of this as much as you, Jerome, remember? I won't simply be shipped back to Scotland as if I'm not."

"That's the problem," he said, his voice drawn. "Ye are a part of this—and I cannae keep ye safe and unravel this plot at the same time."

"Then don't worry about me. I can take care of myself. Let me help you."

"Elaine—"

"Nay," she interrupted feeling her ire rise. "I got myself

safely to France, didn't I? I covered us both with a lie—one that made me look like the most unforgivably foolish girl, I might add. And I've helped you at every step to watch de Soules and gather information. If it weren't for me, you wouldn't even know about him visiting Balliol's estate."

Jerome flinched at that and released her arms. Sensing that she approached a victory, she continued.

"Have you even considered what you would tell King Philip if you sent me back to Scotland while you continued on to Avignon? Or what you'll do with de Soules? How will you get word back to the Bruce about Balliol's plot? And what will you tell him other than the fact that de Soules and Balliol have been meeting?"

"I take yer point," Jerome snapped. "There is much to consider, and much to decide. That doesnae mean I'll leave ye in the midst of this mess, no' when I—"

He cut off abruptly and spun on his heels, giving her his back.

In that moment, she knew the truth like she knew the contours of her own heart. "You care about me," she whispered. "And that scares you—not just because you don't want to see me harmed, but because you don't want to be vulnerable to being harmed yourself."

His broad back was like a wall of unmoving muscle before her, yet the faint sound of his exhale told her she'd struck a nerve.

"It occurs to me," she began, keeping her voice neutral, "that neither one of us could have come this far alone. I alerted you to de Soules's plotting, yet you spoke to him that night he rode off to the Balliol estate. And we both likely avoided his suspicion by pretending to be lovesick fools."

She took a step closer to him, and although he didn't turn, she knew by the tensing of his shoulders that he was aware of her nearness. "Is it possible that we are better off working together?" she murmured. "That we need each other?"

He turned so swiftly that she started. His hands landed on her hips, steadying her.

"Damn it all, Elaine." His voice was so rough that she would have mistaken his tone for anger if her gaze hadn't met his. The rich brown depths of his eyes burned with frustrated desire.

"Dinnae test me. No' when I'm so close to breaking."

She drew in a breath, but she couldn't look away from his scorching stare.

"I know why you are fighting against letting me stay," she said. "You are afraid I'll be hurt. But why are you fighting against *this*?" Carefully, she placed her hand on his chest. His heart hammered wildly against her palm.

He let out a sound that was half-groan, half-growl. "Ye ken why. I cannae risk distraction. I cannae fail."

"But what of all I just said?" she replied. "We are better together. Stronger. Smarter. Whatever this is between us isn't a liability, Jerome. It's a gift."

"What are ye saying?" he said, his voice haggard and wary.

"That I want you to accept this—that I am part of this mission now, and that we both want…"

For all her boldness a moment before, the words stuck in her throat. A hot blush rose to her face.

"What?" he said, taking a half step closer. Her hand on his chest was the only thing separating their bodies now. "This?"

He slid his fingers into the damp hair at her nape and tipped her head back. Then he brushed his lips against hers. The simple, brief contact was over too quickly, yet it still sent a bold of white-hot need through her.

"Aye," she mumbled, her eyes drifting closed. She stood frozen, willing him to kiss her again, praying that he would take what she so willingly longed to give.

"And this?"

His mouth closed on hers again, but this time it was a more demanding kiss. His tongue urged her lips apart and delved into the warm recesses of her mouth.

When he pulled away again, she was panting and swaying on her feet.

"Aye."

He began backing her toward the bed with slow, deliberate steps. She kept her eyes closed, for she was afraid she would see a struggle waging on his hard features against this. Instead, she surrendered her sense of sight, letting him guide her until the backs of her thighs bumped the bed's high edge.

"Tell me to stop," he ground out, his fingers sinking into the dressing robe at her waist. "Do it now, Elaine, before we cannae go back."

"Nay, I won't." Slowly, she opened her eyes. But instead of finding hesitation or even doubt on his face, she found a mask of desperate longing. "I want this. I want *you*."

In the depths of his dark eyes, she saw something snap. Suddenly he was kissing her, but it wasn't the restrained brush of lips or even the controlled exploration from a moment before.

Nay, he was *claiming* her with every heated stroke of his tongue. Elaine's pulse spiked even as liquid warmth began to pool low in her belly.

Abruptly, he scooped her up, but just as quickly he laid her on the bed, caging her with a muscular arm on either side of her. His mouth found hers again, his kiss commanding and hungry. His hands fumbled with the tie on her dressing robe until it loosened and he peeled it away.

Though the chamber was comfortably warm, Elaine shivered, for the chemise she'd found in the armoire was made of the thinnest imaginable linen, spun so finely as to be nigh transparent.

Jerome pulled back, his lust-drunk gaze drinking her in. "Christ," he breathed, propping himself above her.

She took advantage of his distraction to pull his shirt from his belt. She dragged it over his head and down his steely arms, savoring the brush of her fingertips along his heated skin.

His hands found his belt buckle, and when it popped open, his plaid unfurled around them. She lifted her head, unabashedly curious to gaze upon him.

But when her eyes fell on his long, rigid manhood, a maidenly blush warmed her cheeks. Still, no amount of virginal shyness would turn her back now. She wanted this too much, wanted to join with him, take him inside her, just as she had already taken him into her heart.

A heartbeat later, all thoughts of nervousness and inhibition fled, for he lowered his head and took the neckline of her chemise between his teeth. When she heard it rip, she squeaked in surprise and grasped his shoulders to halt his destruction, but she might as well have been trying to move stone.

He snatched her hands away, shackling her wrists in each of his large hands and pinning them to the mattress. She understood why a moment later, for when his hot mouth closed on one of her bare nipples, she nigh sprang off the bed like a startled cat.

She writhed beneath his ministrations, futilely clawing at the air with her trapped hands. White-hot pleasure shot from his mouth straight to the aching place between her legs.

"Jerome, please," she moaned, unsure what she begged for, but knowing only he could give it to her.

One big hand released her wrist to trail down the length of her. Somehow he managed to shove what remained of the chemise away, though in her passion-addled state, Elaine wasn't sure if he ripped the rest of it away or pushed it up and over her head. Her senses were flooded with the feel of his mouth, the warm weight of his body over hers, the rasp of one callused hand on her bare skin.

Then suddenly that hand touched her between the legs, right where she so desperately ached for him. She arched against him, her knees falling apart wantonly.

But she didn't care. Thought had long fled, and there was naught left but feeling.

"I want to taste ye here," he rasped, raising his head as he circled her womanhood with the pad of one finger. "I want to taste ye everywhere, but I cannae wait. I need to be inside ye, Elaine."

"Now, Jerome," she panted. "Please, now."

He rolled fully on top of her, positioning his hips between her legs. But just when she felt his cock nudge her opening, he stilled.

"Are ye sure?"

Somehow through the haze of lust, clarity struck her like a rung bell. "I know what I want—you, Jerome. Only you. Now."

A storm of emotion roiled behind his eyes as he gazed down at her. Slowly, he rocked his hips forward, pushing into her. At first it was only mildly uncomfortable. He was big, though, and as he moved deeper, the dull ache turned into a sharp burn. When she gasped, he froze.

His hand slipped between them and brushed that point of pleasure above her opening. The contact sent a frisson of the old, wonderful heat through her.

"That's it," he murmured through clenched teeth as he stroked her.

Her knees loosened around his hips and again she was arching in pleasure even as he began to inch forward once more.

When he was buried to the hilt, he froze again, except for the slow circle of his thumb against that perfect spot between her legs. His short, sharp breaths rasped against her ear, and she realized distantly that he was barely clutching the last shreds of his control. For her.

Some other time, she longed to see Jerome let go, to surrender to the consuming sensations just as she was. But for now, it took all her concentration just to breathe, to bear the aching fullness inside her.

He withdrew slightly, and she suddenly felt empty where she'd been painfully stretched a moment before. When he rocked back into her, the pain began to ebb, to be replaced with hot need. She felt the tension in her body drain away as new waves of pleasure washed her.

With each of his strokes, something built within her, carrying her higher and higher on a rising tide of sensation. Instinctually, she arched up, willing him to take her more completely, to drive her higher still.

Beneath her hands, his shoulder muscles bunched and he muttered a groan against her ear. His thrusts lost their measured pace—which sent her careening over an invisible edge and into pure ecstasy.

The force of her pleasure had her crying out and writhing beneath him. A heartbeat later, even as she rode the wave of sensation, he shuddered and called her name, driving hard and holding himself deep as he, too, found release.

He slumped over her, their panting breaths filling the quiet chamber.

"God, Elaine." He brushed a few strands of damp hair from her face, his eyes soft in the low light. She gazed up at him, unable to speak or move. She'd known she and Jerome shared a powerful connection, but this had been unlike anything she was prepared for.

As he eased onto the bed beside her, he pulled her against his chest, tucking her head beneath his chin.

"We are bound together in this now," she murmured, unsure if she meant the mission to save the Bruce from the plot against him, their still-unspoken feelings for each other, or both.

"Aye," Jerome replied, his voice a low rumble in his chest. "For better or worse."

She let his words sink in. Some part of him still feared the risks in letting her remain by his side, then—and mayhap the risks to his heart of giving in to his desire.

Elaine could relate. Danger lurked around every corner, but what she feared most were the unknowns that lay between her and Jerome. She hadn't let herself contemplate what would become of them if they made it through this unscathed—and she went back home to Trellham.

As exhaustion nipped at the edges of her consciousness, his words echoed in her ears. *For better or worse.* It sounded to her drowsy, tangled mind like the vows of marriage.

Chapter Twenty-Six

J erome woke to something softly brushing his ribs. He grunted and swatted at it, unwilling to drag himself from warm sleep.

But instead of halting the ticklish contact, his swat elicited a giggle.

His eyes shot open as the events of the previous eve rushed back. *Elaine.*

He found her curled up next to him, her fingers lazily tracing the muscles on his side. Her hair was a love-tussled mane of burnished copper, her creamy skin flushed a bonny pink. Her bright blue eyes were earnest and merry, her lips curving with pleasure as he caught her hand to cease her exploration.

"Morning," he rumbled, dropping a kiss onto those rosy lips. He was rewarded with an even deeper blush.

Damn it all, he was a fool—for her. Things had gone much further than he'd meant last night. He'd come into their chamber with the intention of telling her he was sending her back to Scotland, and instead they'd ended up making love. He would never regret it, but hell if it didn't make everything more complicated.

Still, he'd meant what he said and he would not go back on it. They were in this together, now. Elaine was right, too. They had accomplished far more together than he could have alone. And of course there was no bloody way in hell he was going to let her go after what they'd shared last night. Which meant some tough decisions lay ahead.

"We need to talk," he said gently, releasing her hand.

The teasing glow from her eyes faded and her smile faltered. "About…last night?"

Shite. Without meaning to, he'd made her doubt herself. But of course she was innocent—or had been—and though he'd taken every care with her physically, he'd been too spare with his words.

"Last night was incredible," he said. "I've never kenned a woman like ye, Elaine."

That pretty blush was back. "I didn't know it could be like that."

"With the right one, it can be, so they say—and after last night, I am inclined to believe them."

Her eyes warmed at that, but there was still much left unspoken between them. Jerome had been so set against giving in to his feelings for Elaine that he hadn't considered what would happen if he did.

In fact, naught was as he thought it would be. Instead of threatening to ruin his mission, Elaine's presence was a boon. They were closer than ever to unraveling this scheme against the Bruce. But what could come of their deepening attachment? And what would it mean to care for—*love*—another after so many years alone?

He shook his head to clear it. Whatever de Soules and Balliol were up to still had to remain their focus.

"What I meant was, we need to discuss what comes next. I willnae send ye away, but I damn well need to ensure yer safety however we proceed."

Her russet brows arched. "I've actually come up with a plan."

"Oh?"

"Aye. While you slept."

Jerome would have cursed himself for his laziness if he weren't so occupied with admiring Elaine's ingenuity. "Tell me."

Her teeth sank into her lower lip, and his gaze lingered there despite himself.

"You aren't going to like it," she said with a frown.

He propped himself on one elbow and waited, watching her.

"It would mean getting Kieran involved," she began. "And abandoning your mission to deliver the King's declaration to the Pope."

Jerome jerked upright. "What?"

"Hear me out," she said, clutching the coverlet to her chest to keep it from being yanked away by his abrupt movement. "I believe he can be trusted. And you said yourself that it was only a matter of time before he pieced together the truth."

"And what of me forsaking my mission?"

"I'm sure the Bruce would gladly forgive you if it meant thwarting his overthrow."

Jerome grudgingly eased back onto his elbow, eyeing her. "Go on."

"We cannot let de Soules continue on to Avignon, for who knows what other scheming he might do. But without hard proof against him, nor can we confront him yet—if we did, we'd risk his cohorts catching wind and scattering, and then the Bruce would never know who—or how many—are in on this Balliol plot."

Jerome urged her to continue with a curt nod.

"Therefore we must keep him here in Paris, but we cannot let suspicion—either for him or for what he schemes—to spread. He must be forced to remain at court for some innocuous reason like falling ill. I believe Lady Vivienne can help with that."

"Then where does Kieran come in?"

She worried her lower lip for another moment before going on. "You will give him the Bruce's declaration and he will continue on to Avignon. We'll tell him what we've learned so far, for I doubt he would accept such a change in plans without good reason, but for the rest—including King Philip—I think it would be best to keep our motivations secret."

"And us? Where will we be?"

Elaine drew in a deep breath. "We will go to Balliol's estate and learn whatever we can of his plot. It is dangerous, to be sure, but we can't return to Scone with only a hunch of what Balliol and his supporters are about. De Soules, de Brechin, and whoever I heard him speaking with have infiltrated the Bruce's court all the way to its inner layer. We must learn more of what they plan, and when, if we are to protect the Bruce."

Jerome raked a hand through his hair. Elaine was right—he didn't like it, but they needed to gather more information before sounding the alarm. Continuing on to Avignon would only draw them farther away from Scotland—and Balliol. And they couldn't keep up the ruse with de Soules forever, especially now that they knew he was only a middle-man between Balliol's supporters in the Bruce's court and the would-be usurper himself.

"What will we tell King Philip? And Balliol, for that matter." Even as he asked the question, he knew he would acquiesce to Elaine's plan. It was bold, and risky, but damn it all if it wasn't brilliant as well.

Her lips twitched with mirth. "Tell King Philip that we are having another lovers' quarrel and you've decided once and for all to see me returned to Scotland. It will be enough to explain why we'll leave his court riding north rather than south. Or better yet, tell him that you've decided to make an honest woman of me and need to get me back to Scotland to secure my father's permission before we wed."

Though she smiled, he sensed a question in her eyes. Without thinking, he spoke from the heart.

"The truth is always better than a lie. I'll tell him I'm desperate to keep ye as my own, then. And Balliol?"

She blinked, struck speechless for a moment. "I… yes, Balliol. This will be the most dangerous of all, but I believe we can sell him on it. We'll pretend to be supporters, part of de Soules and the others' scheme. He might just let something slip if he thinks we are sympathetic to his cause."

Damn, if Elaine were a man, Jerome had no doubt she'd be leading armies with a mind that strategic and daring. "Aye," he said slowly, working through each part of the plan. "That just might work."

Elaine opened her mouth to respond, but a soft knock on the chamber door interrupted her. She squeaked in surprise and yanked the coverlet all the way to her chin to hide her nakedness beneath, despite the fact that the door was still securely closed and bolted.

Jerome rose and padded toward the door, snatching up his plaid as he went. Elaine scrambled from the bed and slipped into the dressing robe she'd worn last night before diving under the covers once more. He looped his plaid around his waist as he lifted the bolt and eased the door open a crack.

Lady Vivienne stood on the other side. She remained perfectly composed despite Jerome's state of dishabille, her features trained into polite blankness.

"I brought Lady Elaine a few gowns I believe will fit," she said, holding up a folded stack of brightly colored silks and brocades. "The one she arrived in is still being cleaned."

Jerome opened the door enough to lift the dresses from her hold, but the lady-in-waiting's perceptive blue gaze slid past him into the chamber.

"I trust you found everything suited to your needs last eve," she said, a little too knowingly for Jerome's liking. He glanced over his shoulder to find Elaine blushing to the roots of her russet hair in their tousled bed. He was about to close the door with a curt dismissal when Elaine called out.

"Jerome, wait." She fixed him with a searching look. "Mayhap...mayhap now is the time to speak with Lady Vivienne."

He would have preferred more time to chew on their plan, but time was one of many luxuries they no longer had if they meant to stop Balliol. Jerome opened the door wider and ushered Lady Vivienne inside. She blinked in confusion but stepped in, glancing between Jerome and Elaine.

"Thank you again for confiding in me yesterday about where you'd seen Sir William," Elaine said to the lady-in-waiting. "We have a favor to ask, one that will sound most...strange, until you hear us out."

Lady Vivienne nodded hesitantly, and once Jerome had closed the door, Elaine began to explain everything to the Frenchwoman.

Chapter Twenty-Seven

Elaine tugged absently at the neckline of her emerald and gold-trimmed gown. In the reflection of the polished silver plate propped on the dressing table, she saw Lady Vivienne shake her head and tsk.

"You are too beautiful to be so modest," Vivienne said as she slid the final pin into place to secure the sheer gold veil atop Elaine's head. It covered the loose cascade of curling locks Vivienne had arranged in the style of the most fashionable maidens at French court.

"I'm not used to such finery," Elaine replied, flushing. "Or to revealing quite so much." The pale expanse of her chest was on display in the exquisite gown, her breasts swelling scandalously against the low-cut neckline.

"Ah, *oui*, but this is France," Lady Vivienne said, leaning over Elaine's shoulder with a conspiratorial grin. She, too, wore a beautiful—and revealing—gown, though hers was in a soft lilac with silver threading and a matching silver veil over her flaxen hair.

Elaine chuckled, but then what lay ahead of them tonight made her sober.

"Is everything ready?"

Vivienne's smile faded as well. "*Oui,*" she said. "I will be with the Queen and the other ladies-in-waiting, but I'll join your table when I can. I have what I need already." She patted the bodice of her gown, where she'd tucked a vial of something she'd assured Elaine wouldn't hurt de Soules beyond making him ill enough to keep him in bed—or in the garderobe—while the envoy continued to Avignon.

To Elaine's surprise, Vivienne had taken their request that she incapacitate de Soules with surprising calm. The Frenchwoman seemed relieved to have further confirmation from Elaine and Jerome that she'd done right to tell them of de Soules's dealings with Edward Balliol. She'd been more than willing to help if it meant stopping a nefarious scheme that would threaten France's alliance with Scotland.

Kieran, on the other hand, had been harder to convince. Once they'd explained everything to Lady Vivienne, they'd sent her to fetch Kieran while they hastily dressed and servants brought food and cleared away the tub from their chamber.

When Vivienne had returned with Kieran, the giant Highlander's eyes had already been narrowed with suspicion. He'd listened in grim silence as Elaine and Jerome had explained all they'd learned about de Soules, plus Vivienne's latest revelation about his visits to Balliol's estate.

Kieran took the news of de Soules's plotting with Balliol quite well, simply saying, "I kenned there was something off about him," but when it came to Lady Vivienne's role in detaining de Soules in the French court until the scheme could be exposed, Kieran had exploded with anger.

"Nay," he'd barked. "It's too dangerous to involve her."

Lady Vivienne, in her cool, controlled way, had lifted her chin and somehow managed to stare down at the giant Scot. "I am more than capable, *monsieur*."

He'd turned burning blue eyes on her, but when he spoke, his voice was tight and low. "This isnae work for a refined, gentle-bred lady. I'll do it."

"Do not be ridiculous, *monsieur*," Vivienne had countered. "You are as inconspicuous as a charging elephant, whereas I know how to move without notice. I can drug him tonight during the feast in your honor."

"Ye mean the feast where ye and all the other ladies will be trussed up like peacocks?" Kieran had fired back. "Aye, sounds verra *inconspicuous* of ye."

Lady Vivienne waved dismissively. "It is easy for a lady to make a man look at one thing while she is about something else—especially in a low-cut gown."

Kieran had clenched his fists so hard at that retort that his knuckles had turned white, but before he could respond, Jerome had interrupted their squabbling and returned them to the subject at hand.

When Kieran had at last agreed to their bold plan—including delivering the declaration himself, a task which he'd soberly promised to complete with his dying breath if necessary, he and Jerome had left to see what preparations needed to be made, while Lady Vivienne slipped away to secure the vial she now had tucked in her bodice.

Lady Vivienne had returned to help Elaine prepare for the King's feast that evening, but Jerome and Kieran were still absent. Elaine found herself tugging nervously on her gown once more before Vivienne's tsk stopped her again.

"All will be well," Vivienne said. Though she was only a few years older than Elaine, something about her calm, confident manner put Elaine at ease. "You'll find all the wonders of French court so dazzling tonight at the feast that you will not have time to remain worried."

Elaine smiled weakly at her reflection in the polished silver. "Thank you, Vivienne."

Just as Vivienne rose with a squeeze of Elaine's shoulders, a rap sounded at the door. Without waiting for a response, whoever stood outside pushed the door open.

Elaine turned to find Jerome and Kieran standing in the doorway, clean-shaven and looking surprisingly refined. They both still wore their clan colors belted around their hips, but they'd polished their boots to a shine, and over their plain linen shirts they wore short, well-fitted cotehardies embellished with gold thread and intricate beadwork—gifts from King Philip, no doubt.

Jerome's gaze landed on Elaine, and her heart stuttered against her ribs.

"The feast is already underway," he said, extending a hand to her in invitation.

She rose from the dressing table and glided in her best imitation of Lady Vivienne toward him. His dark gaze pinned her as she went, making her stomach flutter. He actually frowned when his eyes landed on her exposed décolleté, but she assumed he was displeased not with her figure, but at the fact that everyone at the feast would see it.

When she reached him, he drew her arm through his and pulled her close enough to smell the clean, masculine scent of his skin.

Lady Vivienne crossed the room with effortless grace even though a frown creased her brow. "I had best return to the Queen," she said.

"I'll escort ye." Kieran stepped forward, but Vivienne cocked her head at him.

"I am more than capable of seeing myself to my Queen's quarters."

Instead of arguing, Kieran simply snatched Vivienne's slim arm and pinned it under his in a rather blunt maneuver. Vivienne clicked her tongue in disapproval, but Kieran was so much larger and stronger that she couldn't stop him from sweeping her from the chamber and down the stairs.

Jerome followed, though he kept their pace slow enough to allow Kieran and Vivienne to pull away.

"What could have possibly made Kieran detest Lady

Vivienne so much?" Elaine asked as they wound their way down the spiraling stairs.

Jerome chuckled. "It's quite the opposite, I suspect."

Before Elaine had time to ask him what he meant, they stepped into the great hall attached to the tower. But instead of finding it swarming with nobles, it was quiet and dim.

"The King means to show us every luxury tonight," Jerome commented. "He's hosting the feast in the larger hall we saw yesterday."

They crossed the space to a corridor on the far side that allowed the King and his nobles to travel throughout the palace without having to walk outside. When they reached the larger great hall, Elaine could only stare.

It had been wondrously grand yesterday morn when they'd seen it on their tour, but it had been empty and unlit then. Now the light of more than a thousand candles made the space seem as though it were made of pure gold.

The polished marble floors appeared to glow with their own light as they stepped into the hall. Overhead, every elegant curve of the soaring arched ceiling was cast in golden candlelight. The hall itself was filled with a dazzling array of nobles dressed in jewel-toned silks. Long trestle tables filled much of the space, and the guests were being ushered to their seats.

Jerome guided her toward the raised dais, where the King, dressed in his usual ermine-trimmed blue and gold silk, was already seated. Because they were the honored guests of the evening, their table was just below the dais.

As Elaine and Jerome approached, she caught her first glimpse of the Queen. She was of an age with Philip, yet her refined air spoke of timeless grace. She wore a gown of deep royal amethyst to match the rich colors all around, her light brown hair coiled and tucked under a slightly more modest veil than her ladies-in-waiting. Her ladies flocked around her in their pastel-colored gowns like a bouquet of springtime flowers surrounding an inset jewel.

The Queen swept onto the raised dais and dipped into a curtsy to the King. For his part, King Philip played the perfect courtly lover, rising and giving his wife a deep bow, much to the pleasure of the nobles looking on.

As the King and Queen settled themselves in their enormous chairs, the ladies-in-waiting moved to the table nearest Elaine and Jerome's. Elaine made eye contact with Vivienne, who gave her a faint tilt of the head for reassurance before slipping into her place at the nearby table.

Elaine found Kieran already seated at their table, his gaze following Vivienne as well. Bishop Kininmund was there, too, his firm expression unchanging as he took in all the wonders around them. Elaine stiffened when her gaze landed on de Soules, who sat beside the bishop. Of course he would be included in the honors of the evening, but after all she'd learned, she couldn't help seeing wickedness in his seemingly unassuming brown eyes.

Drawing in a breath to steady herself, she took a seat between Kieran and Jerome, across from de Soules and the bishop. Luckily they were spared from having to make conversation, for King Philip rose and lifted his voice in a speech about his great honor in hosting an envoy of the King of Scotland's men, and the long and healthy friendship between their two countries.

After the cheers of the noble guests died down, the King called for food and wine, and the hall came alive with an army of servants, who bustled between the tables in matching blue and gold livery, their arms loaded with steaming platters of food and jugs of wine.

Though merry conversation soon filled the hall, their table remained quiet as they ate, for which Elaine was grateful. It wasn't until the last of the trenchers had been cleared and King Philip had called for his musicians to begin playing that Lady Vivienne approached. She bore a jug brimming with dark wine, which she pretended to nearly slosh when she reached their table.

"And how do our esteemed guests like our French wine?" she said with a little giggle as she moved to fill the goblets on the table.

"Just fine," Kieran replied tightly, watching her. Lady Vivienne shot him a narrowed glance that even Elaine, who was looking right at her, nearly missed. She imagined that if the lady-in-waiting had been close enough, she would have stomped on Kieran's foot in that moment.

"I think I shall retire for the evening," the bishop said, rising. "Revelry and men of God dinnae mix—or at least they shouldnae." He approached the dais and gave his thanks to the King before gliding from the hall.

Vivienne continued filling goblets. When she reached de Soules's, she leaned precariously over the table, giving him a full view of her cleavage. "Do you enjoy music, Sir William?"

De Soules couldn't help but be struck speechless for a moment as his gaze landed on her breasts. "I...that is..."

In that moment, Elaine noticed Vivienne's hand slip from the folds of her skirt to cup de Soules's goblet. A heartbeat later, she flicked her wrist and Elaine spied the tiny glass vial tucked between her fingers before it disappeared once more. She finished pouring de Soules's wine, her hand dropping away as if she'd only been steadying the goblet while she poured.

"I love music, especially when accompanied by dancing," Lady Vivienne said even as de Soules continued to wrestle with his tongue. "Mayhap you can teach me one of your Scottish dances later," she murmured in a low, flirtatious voice.

"I could show ye a thing or two now, lass," Kieran growled suddenly, rising from the table.

Before she could object, he plucked the jug of wine from her hand and set it aside, then swept her off toward the far end of the hall, where the tables were being cleared to allow room for dancing in front of the musicians. Vivienne only had time to dart a glance back at Elaine and Jerome and give them a quick nod—it was done.

A breath frozen in her lungs, Elaine watched as de

Soules lifted his goblet and took a gulp of wine. He stared after Kieran and Vivienne with a frown on his face, but he made no move to stop them, nor did his eyes narrow with suspicion as he took another sip.

The first part of their plan had been set into motion.

Now all she could do was pray that the rest would go smoothly from here.

Chapter Twenty-Eight

"Must you depart so soon, *mes amis?*" King Philip stood at the gates to his private garden, a velvet cloak draped jauntily over one shoulder and his hands planted on his hips.

Jerome bowed his head but kept his voice firm. "Aye, Majesty. The Pope waits for no man. And nor, it seems, will my bride."

His gaze flashed to Elaine, who stood a few paces back with Lady Vivienne. She'd molded her features into a smile, and though he was familiar enough with her to know it was an act, he doubted anyone else noticed.

"But what of Sir William?" the King persisted. "Surely you should wait for your companion to recover his health before leaving."

Just as she'd promised, Lady Vivienne's potion had done its job. Less than a quarter hour after taking his first sip of the tainted wine, de Soules had excused himself from the feast. He never returned, and was found by a servant sometime later locked inside the garderobe.

"I am afraid he will miss Avignon," Jerome replied with a shrug.

Lady Vivienne stepped forward then. "I'll look after your compatriot, *monsieur*. He'll be well tended until he regains his strength." The faintest flicker of one blonde eyebrow confirmed their plan: Vivienne would ensure de Soules was forced to remain at court until Jerome and Elaine could determine exactly how far his treachery went—and what to do with him.

"Many thanks for yer kind attentions, Lady Vivienne," Jerome said with a bow to her. "And to ye, Majesty, for yer hospitality in allowing him to recover here."

"Of course, of course," the King said with an airy wave. "But I cannot help disliking all the changes in plans. With one visit to my palace, your King's envoy has been cut in half. It reflects poorly on me."

"Aye, well, Sir William and I will have to visit Avignon some other time. But Kieran and Bishop Kininmund will see the Bruce's declaration delivered safely." He plastered a conspiratorial smile onto his own features. "After all, a wise man once insisted that when pleasure and beauty present themselves, one had better seize them while one can."

The King's weak frown dissolved into a grin. "That is the silver lining, I suppose. I am so happy for you and Lady Elaine. And I gladly take at least some credit for your impending union—though some must go to *belle*

France herself as well. But won't your King be displeased that you are abandoning his envoy?"

"I'd rather beg his forgiveness than ask his permission in this case. I cannae let aught threaten my chance to secure my bonny love once and for all."

"For a Scotsman, you have a flourish for romance." King Philip pounded Jerome on the shoulder. "Be off with you then, *mon ami*, and give my best to your King. If there is aught else I can do to help him, I am at his disposal."

The King walked with Jerome, Elaine, and Lady Vivienne to the stables, where Kieran and Bishop Kininmund were preparing the horses. Jerome had waited until the last possible moment, but the time had finally come to hand over the declaration.

While the bishop mounted and arranged his robes, Jerome pulled Kieran aside.

"Ye ken there arenae many men into whose hands I would place my fate—and my life," Jerome began, his voice gruff.

"And there arenae many whose duty I would take on as my own, but under the circumstances, I'll do it gladly," Kieran replied quietly.

With a nod, Jerome reached into the pouch on his belt and felt the familiar rasp of parchment against his fingers. He withdrew the carefully folded and wrapped packet containing the Bruce's prized declaration of Scottish freedom.

Jerome held it for a moment, measuring the inconsequential lightness of the parchment against the heft of all it implied—and the weight of his own responsibility to deliver it safely.

It felt like a betrayal of all he stood for to turn it over now. Jerome's whole life had hinged on seeing his duty done, never failing in his loyal devotion to first his Laird and now his King. And now he was willfully deserting his mission.

It was a bitter truth to swallow, but much more than his honor and good name hung in the balance now. In handing over the declaration, he was serving the greater good, he reminded himself firmly. He couldn't simply follow orders anymore. His pledge to protect King and country went beyond that.

And if he had to drag his name through the mud to accomplish his larger goals, he would find a way to survive it. He was strong enough. Elaine had taught him that.

"See it done," he said at last, extending the packet to Kieran.

Kieran wore a somber frown as he accepted the folded parchment. "From one Highlander to another and in the name of King Robert the Bruce—ye can count on me, Jerome Munro."

As Kieran tucked the declaration into his own belt pouch, he extended his forearm to Jerome and they shared a firm shake. In his gruff way, Kieran thanked King Philip for his hospitality, then mounted alongside the bishop. His blue gaze lingered on Lady Vivienne before he gave her a curt nod and reined his horse toward the arching bridge leading off the island-palace.

Jerome watched as they rode into the city and turned

south—toward Avignon—until they were swallowed by the throng of activity in the busy streets. He turned to find Elaine and Vivienne embracing in a farewell. He was close enough to hear what Vivienne murmured to Elaine.

"I'll pray that the peace in both our countries holds," the lady-in-waiting said quietly. "And for your safety, Elaine."

"Thank you, dear Vivienne," Elaine replied, her voice low with emotion. "For everything."

"I am glad to play my part for the greater good." Vivienne withdrew, giving Elaine a faint smile. "The world need not be brought to its knees by the schemes of men like William de Soules." The King approached, so Vivienne drew her mouth into a practiced smile and raised her voice. "Come and visit me anytime, *mes amis*. You've barely tasted the delights of France."

Giving a nod of thanks to Lady Vivienne, Jerome helped Elaine mount the spritely bay mare King Philip had graciously provided for her, then swung onto his steed's back.

With their final farewells and thanks on their lips, they set out toward the bridge. Elaine twisted in the saddle, gazing back at the magnificent palace as their horses clopped across the bridge's stones. The dazzling May sun reflected off the slow-moving river, illuminating her smiling face, yet her blue eyes were clouded with worry.

As they began to wind their way through the cramped Paris streets, Jerome reined his horse close to hers.

"It will be all right," he said simply.

She met his gaze, and though she nodded, her teeth worked her lower lip in apprehension.

"I've been thinking…depending on how favorable the winds were for Captain MacDougal on his voyage back to Scotland, your missive telling Finn that I am with you should have arrived before we reached Paris."

"Aye," Jerome replied, unsure where her thoughts were headed.

"I'm sure he was furious when he discovered I'd fled, and likely isn't too happy to know that I'm in France with you, either—but I realize now that would be assuming he's received your missive."

"And why wouldnae he have?"

Elaine shook her head slowly. "I don't know. It's just…shouldn't we have heard back from him by now? If he is detained in Scone, wouldn't he at least have sent an angry note warning you to look after me?"

Considering all Jerome knew of Finn's character, he wouldn't have been surprised if the surly Highlander had charged straight to France upon hearing what Elaine had gotten up to in his absence. A strongly worded missive would've been the least he could have done.

"Do you doubt Captain MacDougal?" he asked cautiously.

"Nay," Elaine replied without hesitation. "He would have seen your missive delivered, I'm sure of it. I only fear…" She turned fretful eyes on him. "What if Finn hasn't captured David de Brechin yet? Or what if something has happened to him that has prevented him from returning to Scone?"

Jerome clenched the leather reins in his hands tight enough that his horse tossed his head in annoyance. Elaine had every reason to worry for Finn's safety—he was family, after all—but if Finn truly had been waylaid or hindered somehow, they were in far graver trouble.

It was possible that Finn simply hadn't received Jerome's missive yet. The seas could have been rough, delaying MacDougal's ship. Or mayhap Finn had crafted a scathing response, but it hadn't reached Paris yet.

The darker possibility was that Finn might have been ambushed by de Brechin or others who were in on the scheme to overthrow the Bruce. Or de Brechin could be leading him on a merry chase away from Scone, leaving the Bruce vulnerable and unprotected. Either way, Finn's silence didn't bode well.

Damn it all, there were too many unknowns still— what did de Soules intend with Balliol? How many were involved in the plot? And when did they mean to act?

"Finn kens how to take care of himself," he said, though he wasn't sure if the words were meant to reassure Elaine or himself. "I'm sure he's fine. And we are close to unraveling this scheme at last. We'll ken more once we speak to Balliol."

God in heaven, he hoped he was right.

Chapter Twenty-Nine

"**A**re ye ready?" Jerome fixed Elaine with a searching look beneath his furrowed brows.

They had reined their horses off the road only a mile or so from Château de Hélicourt to go over their story one last time.

They'd managed to cover the distance from Paris to Picardy, which had taken them three days with King Philip's slow caravan of wagons, in only a day and a half, thanks to their strong horses. They'd spent much of that time crafting the tale they hoped would get them inside Hélicourt's walls—and in front of Edward Balliol himself.

Elaine swallowed against a tight throat. "De Soules got sick. He entrusted you to take his place in the effort to oust the Bruce."

"Because of my father's history of support for the Balliols and Comyns," Jerome added in an even voice.

She knew it must pain him to have to play the part

of a traitor, to unearth the terrible truths of his past as if they hadn't left invisible wounds on him, yet he was surprisingly calm.

"And I am your…"

"Mistress."

Despite all the times they'd gone over it, the word still stuck in her throat. They hadn't spoken of the fact that they'd made love, and everything had been such a frantic scramble ever since that they'd barely touched, let alone been intimate again.

Elaine knew what lay in her heart for Jerome, and she believed he felt the same. But pretending yesterday morn before King Philip to be heading to Scotland for a hasty marriage, only to act tonight for Balliol as if she were merely Jerome's whore, left her reeling.

Would there ever come a time when there was no more pretending, no more lying and carrying on a charade between them? Would they ever have the chance to simply love each other, be together for no one else's benefit but their own?

She shoved aside the thoughts and the ache that accompanied them. If ever such a time existed, now was not it. They had to sell their story to Balliol convincingly enough to win his confidence. The stability of the Scottish throne depended upon it.

Drawing in a steadying breath, she gave Jerome a curt nod. "I'm ready."

He squeezed her hand before snapping his reins lightly, setting his horse into motion once more. They continued down the road until a narrow dirt path branched off to the right, just as the innkeeper in the nearby village had told them it would.

The path was only wide enough for them to ride one at a time, overgrown as it was with tall weeds. Jerome took the lead, his back reassuringly solid before her.

Dusk had begun to fall, and the darkening trees lining the path seemed to stare menacingly down on them as they rode on. Elaine kept her horse close behind his but forced herself to remain calm. Now was not the time to let her imagination run away with her, no matter the gooseflesh pricking her skin beneath her gray riding dress.

Ahead, the path widened into an open field, though what was likely supposed to be a close-cropped spread of grasses had been left untended and was instead filled with more weeds. The dark outline of a large building sat in the middle of the overgrown expanse. The chateau.

In the failing light, Elaine made out two squat stone towers on either side of a low keep. Each tower was capped with a conical roof in the style of the French and slitted with arrow loops for defense. Still, no stone wall or even a wooden palisade protected the chateau's exterior, and Elaine had yet to see a guard patrolling the keep or the grounds.

When they were nearly all the way to the keep's double doors, two men materialized from the shadows with pikes angled toward them.

"*Arrêtez!*" one shouted, adjusting his metal helm.

Jerome held up his hands. "We mean no harm, *mes*

amis," he said carefully. "We are here to seek an audience with Edward Balliol."

The guards exchanged a look. One shrugged, lowering his pike slightly. The other muttered something in French but lowered his pike as well.

Jerome dismounted then helped Elaine down. Since there was naught to tie their horses to, they simply dropped the reins, trusting that the well-trained animals would happily remain where they were and work on the overgrown weeds. One of the guards pushed his side of the wide keep doors open and motioned them inside.

Within lay a dark, ill-kept hall lit only by a single torch. Elaine moved inside, close on Jerome's heels. The only sound as they entered was the crunch of the crumbling, old rushes beneath their feet.

"Lord Balliol!" One of the guards had stepped into the hall behind them, his shout for his master making Elaine jump. Without waiting for a response, the guard slipped outside once more and closed the door behind him.

A shuffling sounded from what Elaine assumed was the kitchen attached to the back of the hall. The door swung open and a tall, thin man carrying a trencher emerged. He halted, staring at them across the hall.

It took Elaine a moment to realize that he was not another guard or servant, but Edward Balliol himself. Though his clothes were on the threadbare side, he wore an ermine-trimmed cape around his shoulders—the sign of nobility—and a red tunic with what appeared to be a family crest on the chest.

The man angled his pale orange head at them, the

faint red mustache above his lips turning down with a frown.

"Who are you, and what are you doing in my chateau?" he demanded in an accent that sounded more English than Scottish.

Blessedly, Jerome spoke for both of them. "Sire," he said, bowing deeply. "Allow me to introduce myself. I am Jerome Munro, son of Owen Munro of the Highland Munros."

"And her?" Balliol demanded, his dark gaze flicking to Elaine.

"My companion," Jerome said, making his voice drip with dismissive contempt. Elaine had to swallow against the bile rising in her throat.

"What business do you have here?" Balliol asked. He still stood rooted in place, his trencher of food in hand.

Jerome fixed Balliol with an even stare. "William de Soules sent me."

Balliol's shouldered tensed, and for a long, terrible moment, Elaine feared all was lost, but then Balliol lifted a ginger eyebrow at them. "Come. Sit."

Balliol took up the single carved chair on the raised dais facing them. Playing the part of obsequious co-conspirator, Jerome sat on a bench just below the dais so that he had to look up at Balliol while he began to eat the roasted meat on his trencher. Elaine lowered herself next to Jerome, concentrating on pretending to be invisible.

It seemed de Soules's name alone wouldn't be enough to earn Balliol's trust, for he pinned them with a hard stare as he set about his meal.

"De Soules mentioned your name once—you are part of the envoy to deliver King Robert the Bruce's declaration of freedom."

"Aye," Jerome responded casually. "For all intents and purposes, that is how de Soules and I ken each other. But I'm surprised ye havenae heard my name beyond de Soules—or at least my father's."

"Why should I have?"

"News of Owen Munro's actions fourteen years ago traveled," Jerome replied. "For he was given a traitor's death. He supported the Comyn and Balliol bloodline against the Bruce—and would have turned the entire clan in his favor if it hadnae been for Laird Donald Munro."

Now Balliol's eyes sparked with interest. He leaned forward slightly, resting his elbows on the table. "I do recall hearing something of that many years ago."

"Aye, well," Jerome said. "I am that man's son."

Elaine was close enough to see the tick of Jerome's jaw muscle, yet he kept his voice smooth.

"And the apple doesnae fall far from the tree, if ye ken my meaning."

"I think I do, Munro." Balliol eyed him for another moment. "Why did de Soules send you to me?"

"He fell ill in Paris." As they'd discussed, Jerome would omit any mention of the palace or Lady Vivienne's involvement for her protection, but if de Soules and Balliol truly had been conspiring, Balliol would already know that the King had escorted them into the city.

"Ill?" Balliol asked, his eyes narrowing.

"Aye. Glued to the garderobe. Must have been something he ate."

Balliol paused mid-chew, his eating knife poised in the air with a hunk of meat skewered on it. He gave Jerome a nonchalant look.

"And why would he think to send you all this way, Munro? What possible reason might there be for you to arrive at my chateau?"

"Beg pardon, sire, but let's cut the bullshite."

Balliol's eating knife clattered to the table. Elaine sucked in a breath, but before Balliol could speak, Jerome barreled on.

"I'm no' one to dance about with fancy words and coded language," Jerome said, stretching his Highland brogue. "So let me get to the point. De Soules trusted me enough to bring me in on this scheme of yers. He fell ill. So he sent me in his place to ensure that all went smoothly."

For one who claimed not to have a way with words, Elaine noted how carefully Jerome framed their situation. He'd hinted to Balliol that he knew much more than he actually did about the plot, while still remaining vague enough to leave himself some room to wiggle if necessary.

Balliol blinked, shock flickering across his features. "I'm not accustomed to speaking so frankly with strangers."

Spoken with the arrogance of a man whose father had once been a King—albeit briefly.

Elaine realized abruptly that Edward Balliol wasn't so wicked that he enjoyed skulking in the shadows of this dilapidated chateau—nay, he was a proud man, used to a far finer life. It must tweak his vanity to no end to be marooned here in the French countryside, his keep nigh crumbling around him and not enough money to maintain a proper suite of guards and servants.

A man full of pride could be easily controlled by it. Balliol likely wasn't the nefarious mastermind behind the scheme to dethrone the Bruce after all—nay, he was a pawn for de Soules, de Brechin, and whoever else conspired with them to accomplish their goals.

She dared a glance at Jerome. From the quick look he shot her, he'd realized the same thing.

"Forgive me, sire," Jerome said, making his voice conciliatory. "De Soules gave me little information to go on, but it was my understanding that ye'd ken how to direct me once I arrived. And dinnae mind her." He waved dismissively at Elaine. "She's naught more than a doxy, trained to keep her mouth shut and her legs open."

Elaine bit back a gasp at the crude description, but they'd agreed it would be best to make her seem as unimportant as possible. It riled her to have to play the part she most despised—that of no more than a foolish female—but she would not allow her ego to thwart their aims.

Balliol shifted in his seat, watching them down the length of his prominent nose.

"I'm committed to the cause to be rid of that usurper the Bruce and put ye in yer rightful place, sire," Jerome offered when the silence stretched. "I only need to be pointed in the right direction."

Those seemed to be the words that lowered Balliol's guard, because he sniffed and nodded. "My rightful place is on the Scottish throne," he said tartly. "Not crushed under the weight of bloody King Philip's taxes and without the aid of King Edward of England." He waved at the dilapidated hall to illustrate his financial hardship.

"King Edward hasnae assisted ye in yer claim?" Jerome tsked in a show of sympathetic disgust.

"You know, Edward's father and mine had an agreement—one which my father honored until his death." Balliol's mouth curled in disdain behind his orange mustache. "But Edward is a fool. He'd rather make war against Scotland than support my claim, even knowing I would be a willing partner in peace with him."

On the bench between them, Elaine saw Jerome's hand close around the wood so hard that his knuckles blanched. Somehow, he managed to keep his features easy, though.

"Edward isnae the man his father was—and Scotland's the worse for it. While the Bruce poisons the people's minds with thoughts of freedom, what we need is a leader who kens that peace often requires bowing before the stronger force."

"Exactly," Balliol said. "It's what my father tried to do—and what I will do once the Bruce is removed and the Balliol line is restored to its rightful place."

"De Soules was wise to send me in his stead, for it seems we are of a like mind," Jerome commented. "I only wish he'd given me instructions beyond coming here."

Jerome waited for Balliol to walk into their trap and tell them what he knew, but to Elaine's surprise, the man sighed and sat back.

"I doubt I'll be much help. I know he has associates, but I only ever spoke directly with de Soules. Why didn't he tell you what you were to do after you spoke to me?"

Jerome shrugged casually. "He said something about keeping each player in the scheme isolated enough that no individual's capture or failure would destroy the entire effort."

Balliol nodded thoughtfully at that. "Sound reasoning. No wonder he never told me who else supported me or how they planned to do it. All I know is that I am to remain here until I am sent for—once the Bruce is dead."

The words hit Elaine like a blow. The room dimmed for a moment as her mind tried to comprehend what Balliol was saying.

"Once the Bruce is…" She heard Jerome clear his throat beside her. "Dead." He cleared his throat again. "Aye, of course." His voice sounded strained and distant in her ears, yet he was at least attempting to cover his shock. She could only pray her face hadn't given her away already.

Balliol was saying something about how after the Bruce was gone, he'd promised to reward de Soules and his compatriots with grants of land—which they apparently felt they'd been denied under the Bruce. Elaine trained her gaze on the floor, but inside her mind, a storm raged.

Why hadn't they considered the fact that any

attempt to dethrone the Bruce might involve his assassination? Somewhere between learning of de Soules's contact with Balliol and realizing that it most likely meant an overthrow of the crown, Elaine hadn't considered what would actually happen to the Bruce.

And from Jerome's tight voice, neither had he. They'd both been so focused on unraveling de Soules's plot that they hadn't contemplated the obvious—that the easiest way to be rid of a King was to kill him.

Balliol droned on with his complaints about his birthright being stolen and all he would accomplish as King of Scotland. At the first possible break in his musings, Jerome interjected.

"We've taken up enough of yer time, sire," he said, rising. "Besides, if we are to get ye on the throne, I'd best return to Scotland and see how I can help with the cause. Surely I'll be able to find our other allies using de Soules's name."

The pretender-King rose, pushing aside his trencher. "I appreciate your loyalty, Munro, and the sacrifices your family has made in my name."

Jerome bowed to hide the way his lips curled back in disgust.

"I only wish I could provide more guidance," Balliol said. He paused. "De Soules always said 'The unicorn will fall to the lion,' if that is any help."

Elaine fought to keep her features smooth even as she internally grimaced at the saying. It made sense, of course. Growing up in the Borderlands, she was all too familiar with the symbolism. The lion, proud and fierce, was thought to represent England. The unicorn, a mystical, noble creature, was considered the natural enemy of the lion—and the adopted symbol of Scotland.

De Soules and his conspirators clearly hated the Bruce so much for supposedly slighting them when it came to distributing lands that they were willing to ally with an English-sympathizing ruler to bring their own country to its knees. Elaine swallowed against another wave of disgust.

"I willnae fail ye, sire," Jerome said with another hasty bow. He began backing toward the hall's doors, gripping Elaine by the elbow as he went.

"Farewell, and best of luck," Balliol called after them, his voice bouncing off the bare stone walls as they retreated.

Jerome pushed open the doors, his face a mask of indifference as they strode past the two guards. Yet his fingers bit into her arm where he held her.

"Jerome," she breathed as his pace increased toward the dark outlines of their grazing horses.

"Hush," he hissed. "The guards can hear us."

When they reached their horses, he gripped her waist as if to lift her into the saddle, but instead he lowered his head until his breath brushed her ear.

"There isnae time to gather more clues or hunt down de Soules's associates," he whispered. "The Bruce is in grave danger, and only we ken it."

Elaine nodded, frightened tears burning her eyes. She blinked them away, commanding herself to maintain her composure.

"We'll ride through the night to Calais and board

the first ship bound for Scone," Jerome continued, his voice so low it was barely audible even right against her ear. "I...I need ye to be strong, Elaine. I cannae do this alone. We are in this together, remember?"

His words sent steel into her spine. They'd made it this far. Now, with the King's life hanging in the balance, she couldn't succumb to fear, for she and Jerome were the only ones who might stop this traitorous scheme.

"Aye," she replied, giving him a nod.

He hoisted her into the saddle and mounted his horse, snapping the reins and leading them back down the overgrown path.

Elaine followed, her mind filled with a single prayer.

Please, God, let me be strong enough.

Chapter Thirty

Jerome stared out at the inky North Sea. He silently cursed the gentle wind rippling off the water, for it barely filled the sails of their ship as they glided along through the dark night.

Toward Scotland. But not bloody fast enough.

He felt a tentative hand come to rest on his back and turned to find Elaine standing behind him.

"I hope I didnae disturb ye in coming up here," he said.

Thanks to Jerome's liberal use of the last of his coins in Calais, they'd managed to secure passage on a cargo ship set for Scone. The captain, a Spanish trader who sailed between France, Scotland, and Spain with silks, wools, and linens, had agreed to give them a small cabin below deck to use as their own. But now that they were only a day away from Scotland's shores, Jerome found he couldn't sleep.

"Nay," Elaine replied, moving to his side to gaze out

at the water beyond the gunwale. "I wasn't sleeping either—not truly."

Jerome clawed his hair away from his forehead. "Damn it all, but this journey seems interminable. I cannae stand to be bobbing on this bloody ocean another day, no' kenning if the Bruce is well or if—"

"Don't say it," Elaine cut in. "You're only torturing yourself when there is naught we can do from here anyway."

She was right, of course, but it didn't ease the knot of sickening fear that had tangled Jerome's insides since they'd spoken with Balliol and learned of the assassination plot.

He let a long breath go. "I ken it, but it doesnae make the waiting any easier."

"All will be well," she murmured, though he saw out of the corner of his eye that her brows were creased with worry. "We will reach the Bruce in time—I have to believe that. And we'll find a way to stop de Soules's co-conspirators." She turned to him, her eyes catching the moonlight. They glowed like liquid pools of sapphire. "I believe in you, Jerome—in us. No matter what happens, we'll find a way through. And afterward…"

Her voice trailed off, and Jerome couldn't help but flinch. They still hadn't spoken about what would happen once they ended the threat to the Bruce once and for all—for Jerome feared they'd never reach that point. But he couldn't ignore what he bore in his heart for Elaine. Not anymore. Not when this might be their last night together before all hell broke loose.

"Come below deck with me," he said gently. "We

both need rest if we are to be sharp when we arrive in Scone tomorrow." And he had something to tell her that the sailors on the night watch needn't eavesdrop on.

Elaine let him guide her to the ladder that led below deck. They climbed down and wove their way through the cargo crates and the swinging hammocks of the sleeping sailors to their wee cabin in the nose of the hull.

Once Jerome closed the door behind them and lit one of the hanging lanterns, he turned to find Elaine perched on the edge of the nailed-down cot in the corner.

"Elaine…" He approached, lowering himself on the cot beside her. "I need to tell ye something." He swallowed. "If we dinnae make it out of this…"

"Nay, don't."

"Hear me out, lass. We dinnae ken what fate holds in store for us when we reach the Bruce's court. And I would never forgive myself if I didnae speak my heart's truth to ye before then."

She stilled, gazing at him. He let his eyes trace every lovely angle of her face, from her coppery brows to her pert nose and those lush, berry-colored lips. She'd plaited her russet locks to tame the effects of the salty breeze. He took up the end of the braid and loosened it with his fingers until her hair fell in rich waves around her shoulders.

"God, how I love ye, lass," he murmured, devouring the sight of her like a man half-starved.

She pulled in a breath, but before she could speak, he went on.

"I think I've loved ye since the moment I saw ye, but

I was too stubborn and blind to realize it." He stroked her velvety cheek with his thumb. "I'll never forget that first sight of ye. Ye were all windblown and looking as wild as a banshee. Ye burst over that ridge and barreled straight for me as if God himself had shot ye from a bow, aiming ye right at my heart."

"Jerome." Her voice cracked with emotion.

"I should have told ye right then," he continued. "Or after our first kiss at Trellham. Or when we said farewell—for what might have been forever—in Scone. And I damn well should have told ye the night we made love, for I kenned with certainty then, but I was afraid."

"Of what?" she murmured, gazing at him with those vibrant, emotive eyes.

He shook his head. "Afraid I'd lose ye somehow, I suppose. Afraid to let myself care when I never have before. Afraid I wasnae worthy of ye. And afraid I'd go so mad with wanting ye that I'd fail my mission and prove those clansmen who said I was no different from my father right."

She cupped his bristled cheek with one hand, her eyes riveted on him even as they began to shimmer with unshed tears.

"I hope that by telling ye now, it's no' too late," he said. "There hasnae been enough time to do things right. With the mission and de Soules and Balliol and—"

"I know," she interrupted. "There is never enough time. But you're not too late."

He swallowed. "I dinnae ken what lies ahead. All I

ken is that I want to spend every moment we have together telling ye and showing ye how much I love ye."

"I love you, too," she replied, tears spilling down her cheeks.

Jerome's heart soared even as the shadow of all that lay ahead still cast them in darkness.

"Then promise me something."

She nodded. "Anything."

"Promise me that if we get through this and live to tell of it, ye'll make me the happiest, luckiest man that ever lived and marry me."

Elaine's eyes widened and her lips parted.

"Dinnae think of the Bruce or Finn or yer father or yer life in Trellham or aught else. Ye said that all would be well and that ye believed in us. I believe we can find a way, Elaine. Say aye."

A heartrendingly sweet smile broke over her face, warm and promising as the dawning of the sun.

"Aye."

He pulled her into his arms then, burying his face in her hair. She clung tightly to him, squeezing as close as she possibly could. Her breasts crushed against his chest, her slim arms looping around his neck.

"Ye are my heart and soul, Elaine," he breathed.

"And you are mine."

He drew back, but only enough so that his mouth could find hers for a desperate kiss. Whatever awaited them, they only had this moment—and he intended to use it well.

"If this is to be our last night before whatever we'll

face tomorrow, let us spend it joined as one. No more distractions. No more doubts or fears. Just us."

She answered by kissing him once again, showing him wordlessly that her passion and love matched his own.

Like a fanned flame, desire blazed inside him, firing his blood and making him hard with wanting. He longed to shove their clothes aside and join with her swiftly, but they had all night, and he would not allow himself to rush this. The first time they'd made love, he hadn't given himself time to savor every beautiful inch of her. This time he would not make the same mistake.

He let his lips trail from her mouth to her cheeks and throat, then to where her ear lay buried in the waves of her hair. He nibbled gently, then traced the outside of her ear with his tongue, eliciting a shiver from her.

Her hands flew to his shirt and began tugging it from his kilt. He let her pull it up and over his head, but then he returned to his ministrations, trailing kisses down her neck to the neckline of the stout wool dress she'd selected at King Philip's palace for their travels.

Gooseflesh rippled beneath his lips as he kissed the sensitive skin at the top of the gown's bodice. She sighed, her fingernails grazing his bare back in wordless encouragement.

His fingers found the ties at the back of her gown and he worked them loose, all the while raining kisses on her. When the dress sagged from her shoulders, he eased her down onto the cot and slid the wool away, leaving her in her chemise. She lay back, watching him as he tossed the gown aside and moved over her.

"I want to see ye—all of ye," he murmured, reaching for the chemise. The fine linen whispered against her creamy skin as he pulled it away, revealing each perfect inch of her.

God in heaven, what had he done to deserve her? He was nobody, a man from a disgraced family, a warrior from a small clan who had naught more than his pledge of loyalty to his name. If his Laird hadn't agreed to send him into the King's service, and if the Bruce hadn't selected him to collect the seals for the Declaration of Arbroath, his path never would have crossed Elaine's.

And yet staring down at her, his brave, bold, beautiful woman, some part of him knew it couldn't have been mere coincidence that had drawn them together. Whether it was fate or God or some other unseen force, his soul and hers were bound to meet and intertwine for whatever time they had.

"Jerome," she murmured, her eyes tracing him like a caress. "Touch me. Please."

He was all too eager to comply. He skimmed up her arms and over her shoulders until he was cupping each perfect breast. Her dusky pink nipples drew into pearls and she moaned as he swept them with his thumbs.

He couldn't hold back then. He leaned over her, closing his lips around one of those perfect, taut nipples. She gasped and arched against his mouth. But he wanted so much more. He slid lower, dragging his lips along her ribs and flat stomach until he reached the curls hiding her womanhood.

She sucked in another breath when he kissed her

there. But instead of tensing or pushing him away, her legs parted in invitation. Her trust shook him to his core and fired his lust until his cock ached with the need to be inside her.

But not yet—not until he'd tasted her and brought her this selfless pleasure. He spread her wide with his tongue, swirling and teasing until her knees trembled around his shoulders and every panting breath was a moan.

Abruptly, she shattered beneath his mouth, crying out her pleasure as she arched off the cot. When the last quakes of ecstasy began to ebb, he rose up on his haunches and ripped off his belt and plaid.

She opened lust-hazed eyes and gazed at his naked form as he loomed over her. But instead of lowering himself between her legs, he lifted her up and settled onto his back. She made a surprised noise as he positioned her above him, her knees straddling his hips, but when his desire-hardened cock nudged her opening, understanding dawned across her features.

Desperate to be inside her but longing to make the moment last, Jerome gripped her hips and slowly began to lower her onto his length. Elaine let her head fall back, her russet locks cascading over her shoulders and breasts.

He gritted his teeth against the nigh blinding urge to thrust hard and fast. God, he never wanted to forget this moment, never wanted to be anywhere else but here.

Praying for his control to last as long as possible, he began to move, showing her the way with his body. She found her own rhythm, and soon his hands rose from her hips to her breasts.

When he dropped one hand to brush that point of pleasure just above where they were joined, Elaine came undone with another hard release. She went taut and cried out his name over and over as she rode him.

It was his undoing. The final thread of his restraint snapped and he sank his fingers into her hips, driving into her with ferocious abandon. A powerful release broke through him. He groaned, emptying himself into her until they were both left panting and spent.

Elaine folded over him, coming to lie on his chest. He dragged a blanket over them both, stroking her back until her breathing slowed and she turned soft and limp in his arms.

"I love ye, Elaine," he murmured, his voice low and tight with emotion.

She was already asleep, but oblivion eluded him. He couldn't seem to let himself drift away when he held her in his arms. So he lay in the gently swaying cabin, listening to her breathe and feeling his heart beat in its steady, strong rhythm—for her. Only and forever for her.

Chapter Thirty-One

E laine gripped the ship's railing as they glided the last hundred yards to the docks along the River Tay. At last, they would put their feet on Scottish soil once more.

Time seemed to stretch cruelly as she watched the men slowly ratchet down the anchor and lower the crates of valuable cloth into the waiting dinghies by rope.

But when Jerome's warm arm looped around her waist, holding her close, she felt herself relax a hair's breadth.

"Remember yer words to me, lass—all will be well."

His touch was like a balm to her ragged nerves. Her mind flooded with memories of the night before—Jerome's kiss, his touch, their joining so fierce and passionate, yet so filled with love at the same time.

They'd woken early in each other's arms and made love again that morn, slow and tender. By the time they'd emerged from their cabin, Scotland had already been sighted, her green shores cloaked in mist.

But without any way to speed their progress, the morning had dragged with naught to do but wait and worry about what lay ahead.

Even once they disembarked, they would still be an hour's ride from Scone Abbey and the Bruce's court. And the uncertainty of what they would find there left Elaine pulled taut with fear.

At last, the cargo had been unloaded and the captain motioned for them to climb down the ladder to the waiting dinghy. They sat in silence while one of the crewmen rowed them the short distance to the wooden docks along the riverbank, which bustled with trade and activity.

Despite the milling seamen, the smells of fish and unwashed bodies, and the commotion from the other anchored ships, when they stepped on solid Scottish ground once more, Elaine let out a breath of relief.

"The town of Errol is nearby," she said as she and Jerome began to trudge away from the noisy docks. She flashed him a smile. "It's where Captain MacDougal took my horse to be traded for coin—which is how I gained passage to France for myself. I imagine we can secure mounts there."

Jerome gave her a warm look. "Ever resourceful, arenae ye, lass?"

She slid her hand in his as they began climbing a low, grassy rise on the north bank of the river. She wasn't sure exactly how far Errol lay, but there was no other option than to walk, as they had no coin and didn't wish to draw attention to themselves or why they were there, even this far from Scone. They'd have to come up with some way to procure horses—steal them, if necessary—and trust that once they reached the Bruce, all would be forgiven.

Just as they entered a dense forest, a cool spring rain began to fall, pattering softly on the leaves overhead.

If it hadn't been for the murmur of the drizzle in the trees, Elaine might have heard it sooner.

Footsteps closing in on them. Jerome dropped her hand and spun, reaching for the sword on his belt, but it was already too late. Two men tackled him to the ground while a third raised the hilt of his sword toward his head.

Elaine screamed, but a hand closed over her mouth, muffling the sound. She watched in horror as the man looming over Jerome brought his hilt down with a sickening thud against Jerome's skull. Jerome's eyes rolled back in his head and he went limp even as dark red blood began to ooze from his scalp.

Elaine screamed again, uncaring that no one would hear her. She fought wildly against the man holding her from behind, kicking and thrashing. But the brigand who'd struck Jerome rose up and slowly approached, his weapon raised to deliver a similar blow.

"Gentler this time, Orrin," the man holding her said.

Through the shroud of panic and fear enveloping her mind, cold clarity hit Elaine like a splash of ice water.

She knew that Lowland-intoned voice.

"We need them both alive, remember?" the man continued.

Orrin closed in and lifted the hilt above her head. One thought rang through her before all fell to blackness.

David de Brechin was alive—and now they were his captives.

JEROME CLAWED against the pull of unconsciousness, but the darkness kept hauling him down. It wasn't until he smelled smoke and felt cold, hard stone beneath him that he managed to drag his eyelids open.

His head ached, a dull, sickening pulse everywhere and a sharp, hot pain where he'd been struck. He squinted against the light of a fire and winced at the sound of steady dripping somewhere in the distance.

Slowly, he realized he was in a cave of some sort, for the firelight flickered off damp stone all around. He rolled his head slowly, trying to see more.

When his gaze landed on Elaine, he fought against the rope binding his hands and feet behind his back and tried to sit up, but a wave of nausea kept him on his side.

She was unconscious, propped up against one of the cave walls with her hands bound behind her as well.

"Elaine," he hissed, his voice echoing painfully loud. "Elaine, wake up."

She stirred, her head lolling to one side and a groan slipping past her lips, but before Jerome could do aught else, a pair of boots filled his vision as a man stepped between them.

"Ah, ye're awake. Good."

Jerome looked up to find David de Brechin standing over him, a smile that didn't reach his eyes quirking his lips.

"Jerome?" Elaine's pained, thin voice drifted from behind de Brechin.

"Both of ye," de Brechin commented, glancing back at Elaine. "Even better."

"Let her go, de Brechin, and I might consider giving ye a swift death rather than the slow and painful one ye deserve," Jerome snarled.

De Brechin chuckled, cocking his sandy blond head at Jerome. "Blockheaded Highland brute. Arenae ye the one bound and bloody on the floor and I the one in control?"

Jerome bit back a curse and instead focused on catching Elaine's eye around de Brechin's boots. "Are ye all right, lass?"

Before Elaine could answer, de Brechin interjected. "She'll be fine—*if* ye cooperate, Munro."

"Cooperate with *ye*? A traitor?" Jerome replied, then spat on de Brechin's boots.

It earned him a swift kick to the ribs. He grunted in pain, but he refused to back down. "We ken all about ye and de Soules's little plot with Balliol."

"I ken that," de Brechin said testily. "Otherwise I wouldnae have taken ye."

"How?" Elaine asked. "How could you possibly—"

De Brechin cut her off with a wave. He strode around the fire and held his hands out to it.

"Finn Sutherland."

Elaine gasped. "What did you do to Finn?"

"Oh, he gave me a merry chase, I assure ye," de Brechin replied, his voice filled with venomous mirth. "He hunted me nearly to the Borderlands before I managed to assemble enough men to take him down."

"Nay!" Elaine cried.

Jerome's heart broke for her, but there was no time to mourn the great warrior now.

For the first time, Jerome noticed that de Brechin looked haggard. Unlike the last time he'd seen the man, when he'd been all fine silks and courtly manners, de Brechin's blond hair was disheveled and his clothes torn and dirty.

His appearance spoke of desperation. At least Finn had given the man a hell of a chase and put the fear of God in him.

"And after ye set yer men on Finn, ye made yer way back to Scone," Jerome surmised. His head still throbbed, but he willed himself to concentrate. If he could wheedle enough information out of de Brechin, who'd always seemed a man with too loose a tongue, mayhap there would be an opening to save Elaine.

"I've been waiting at the docks for nigh on three days for word from de Soules," de Brechin commented. "But even before then, I kenned something was amiss the moment I realized Sutherland was after me. When the missive of confirmation never arrived from de

Soules, I thought all was lost, but then I spotted the two of ye disembarking."

De Brechin strolled back around the fire and crouched between Jerome and Elaine.

"With the lass's connection to Sutherland and ye supposedly in France, Munro, I guessed that ye had some part in all of this. And now ye've just confirmed it. I dinnae ken how ye came to learn of our plan, but now that ye have, ye'll play yer part—or yer bonny English whore will suffer."

Jerome's blood ran cold as de Brechin cast a glare at Elaine. "What do ye mean, play my part?"

"I cannae get close to the Bruce's court—thanks to whoever found me out and sent Sutherland on my heels," de Brechin replied testily. "But ye can."

"And why would I?" Jerome demanded.

"Because tonight is the night." De Brechin's thin lips curled in a smile. "The Bruce is throwing another feast to honor more of his nobles. It will be the perfect opportunity to strike him down."

Through the pain and worry clouding his brain, realization struck. "And ye want me to be the one to do it."

"Who better than ye, Munro? Ye're the son of a traitor, the perfect symbol of our revolution. They tried to crush us, to eradicate us from Scotland. They killed good men like yer father, men who understood that the Bruce never should have gained the throne, yet we will rise again."

"My father was a coward and deserved his death," Jerome spat. "I'll never follow him—or ye. Ye're mad, de

Brechin. Balliol willnae save ye. He's a greater fool than ye."

De Brechin snorted. "I never said Balliol was a great man. But he'll play his part too, just as his father tried to before the whole country went mad and cast him aside."

"Ye mean before we realized that freedom was worth more than the supposed protection of an English King who would've rather wiped every last Scot from our own lands than leave us be?"

"Enough!" de Brechin shouted, slamming his hand against the cave floor. He took a breath, smoothing his hair back. "I dinnae need to debate politics with ye when ye are completely at my mercy. Aye, ye'll play yer part. Ye'll be the one to take the Bruce down, for he trusts ye. He'll let ye close enough, never suspecting that ye will betray him."

Jerome ground his teeth until the throbbing in his skull forced him to stop. "Never."

"Nay," de Brechin replied. "*Tonight*. For if ye dinnae, she'll bear the cost."

De Brechin rose and strode slowly to Elaine. He casually pulled a dagger from his boot and inspected it. Then without warning, he plunged it into her upper arm.

Her scream of pain clashed with Jerome's rage-filled roar. *God, nay!* He thrashed against his bonds, but the rope held his wrists and ankles fast. When de Brechin turned back to him, holding up the bloodied dagger, Jerome growled like a feral animal.

"It's simple," de Brechin said. "Her life or the Bruce's. Choose, Munro."

Jerome lay panting on the floor, his gaze locking with Elaine's. His heart rent in two when he saw the fear in her eyes. She shook her head ever so slightly, then mouthed *I love you*.

Damn it all, this was not how it would end! He could not let de Brechin hurt her. But nor could he kill his King.

"Ye're taking too long, Munro," de Brechin said. In a flash of movement, he was before Elaine once more. He drove the dagger into her other arm in a swift, cruel stroke.

"Nay!" Jerome bellowed, his gaze riveted on the twin spots of blood darkening the sleeves of her dress. His beloved Elaine's blood. There had to be a way to save her and protect the Bruce. But he couldn't think straight, not while staring at her tear-streaked, pain-drawn features.

He needed more time. More time, and he might be able to come up with a way… But he was out of time, for de Brechin was raising the dagger again, pointing its dull, blood-stained tip at Elaine's beautiful face.

"Stop!" Jerome cried.

"Jerome, nay!" Elaine moaned on a sob.

"I'll do it," he shouted, ignoring Elaine's plea. "I'll do it, damn ye. Just dinnae hurt her."

A slow smile broke across de Brechin's face.

"Excellent."

Chapter Thirty-Two

Elaine saw the exact moment when Jerome made up his mind. His strong features twisted with pain even as something inside the depths of his dark eyes went dead.

She screamed at him, but then he was saying the words that would seal his fate.

He would kill Robert the Bruce.

Elaine struggled against her bonds, but her arms were numb with pain and the rope bit into her wrists.

Jerome stared at her, his eyes, once so full of love, now desolate and empty.

De Brechin crossed to the mouth of the cave and called to his henchmen. While he was out of earshot, Jerome spoke softly.

"Forgive me, Elaine."

"Jerome, nay, you cannot—"

"I'll do everything in my power to find another way," he cut in, his voice flat. "I still need to be taken to Scone and get close to the Bruce. I might be able to…" He shook his head, squeezing his eyes closed for a moment. "But if I cannae…"

"My life isn't worth his," she sobbed. God, she didn't want to die. But she couldn't let Jerome kill the Bruce, for it would not only rip all of Scotland apart, but it would certainly mean his own life as well.

"I love ye," he said simply.

She opened her mouth, but there was no time to say more, for de Brechin strode back inside with Orrin and the two others who'd tackled Jerome.

"Be careful with this one. Keep him bound until ye reach the abbey," de Brechin said, waving at Jerome's prone form. "And train yer weapons on him when ye free his hands and give him the dagger. He may be weakened, but he's still a trained warrior."

De Brechin removed a jewel-encrusted dagger from his belt and handed it carefully to Orrin. Elaine caught a glimpse of a lion's head inlaid in sparkling gemstones into the hilt. The flickering light of the fire made the lion's ruby eyes seem to dance.

"Ye," he said, looking down on Jerome. "Dinnae try aught. My men will be watching yer every move until ye reach the abbey, and once ye're inside, my allies will ken if ye dinnae play yer part. I have eyes and ears everywhere, Munro, and if word reaches me that ye faltered in any way, yer bonny whore will pay for it in flesh."

Abruptly, de Brechin drove his foot into Jerome's stomach, making him sputter in pain.

"Understand?"

"Aye," Jerome croaked.

The two outlaws lifted Jerome under the arms and dragged him to the mouth of the cave.

This was it. The last time Elaine might ever see him. She screamed and tried to stagger to her feet, but de Brechin stepped in front of her and shoved her to the ground. She landed on her backside, breaking the fall somewhat with her bound hands, but a sharp rock jabbed into her palm, making her cry out again.

Orrin hesitated at the mouth of the cave. "Are ye sure we should leave ye alone with her, milord? One of the men could stay back if—"

De Brechin snorted. "Are ye jesting? Look at her." He flung his hand toward her. "She's just a foolish wee lass."

Something stilled inside Elaine then. Her mind went very quiet as clarity swept over her.

De Brechin was wrong.

She was not a mere weak and silly girl—she'd proven that to herself. Yet he'd underestimated her, sending all of his men with Jerome and leaving himself vulnerable without even realizing it.

What was more, Jerome still lived, which meant she wasn't through fighting for him—or herself—just yet. All was not lost. He would do all he could to find another way to free them from this bind, but she had to do her part as well.

Behind her, she groped for the sharp rock that had pierced her palm a moment before. When she felt its jagged edge, she curled it into her grasp and began working it against the ropes on her wrists.

With a curt dismissal, de Brechin sent Orrin after

the others and Jerome. He rounded on Elaine and she froze, but there was no way he could see the rock in her hand.

"And now, my sweet Elaine, we wait," he said, prowling around the fire.

Cautiously, she dragged the shard of rock against the rope. The motion made no noise and de Brechin didn't seem to notice the ever so slight movement of her arms. So she kept working the jagged shard against the rope, feeling the first of its threads pop.

"What a shame it's come to this," he said, clasping his hands behind his back and watching her through the flickering flames. "Ye should never have gotten involved with a man like Munro, Elaine."

She glared at him. "And I should have chosen *you* instead? A traitor and a coward?"

He smiled, but it was more a cruel twist of his lips than a true show of mirth. "Watch yer tongue, or I'll cut it out."

Another thread snapped, but the rope didn't loosen. She was still a long way from freeing her hands, and even once she did, she'd have to somehow overpower de Brechin. That was, assuming he didn't lose his temper and simply kill her first.

She walked a knife's edge between needing to buy more time to cut the rope and avoiding de Brechin's wrath. She would have to keep him talking—but carefully.

"Ye should have been mine," he continued, stalking around the fire toward her. "But ye let that bastard Munro touch ye instead. Aye, I saw ye holding hands as ye left the docks. I should have never let him come between us that first night in Scone."

His blue eyes gleamed with vicious intent as he approached. Foreboding lanced her. She pushed herself backward until she bumped into the damp cave wall, her hands pinned against the stone. She wriggled to create enough space to continue her work on her bindings, but still de Brechin drew closer.

"But I neednae be constrained by courtly etiquette now. Ye see, that is the beauty of this revolution," he continued, crouching before her. "All these years, de Soules and I—and countless others—have been hanging on the Bruce's hem, begging for scraps, when we should have been doing what he did from the beginning. He *took* what he wanted, stole the Scottish crown without asking permission. And once we are rid of him and have our chosen King in place, we will do the same."

He drew the dull dagger he'd used on her arms from his boot once more. It still bore her blood on its edge. Sickening terror rose in her throat as he slowly waved it before her face.

"That is what this coup is truly about," he murmured, smiling faintly. "*Taking.*"

"Y-you promised not to hurt me if Jerome did as you bid," she breathed, her eyes fixed on the dagger.

"It will only hurt if ye struggle."

He notched the dagger's point against her throat, then slowly moved in. When his lips crushed hers, she forced herself to remain perfectly still—except for the hand behind her back that sawed the rope.

She felt another thread pop, and her hands separated a fraction of an inch. Her arms screamed in protest where he'd stabbed her, but she kept the shard moving, each impossibly small scrape bringing her closer to freedom.

De Brechin drew back with a satisfied grin at her passivity. "There's a good girl," he said, lowering the dagger from her throat. He slid it back into his boot, then reached for her.

She nearly howled in outrage and disgust when his hands closed on her breasts, but instead she squeezed her eyes shut. A few more seconds. She could do this. She had to be strong for Jerome. For herself.

His mouth covered hers once more, his tongue probing forcefully. Suddenly the rope snapped and her hands sprang free. There was no time to think—only to act.

She tightened her grip on the jagged rock in her palm even as she jerked her arms free. With all her strength, she drove the shard into the side of de Brechin's neck.

He jerked, his mouth and hands coming away from her. His eyes widened in shock and he coughed wetly.

"Ye bitch!" he hissed, tumbling onto his backside. But instead of going limp, he reached for the piece of rock protruding from his neck.

Without thinking, Elaine dove forward and yanked the dagger from his boot. He kicked her viciously, but she managed to hold onto the hilt even as she went careening across the cave's floor.

"Ye'll pay for that!" he howled, but when he tried to

pull the rock shard free, his fingers slipped in his own blood.

Elaine scrambled to her feet, brandishing the dagger before her. De Brechin staggered up, too, lurching toward her. Yet his movements were clumsy and she knew he was already weakening.

She darted out of his path and around the fire. To her horror, instead of chasing her from one side, he simply leapt over the flames. He plowed into her, driving them both to the ground. His bloody hands closed around her neck, his eyes wild. But so focused was he on squeezing the life from her, he left her hands free.

She drove the dagger up, feeling it sink into his flesh. He shrieked in rage, gripping her throat tighter, but she stabbed again and again until at last his hands loosened.

He coughed, this time splattering blood on his lips. He suddenly sagged on top of her, his weight pinning her to the ground. With a cry, she shoved him away and scrambled out from under him.

He flopped on his back, his eyes fixed on the ceiling. His breath came short and shallow for three terrible, long heartbeats, until at last his chest stilled and his eyes clouded with death.

A high, shaking sob echoed through the cave. It took Elaine a moment to realize the noise had come from her. De Brechin's dagger slid from her trembling, bloodied hands and clattered to the ground. Her vision spun and her stomach lurched. Abruptly, she turned her back on his body.

There would be a time to cry, to shake, to curl into a

ball and try to understand what it meant to take a life, even in self-defense, but now was not that time.

Jerome was still alive—she prayed—and he needed her.

She stumbled from the cave to find an unfamiliar, night-dark forest surrounding her. A solitary horse stood tied to a nearby tree. It must have been de Brechin's.

Elaine hastily gathered the animal's reins and dragged herself into the saddle. She guided the horse toward the wooded rise off to the left. At the top of the rise, she studied the sky. Though darkness had fallen, a band of pale blue still clung to one horizon—west. In the distance to the south, she saw the glimmer of faint moonlight on water. The river.

Her gaze traveled east until far off she made out several pinpricks of orange light. They must have been the torches at the docks. Which meant she was closer to Scone that she could have hoped. She pointed the horse southwest, knowing that once she ran into the river, she could follow it westward all the way to Scone.

Digging her heels into the animal's flanks, she prayed she would get there in time.

Chapter Thirty-Three

J erome groaned in pain as he bounced face-down against the horse's back. With his hands and feet still bound, he was lucky he hadn't tumbled off the animal and broken his neck by now.

After what felt like an eternity of rib-crushing jostling, his horse suddenly came to a halt. Rough hands dragged him from the saddle and dumped him unceremoniously on the ground. The hiss of steel against leather had him raising his head. If he was going to die, he wasn't bloody well going to go without being on his feet.

The three henchmen had their swords pointed at him, but instead of striking him down as he struggled to stand, they merely watched in silence. The apparent leader, whom de Brechin had called Orrin, stepped closer cautiously. With the tip of his sword, he sliced the bindings on Jerome's ankles.

Jerome gained his footing and braced his legs, but still they didn't move to cut him down.

"Ye remember what de Brechin said." Orrin pulled the jeweled dagger from his belt and approached once more. "Try aught and the woman dies. We'll watch ye all the way into the palace, and once ye're inside, we'll have eyes on ye at all times. If the task isnae complete in half an hour, I'll send Maurice here back to de Brechin and the lass will pay."

He had half an hour, then, to find a way out of this. Though adrenaline coursed through Jerome's veins, giving him a surge of strength despite his throbbing head and battered body, it would be three armed men against one if he tried to strike now. So he nodded warily at Orrin.

Orrin pulled a cloak from his saddlebags and tossed it to Jerome, who caught it with his bound hands.

"Put that on to hide yer bloodied clothes," Orrin commanded.

As Jerome settled the cloak around his shoulders, Orrin unsheathed the dagger and approached. He cut the rope on Jerome's wrists, then re-sheathed the dagger and handed it to him.

Jerome tucked the dagger into his belt and nodded again, but inside his mind scrambled frantically for a plan. If de Brechin truly had eyes and ears inside the Bruce's court, he would never be able to alert the guards to this scheme before word reached Orrin—and then de Brechin—that Jerome had broken their agreement.

He could only pray that some alternative would

present itself once he was inside, or else he'd be forced to do the unthinkable.

Orrin took his arm and pulled him through the trees while the other two outlaws trailed after them, weapons pointed at Jerome's back. The palace's wooden palisades loomed through the darkness ahead. They were approaching from behind, where a smaller gate was set into the palisades.

Just before they reached the tree line, Orrin halted. "We'll be waiting, Munro." He released Jerome's arm and shoved him toward the palisades.

Gripping the jeweled hilt of the dagger in his belt, Jerome approached the gate, where two of the Bruce's guards stood on duty. He drew up the hood of his cloak to cover his bloodied hair, but left his face visible. As he stepped into the light cast from the torches on the palisades, the guards hailed him.

"Jerome Munro to see the King."

The guards nodded and immediately moved aside, for Jerome had been a fixture at the Bruce's court for several months before he'd been sent to collect seals. He crossed the torch-lit yard swiftly, passing the abbey and moving straight for the great hall, where he assumed the Bruce was hosting his feast.

Entering from the back forced him to weave his way through the winding corridors attached to the hall. As he drew nearer, the sounds of merriment drifted to him. Musicians were playing, and laughter and chatter hung in the air.

Ahead, warm yellow light spilled into the mouth of

the corridor. He ducked into the shadows, leaning against the arched entryway that opened to the hall.

Sure enough, the room was abuzz with nobles, just as it had been the night before he'd departed for France. Though the Bruce's court couldn't rival King Philip's for opulence and luxury, the room still glowed with candlelight that made the ladies' jewels sparkle. All the rich silks appeared to shimmer as nobles spun with the music or stood holding goblets of wine and chattering.

And the Bruce sat at the raised dais on the opposite side of the hall. He was watching the festivities, a smooth smile plastered on his face.

The jewels encrusting the dagger's hilt dug into Jerome's palm. He was running out of time.

Drawing in a ragged breath, he forced himself to step from the shadows and into the hall. A few of the nobles cast surprised looks at him as he began to weave his way toward the dais, but most were too drunk or focused on each other to notice him.

But as he continued across the hall, he began to feel eyes following him. He glanced at a nobleman dressed in a red tunic and breeches in the style of the Lowlands, only to find the man's gaze fixed on the dagger in Jerome's belt. The man wore a pendant on his chest, a lion cast in gold.

The lion. It was the symbol of England. *The unicorn will fall to the lion.* Balliol's words cut through the haze in Jerome's mind. It must have been the adopted symbol of de Soules's conspiracy.

As he slipped by, the man gave Jerome a subtle nod,

and Jerome knew—he was one of de Brechin and de Soules's co-conspirators.

He weaved past a noblewoman wearing a brooch made of rubies—in the shape of a lion's head. His gaze darted around the room. How many more were there? He saw at least one other man with a lion etched into the hilt of his ornamental sword.

So de Brechin had been telling the truth—he had eyes even in the heart of the Bruce's court. Which meant Jerome was good and cornered in his task.

He ducked his head, praying for some solution, some way out of this bind, but instead his mind filled with images of Elaine. Bleeding. Screaming. Dying.

Before he realized what he was doing, he'd stepped onto the dais before the Bruce. He lifted his head, letting the candlelight fall on his face.

The Bruce's gaze locked on him, his keen brown eyes widening.

"Jerome. What the hell are ye doing here, man? Ye are supposed to be in France."

The moment had come, and yet still Jerome silently begged for an answer. If he could trade his life for the King's, or for Elaine's, he would do it in a heartbeat. Yet cruel fate had given him no such option.

He searched the Bruce's confused features. This was the man who had united Scotland, who had shed blood on countless battlefields against the English for his people's independence. He was more than a King. He was the country's hero.

Jerome couldn't do it. But not because of his pride, his determination not to become a traitor like his father, or even his loyalty to the King. He knew that if Elaine somehow made it through this, she would never forgive him for destroying the cause she believed in most —freedom.

An idea came to him then, one last chance to save Elaine, if not himself. If he appeared to *attempt* to assassinate the Bruce, yet failed, would de Brechin still harm Elaine? He would have to make it convincing to ensure that de Brechin's co-conspirators in the hall would believe he was in earnest.

It was the thinnest imaginable plan, but it was his only hope. He pulled the jeweled dagger from its sheath and pointed it at the Bruce.

"Jerome?" The Bruce pushed back from the table and stood slowly from his chair. "What are ye doing?"

"I pray that you'll trust me, Robert," Jerome said. "And that God forgives me." He closed his eyes, letting the hall and the crowd and the Bruce fall away. "Elaine, I love ye."

He lunged across the table, but instead of driving the dagger point forward, he used his other hand to shove the Bruce into his chair. He pushed the King so hard that he and the chair tumbled backward and landed with a clatter on the dais.

"He's got a weapon!" someone shouted behind Jerome.

Suddenly the hall erupted into shrieks of terror. Guards exploded through every door and entrance, shoving their way through the nobles to reach the dais. The nobles scrambled in every direction, some trying to flee to safety, others attempting to see what had happened to the King.

When the guards reached Jerome, they threw him onto the table roughly. The dagger went flying from his hand to land a few paces away on the dais. Several of the guards bellowed at him to surrender, though he didn't struggle against them. Others searched him for another weapon while still more circled the King where he'd toppled to the ground.

Jerome's ears rang with the panicked screams of those in the hall and the shouts of the guards. He could only pray that in the pandemonium, none of de Brechin's allies would be able to tell if he'd succeeded in killing the King or not. With any luck, de Brechin wouldn't hurt Elaine and she would find a way to escape somehow.

He closed his eyes once more, letting the guards roughly search him. He expected at any moment to feel the sharp bite of a blade giving him a swift traitor's death for the attempted assassination. But one voice, high and urgent, pierced the fog in his mind.

Someone was shouting his name over and over again. A woman.

Nay. It couldn't be. Jerome's head jerked from the tabletop and his gaze darted between the guards' bodies and into the roiling throng of nobles.

There, at the hall's main entrance, he caught a glimpse of long copper hair as someone fought against the tide of nobles trying to flee.

Elaine.

She was clawing her way toward him against the crush of bodies going the opposite direction.

"Jerome!"

She was alive and unhurt. Somehow she'd managed to escape de Brechin.

Which meant de Brechin's plan had crumbled. They had to stop his allies before they disappeared into the woodwork once more.

Jerome suddenly surged against the guards holding him down.

"The lion!" he shouted. "Stop them! Dinnae let them get away!"

Distantly, he knew he sounded like a raving lunatic, but he didn't care.

"Elaine, the lion!"

Suddenly the King sprang to his feet and loomed over Jerome.

"What the bloody hell is going on?" he roared.

"Robert, there is a plot to kill ye."

"I surmised that," the Bruce snapped.

"They forced my hand. I can explain aught, but ye must stop yer guests. At least three here tonight are part of a conspiracy against ye. They bear the symbol of the lion."

Jerome stared up at the Bruce, panting raggedly and praying he would believe him. The Bruce lifted his gaze from Jerome to the throng of nobles scrambling about the hall. With a muttered curse, he turned to his guards.

"Release this man and halt everyone from leaving," he ordered.

The guards' eyes rounded in confusion, but they

were well trained enough to obey without question. They abandoned Jerome and began plowing back into the sea of people, shouting for the doors to be closed and the palisade gates sealed.

Just then Elaine broke through the crowd and reached the dais. Jerome sprang from the table and collided with her so hard that he brought them both to the dais's wooden surface.

"Ye're alive."

"So are you."

He buried his face in her hair, squeezing her so hard that she made a pained noise after a moment. Reluctantly, he released her, only to find the Bruce standing over them with a baffled frown on his face.

"Ye two have some explaining to do."

Jerome rose on shaky legs and helped Elaine up. The Bruce motioned to one of the nearby guards.

"See that the entire palace and abbey are completely sealed," he said. "And secure *that*." He pointed at the discarded lion dagger that lay a few feet away. He turned back to Elaine and Jerome. "Ye two —follow me."

Chapter Thirty-Four

"What in the bloody hell is going on?" the Bruce demanded for the second time that night when the door to his small meeting room had been closed tight.

At his harsh words, the last of Elaine's composure snapped. She sank into a chair, buried her face in her hands, and wept.

Jerome was instantly by her side.

"Are ye hurt, lass? What is it? Please, speak to me."

"Nay," she mumbled into her palms. "I am not hurt —not truly. I am just so *tired*."

She'd driven herself beyond what she'd ever thought possible tonight, clinging to the hope that she would be in time to save Jerome.

And she had been. Jerome and the King were both alive and well. They'd stopped de Brechin and de Soules's plot. Yet Elaine had used every last drop of strength she possessed.

Suddenly Jerome was lifting her in his arms. He cradled her against his chest and sat in the chair she'd occupied a moment before, settling her in his lap.

"It's over," he murmured, his voice low and soothing. "Ye did it, lass. All is well."

For a long while, the small chamber was quiet except for Elaine's soft sobs. When at last the worst of her tears abated, the Bruce spoke again, this time gentling his voice.

"What happened?"

Jerome's arms tightened reassuringly around her. He drew in a breath and began.

He told the Bruce of the uneventful voyage to France, but before he continued, the Bruce interjected.

"And what of ye, Elaine? When I realized ye were missing, I feared the worst."

Elaine lifted her head from Jerome's chest and looked up at the Bruce. "I-I bought passage for myself to France as well. I left the same night Finn did."

"Why on earth did ye do that?"

She swallowed. "Finn said that if he had another man he could trust, he'd send someone after the envoy to warn them of what I overheard that night. I only thought to help, to save the mission to deliver the declaration."

The Bruce let out a long breath and sank into a chair opposite them. "Why didnae ye at least send word? We were worried for ye—especially Finn."

Confusion crashed over her. Her heart splintered at the mention of Finn. "We did—we sent a missive to be delivered only to Finn's hands explaining what I had done, but it must never have reached him. I only wish..." Tears clogged her throat once more, but she forced herself to swallow them. "I only wish he would have gotten it before de Brechin's men killed him."

The Bruce's brows shot together. "But Finn is here, lass."

"Ye mean...ye buried him here at Scone?" Jerome asked, uncertainty lacing his voice.

"Nay," the Bruce replied. "I mean he's here in the palace. He's alive."

Elaine bolted from Jerome's lap. "What?"

"My guards found him no' far from here yesterday morn. He'd been badly beaten, but he nearly took out a few of my men for trying to bring him to the palace. He said he'd tracked de Brechin back to Scone and was determined to hunt him down."

The Bruce rose as well and moved to the door. He spoke quietly with one of the guards posted outside, instructing the man to bring Finn to the chamber.

Elaine listened in disbelief. "De Brechin said he'd set his men on Finn and killed him," she said to the Bruce as he stepped back inside.

"Aye, Finn said he'd nearly caught up with the bastard in the Borderlands when half a dozen of de Brechin's men attacked and de Brechin himself slipped away," the Bruce replied. "Still, Finn managed to best the men, and even with a broken arm and more than a few cuts and bruises, he tracked de Brechin all the way back here. As I said, he was none too pleased that he was forced to return to the palace, but my men thought he might drive himself into his grave in his search for de Brechin."

Happy tears blurred Elaine's vision. "Aye, that sounds like Finn."

Just then, the door swung open and there he was, her surly, scowling brother-in-law, his arm in a sling and his face covered in half-healed bruises and scratches.

"Finn!" Elaine launched herself at him, uncaring of either his injuries or her own.

"Lainey!" His eyes widened in shock just before she reached him for a hard hug. "Where the bloody hell have ye been? The Bruce told me ye've been gone since I went after de Brechin."

She drew back, sobering. "I went to France to warn the envoy about de Soules."

His battered features darkened and he opened his mouth to deliver what Elaine was sure would be a blistering lecture, but before he could speak, the Bruce interjected.

"I want to hear the rest of it. How did ye managed to reach France and find the envoy?"

Once everyone was seated, with Elaine in her own chair this time instead of Jerome's lap, she picked up the story. She explained how she'd secured passage on the Bonny Berta, and Captain MacDougal's kind treatment of her. Jerome told of how she'd arrived in Calais at nearly the same moment as King Philip, and that they'd taken on the act of being lovers for the King's benefit.

At that, Finn cast a narrow-eyed glare at Jerome, but Jerome continued on, describing how Elaine had apprised him of what she'd overheard, and their shared suspicions about de Soules. He spoke of their journey to Paris, and how they'd caught de Soules slipping away. When he explained Lady Vivienne's revelation about de Soules being seen on Edward Balliol's estate, the Bruce jerked forward in his chair.

"Bloody hell," he muttered.

"Aye," Jerome replied. "That was when Elaine devised the plan to coerce information out of Balliol about the plot against ye, Robert." He turned warm eyes on Elaine and she felt her chest swell with pride.

Elaine explained how Lady Vivienne had helped them detain de Soules in France, and that Kieran had taken charge of the mission to deliver the declaration. When she described their meeting with Balliol, the Bruce muttered a few more choice curses under his breath.

"Bloody bastard," he said. "Damn pretender, thinking he deserves my place just because he's willing to sit on King Edward's lap."

"We believe Balliol is merely a puppet in this scheme, as his father was before him," Jerome said gravely. "He was chosen as yer replacement because he would have acquiesced to the demands of English-sympathizing nobles like de Brechin and de Soules. They were the true masterminds behind this plot."

"But when we learned that they didn't just mean to dethrone you, but assassinate you, we returned to Scotland as fast as we could," Elaine went on. She explained their plan to reach Scone, but that de Brechin and his men had attacked them and taken them hostage.

"De Brechin said he'd been waiting for word from

de Soules when he spotted us instead," Jerome said. "He vowed to kill Elaine unless I carried out the assassination, since he couldnae show his face near the palace anymore. I agreed to do his bidding on the promise that he wouldnae hurt Elaine."

Elaine looked down to find Jerome gripping the arms of his chair so hard that his knuckles had turned white. She caught Finn eyeing Jerome once more, but instead of a frown, he wore an assessing look, and his dark eyes shone with guarded respect.

"His men brought me here and warned me that if I failed, they'd send word to de Brechin and Elaine would be killed. My only hope was to make it seem as though I'd attempted to stab ye, Robert, and cause enough chaos and uncertainty that Elaine would be safe. But then she was here."

He turned to Elaine then, searching her with his gaze. "How did ye do it, lass? How did ye escape?"

She felt both the Bruce and Finn's eyes lock on her as well. She drew in a steadying breath.

"De Brechin thought me naught more than a weak girl. He assumed he could handle me on his own. He was wrong."

Memories of her fear, of de Brechin's hands on her, and then his sightless eyes and all the blood everywhere, made her shudder and squeeze her eyes shut for a long moment. But then she willed herself to continue. "I managed to free my hands and stab him in the neck. We struggled, but I bested him. He is…" She had to swallow before going on. "He is dead."

Jerome's warm, gentle hand closed over hers, and she looked up to find his dark eyes full of emotion.

"Ye are the bravest woman I've ever kenned," he said softly.

The chamber fell silent for a long moment before Elaine managed to go on. "I found my way to the palace just in time to see your guards take Jerome down, sire."

Jerome frowned, turning back to the Bruce. "Ye said ye'd surmised that there would be an assassination attempt, Robert. How?"

"When my men found Finn in the woods, he insisted that de Brechin was close, which made both of us suspect that some sort of attack was imminent."

"I might have been able to stop him before all this if ye hadnae insisted on dragging me back here," Finn growled.

The Bruce cocked a russet eyebrow at him. "Ye were closer to dead than alive when my men came upon ye," he replied. "A simple thank ye for saving yer life, setting that arm of yers, and giving ye food, water, and shelter would suffice."

Finn muttered something under his breath that the Bruce pretended not to hear. He returned his gaze to Jerome and Elaine.

"Regardless, de Brechin's presence in the area had us prepared for a strike—hence all my guards at the ready just outside the hall. But what were ye shouting about a lion, man?" he asked.

Jerome quickly explained what Balliol had said about de Soules's saying, the jeweled dagger, and the lion symbols he'd seen on three of the nobles in the hall.

The Bruce's face grew darker with each word. When Jerome finished, the King pounded his fist against the arm of his chair.

"Even though they've failed, their very existence— and right in my midst, no less—is an assault against my reign. I'll weed out every last one of the bastards, I vow it. This madness cannae go unpunished."

"What will ye do?" Finn asked quietly, all seriousness now.

"As we speak, my guards are gathering those who were in the hall tonight," the Bruce replied. "With yer help, Jerome, we'll identify the three ye saw earlier and determine if there were more present this eve." He stroked his russet and gray beard in thought for a moment. "With the threat of a public drawing and quartering over their heads, I imagine a few will turn on their compatriots and give up any other names."

"What of de Soules?" Jerome murmured.

"I'll send word to Avignon instructing Kieran to fetch de Soules from Paris on his return from delivering the declaration. Kieran will bring him to Scone—as a prisoner of the Scottish crown under charges of treason. We'll see what he has to say for himself when he arrives."

"And Balliol?" Elaine ventured. "What will you do about him?"

The Bruce clucked his tongue in annoyance. "If the man is aught like his father, the moment he realizes the plot has fallen through, he'll seek refuge with King Edward. Unless I want to march all the way to London for his head, I'm afraid we'll have to ignore him for the time being."

"If that is all, Robert, I would have the healer see to Lainey and let the lass rest," Finn said, eyeing her.

Elaine glanced down at herself to find her gray wool gown covered in dirt and blood. Her wrists were chafed from the rope and her arms ached dully where de Brechin had stabbed her. She imagined that her face was tear-stained and drawn with exhaustion as well.

"Aye, of course," the Bruce replied, giving Elaine a somber nod. "Yer King and country owe a great debt to ye, lass—to both of ye. I willnae soon forget all ye've done for me."

Pushing himself from his chair, the Bruce fixed Jerome with a measuring look. "If ye are up to it, I'd have ye begin assessing my guests right away. The thought of traitors in my midst is making me twitchy."

"There is one more thing, Robert," Jerome said. He took Elaine's hand in his and drew in a breath. "I'd like yer permission to marry this woman."

Elaine felt her eyes go round. Aye, she'd agreed to marry Jerome if they made it through this alive, but she hadn't expected him to take the first possible opportunity to pursue the matter. Her heart did a little flip in her chest.

The Bruce, too, blinked in surprise. He opened his mouth, but to Elaine's shock, Finn spoke before the King could.

"I give ye my blessing," he said evenly. "In truth, it is yer father's place to do so, Lainey, but I dinnae mind speaking in his stead to say that Jerome Munro is a good man worthy of ye—that is, if ye'll have him."

Her vision blurring with happy tears, she turned to Jerome. "Aye," she said, her voice thick with emotion. "I will."

Epilogue

Late July, 1320
Two months later
Scone, Scotland

"Kieran MacAdams approaches, sire!"

Jerome's head snapped up at the guard's announcement. His gaze met Elaine's across the King's table on the raised dais. All thoughts of the trade agreement with France they'd been discussing with the Bruce over the morning meal fled.

Elaine's bright, excited eyes reflected his thoughts. Kieran brought William de Soules with him—which meant the last conspirator against the Bruce would finally face justice.

And they would finally be wed.

A few days after de Brechin's thwarted assassination attempt, Finn returned to Trellham Keep to allow his arm to heal and to be with Rosamond when she delivered their bairn—another healthy boy to join Rand. But the Bruce had requested that Elaine and Jerome remain at Scone to assist him in the process of hunting down and questioning those who'd been involved in the plot.

The three guests Jerome had seen that night at the feast, along with Orrin and the other two men who'd served de Brechin, had all been taken into the King's custody. The nobles were Sir John Logie, Sir Gilbert Malherbe, and Countess Agnes of Strathearn. The Countess had immediately come undone under the threat of being drawn and quartered. In exchange for a life of imprisonment rather than death, she'd turned over Sir Richard Broun and Roger Mowbray, as well as a few lesser nobles.

All the co-conspirators were land owners who'd once supported Balliol and English control over Scotland instead of the Bruce. When the Bruce had come into power, they'd all reluctantly pledged their fealty to him, and he'd willingly forgiven their past opposition. Yet despite several of the traitors' public support of the Bruce—some had even attached their seals of approval to the Declaration of Arbroath—they'd secretly turned against him, imagining they'd been passed over for more lands and titles. Greed was a powerful poison.

Roger Mowbray, who had already been ailing, died in the King's custody. The others remained locked in Scone's dungeon, awaiting the Bruce's final judgement.

But with the matter unresolved until de Soules, the conspiracy's architect, could be brought to Scone, the Bruce had requested that Elaine and Jerome hold off on their nuptials so that they could remain focused on fully unraveling the plot against him. Elaine had also wished to delay their wedding until Rosamond was recovered enough to travel with the whole family to Scone for the event.

The waiting had been torture. Now that Elaine held Jerome's heart, and he hers, he wanted naught more than to bind them together before the eyes of God, the King, and Elaine's family. Luckily, the Bruce and all those in the palace had turned a blind eye to the fact that Elaine had stolen off to Jerome's chamber every night for the last two months.

Yet Kieran's arrival with de Soules in tow would put an end to all their clandestine meetings. Jerome would finally be able to say that he had the bravest, boldest, bonniest wife in all of Scotland.

But first de Soules had to be dealt with.

The Bruce ordered the great hall emptied except for Elaine, Jerome, and a handful of guards. Their meal was cleared away, as were the other tables and benches below the dais.

Just as the last of the servants slipped out, the double doors opened and in strode Kieran, pulling a bound William de Soules by the arm after him.

Never one for formalities, Kieran sketched a faint bow to the King, then unceremoniously shoved de Soules to his knees before the dais.

"As requested, sire," Kieran said. "The traitor."

Gone were de Soules's obsequious, overwrought manners and in their place was a defiant sneer. His once-fine clothes were tattered and stained, yet even on his knees, and even after his spectacular failure, his brown eyes burned with hatred as he stared up at the Bruce.

"Do ye have aught to say for yerself, man?" the Bruce asked evenly.

De Soules spat on the ground. "Ye may have won this battle, but the war is far from over. There are others like me, others who are tired of kissing the hem of a pretender-King, and when they rise again——"

"Oh, aye," the Bruce cut in. "Havenae ye heard? Nay, I suppose ye wouldnae have. We've already apprehended all yer co-conspirators."

As the Bruce began rattling off the names of the others they'd captured, de Soules's eyes grew wider and wider in disbelief.

"And the lass here killed yer friend David de Brechin with her bare hands," the Bruce added blithely, gesturing toward Elaine. She stared at de Soules with the closest thing to hate Jerome had ever seen in her vibrant eyes.

"Nay," de Soules hissed. He shot Elaine a detestable look. It took all of Jerome's self-restraint to keep from vaulting over the table and pummeling de Soules into oblivion just for laying eyes on her.

"Aye," the Bruce countered calmly. "In a matter of days, I am set to pass final judgement on them all."

"Some are already calling it the Black Parliament," Jerome commented, fixing a hard stare on de Soules. "For death promises to be the outcome for those who would seek to assassinate their King."

De Soules's eyes darted from Jerome to the Bruce.

"Ye can kill me, but it will only serve to make me a martyr in the eyes of those who sympathize with me."

The Bruce waved as if de Soules's threat was naught more than the buzzing of a midge.

"Oh, the others will receive a traitor's death—except for Agnes of Strathearn, who turned so quickly on the others. But I'm inclined no' to grant ye the same fate."

De Soules lifted his chin defiantly, but Jerome didn't miss the fact that he swallowed hard.

"Aye," the Bruce continued evenly. "I'm inclined to make an example of ye instead. But no' by displaying yer entrails in a public execution or mounting yer head on a pike outside Scone."

He leaned forward, his tone sharpening. "Nay, I think I'll let ye live. That way, every day ye sit in my dungeon will serve as a reminder of yer failure to best me. Every breath ye draw will be a token of my perseverance. Ye'll become an example to others who think to cross me—and yer punishment will be to remember yer ruin for the rest of yer long life."

"Nay," de Soules breathed again. He stared in disbelief at the King, who motioned to two of the guards to remove de Soules. As the guards began dragging him from the hall, he screamed at the Bruce, alternating between curses and pleas, until the doors closed behind him and the hall fell silent.

The Bruce let a long breath go. "That was more satisfying than I'd imagined," he said. He gave himself a little shake and fixed his attention on Kieran, growing sober once more. "What news from France?"

Kieran clasped his hands behind his back. "We success-fully delivered the Declaration of Arbroath to the Pope," he began. "Thanks to Bishop Kininmund, who spoke on yer behalf, sire, the Pope seemed receptive to reversing course and acknowledging Scotland as sovereign from England."

The Bruce slapped the arm of his chair, a wide grin breaking out behind his beard. "Excellent!"

"In fact, the Pope asked Bishop Kininmund to remain in Avignon to discuss the role of the Scottish Church in yer efforts for freedom. And he indicated that he would be writing to King Edward to urge him to cease his war against Scotland once and for all."

"That is better than I'd let myself hope for," the Bruce said, shaking his head in amazement.

"I would have remained longer, too, but when yer missive about the attack against ye reached me, I made haste for Paris," Kieran said. "Apparently word of the assassination attempt traveled just as swiftly as yer missive, for when I reached the French court, King Philip had already secured de Soules in his dungeon. If it makes ye feel better for allowing the man to live, Vivi-enne, the lady-in-waiting who aided us, kept de Soules drugged and miserable for nearly a fortnight before the King finally learned of his role in the attempted coup and locked him away."

"Aye, that is a pleasant thought," the Bruce mused.

Kieran's mouth quirked into a wry smile before he returned to his serious demeanor. "By the time I passed through Picardy with de Soules, Balliol had already fled to England."

The Bruce nodded. "Aye, he is said to be at Westminster hiding behind King Edward's robes."

"King Philip was none too pleased to learn that the pretender had sheltered in France and that treasonous plotting against his ally had taken place on his soil. He has seized all of Balliol's land, as well as de Soules's, and is even considering rescinding King Edward's French titles and lands for harboring Balliol." Kieran shrugged. "Philip is eager to show ye that he counts ye as a friend, sire, and that yer alliance remains strong."

"I never doubted Philip," the Bruce replied. "I'll write to him immediately to let him hear it from me."

"There is…one final matter I wish to discuss with ye, sire." Suddenly Kieran's normally confident air was replaced with hesitancy.

The Bruce frowned. "What is it?"

"Given the fact that de Soules fomented his plot no' only in Scotland but also on French soil, King Philip is determined to ensure that if any of the man's sympathizers remain in France, he'll weed them out. Still, Lady Vivienne's role in incapacitating de Soules is now public knowledge in court. If any of de Soules's co-conspirators still lurk in France, she could become a target for helping ye."

"What are ye suggesting?" the Bruce asked.

Kieran made his features expressionless. "I'd like permission to return to France, collect Lady Vivienne, and stow her someplace safe until we can be sure the threat has passed."

Jerome's gaze shot to Elaine. Her brows rose in

surprise, but then she met his eyes with a knowing look on her face.

The Bruce, however, who hadn't witnessed the taut bickering between Kieran and Vivienne—and wasn't privy to Jerome's suspicion that something other than animosity sparked between the two—merely nodded slowly.

"Aye, indeed. All those who have aided us must be ensured safety and protection." The King straightened in his seat abruptly. "Have ye heard of my Bodyguard Corps, man?"

Kieran jerked in surprise. "Aye, of course." His gaze flicked to Jerome. "They are the band of yer most trusted warriors, pledged to protect the innocent and serve yer cause in every way they can."

"If ye are to watch over this Lady Vivienne in my name, it seems only fitting that ye should enter the ranks of the Corps." The Bruce rose, dropping the last vestiges of formality as he stepped from the dais. He extended his forearm to Kieran. "What do ye say, man? Will ye join?"

A rare smile flashed over Kieran's normally hard features as he clasped the Bruce's arm. "Aye, it would be my honor, sire."

"Robert," the Bruce corrected. "Ye are part of my inner circle now. I ken ye're eager to be off, but before ye return to France, I'll arrange for ye to meet with Ansel Sutherland and a few of the others in the Corps. For the time being, Jerome here can fill ye in on what it means to become a member of the team."

Jerome rose and stepped from the dais, giving

Kieran a firm forearm shake. "Welcome to the family," he said. "I cannae think of another man I'd trust more."

Elaine joined them as well. "Give my best to Lady Vivienne when you reach her," she said warmly. "And keep her safe."

Kieran sobered. "I will."

The Bruce turned to Elaine and Jerome. "And as for ye two, I ken Scone must seem humble compared with King Philip's court, but I'm keen to keep ye here."

Elaine blinked in surprise. "You…you wish for us to stay?"

Though she and Jerome had spoken about their future, much had been unknown these past two months —other than the fact that whatever came, they would face it together.

Elaine loved her family, but she didn't wish to spend the rest of her days at sleepy Trellham Keep. Jerome would always have a place in his clan thanks to his devotion to Laird Munro, but he didn't hold land of his own in the Highlands. And though Elaine had been dazzled by France, she'd said she couldn't imagine living anywhere but Scotland now, much to Jerome's gratification.

But with so much uncertainty until de Soules's conspiracy could be resolved once and for all, they hadn't let themselves hope for any one outcome.

Yet judging from the way Elaine's eyes shone with eager anticipation, remaining at the Bruce's court was her deepest desire.

"Of course I want ye to stay!" the Bruce replied. "We still have this trade agreement with the French to nail down, and then there is the matter of redistributing the lands of de Soules and his allies."

"And after that?" Elaine asked hesitantly. "Jerome has the skills of a warrior to offer you, sire, but I have no special talents or abilities."

The Bruce folded her hand in both of his. "What was it Munro here said about ye the first time we met, lass? That ye were my fiercest supporter and most loyal subject?"

Jerome swelled with pride, for the words were more apt than ever. For her part, Elaine's cheeks turned rosy with a modest blush.

The Bruce fixed her with a serious look. "Ye may no' come with any fancy skills, but ye do possess the most valuable thing of all—loyalty." He shifted to encompass Jerome with his gaze as well. "I couldnae ask for more after all ye've done. Stay, and honor me with yer presence."

Jerome had to clear his suddenly tight throat before he could answer. He looked to Elaine, whose eyes brimmed with happy tears. At her nod, he spoke. "The honor is ours, Robert."

The Bruce squeezed Elaine's hand before releasing it, a pleased smile on his face.

With the matter settled, Jerome drew a deep breath. "If ye dinnae need us for the moment, Robert, Elaine and I have some business to discuss."

"We do?" she asked, giving him a quizzical look.

"Aye. We have a wedding to plan."

The Bruce threw his head back and laughed. "Off

with ye then. I have an inkling just what this 'planning' will involve."

Kieran snorted and Elaine sucked in a scandalized breath, her cheeks burning red once more, but Jerome didn't rise to the Bruce's bait. Instead, he took Elaine's hand and rushed them from the hall down one of the many branching corridors toward his chamber.

"You can't truly mean to—" Elaine huffed as he pulled her into his chamber and closed the door.

"Why no'? We are finally free to wed. What better way to celebrate than this?" He dropped a searing kiss on her lips. To his satisfaction, he felt her instantly melt in surrender. He, too, yielded to the desire rising like a storm within him.

"I love ye, Elaine," he breathed, drawing her close. "I cannae wait to spend the rest of my life showing ye."

And he did just that.

The End

Author's Note

As always, it is one of my great joys in writing historical romance to combine a fictional romantic storyline with real historical details. This book offered a rare and special opportunity particularly when it came to the history, because so much of the real events at this time were more remarkable than fiction!

The drafting and delivery of the Declaration of Arbroath provided an amazing—and true—backdrop for my story. Considered the prototype for the United States Declaration of Independence, this document outlined the atrocities committed by the English against the Scots. It petitioned the Pope to acknowledge Scotland as an independent nation and reverse his decision to excommunicate Robert the Bruce.

There were thought to be about fifty signatories on the declaration, including not only the Bruce's noble allies, but also some who had been resistant to his reign. Not all the signatories could travel to add their seal in person, so many sent their seals to Scone, where the Bruce ran his parliament. I altered those events slightly, inventing the character of Jerome Munro to collect the seals rather than having the nobles simply send them themselves.

A side-note on Scone—Scone Abbey has long been the site for the crowning of Scotland's Kings. The famous Stone of Scone (or Stone of Destiny) was a large rock that had historically been used for the coronation of Scotland's monarchs. In 1296, King Edward I of England stole the stone and had it moved to his court in Westminster. There he had it fitted into a wooden throne for England's monarchs to sit on, symbolically indicating that England's Kings were now rulers of Scotland as well. The stone remained in England for six centuries until it was ceremoniously returned to Edinburgh in 1996, where it remains—except in the event of a British coronation.

Despite the removal of the stone, Scone Abbey served as the location of Scotland's parliament for much of the medieval era. The original abbey, along with the palace added to accommodate the Bruce and other monarchs when they were at Scone, no longer exists. However, a depiction on the abbey's seal, plus some architectural fragments, give historians a vague idea of what Scone would have looked like in the Bruce's lifetime.

It was built in the Romanesque style, with a central tower topped with a spire. It was likely surrounded by a ditch and wooden palisade for defense. An archaeological dig in 2008 revealed three complete human skeletons buried on the abbey's ground, but they have not been identified. A newer abbey and palace now rest atop the ruins of the old, making the history of Scone all the more layered.

Returning to the Declaration of Arbroath—the lines I incorporated from the declaration, including the most-often quoted section ("As long as but a hundred of us remain alive, never will we on any conditions be brought under English rule. It is in truth not for glory, nor riches, nor honors that we are fighting, but for freedom—for that alone, which no honest man gives up but with life itself.") came from a popular translation of the original Latin document. Those lines are displayed on the walls of the National Museum of Scotland.

Once the declaration was drafted at Arbroath Abbey by Abbot Bernard of Kilwinning and the seals affixed, the Bruce sent the document, along with letters from himself and four of his bishops, to the Pope. The Papal court at this time had been established in Avignon, France, though to my knowledge the envoy did not receive a royal escort from King Philip V (called Philip the Tall) of France. I did, however, include a nod to the original members of the envoy: Bishop Kininmund, Sir Odard de Maubuisson, and Sir Adam Gordon (I gave Kieran the surname MacAdams in honor of Adam Gordon).

Researching medieval France provided a fun challenge. Calais was indeed an important and bustling trading port at that time. Paris was a large city of roughly a quarter of a million people, and rapidly growing. As I described in the story, Paris was walled several times, each time growing larger to accommodate the expanding city. The land north and east of the Seine was dominated by trade and commerce, while the south-west side contained universities and scholars.

The *Île de la Cité*, the Island of Paris, served as both the governmental and religious heart of the city. With the soaring, majestic Notre-Dame Cathedral on one end and the King's palace on the other, it was a reminder to Paris's rulers to balance the powers of church and state. Though the medieval palace no longer stands in its entirety, some of its most famous buildings, including the Sainte-Chapelle and the Hall of Soldiers, one of the many great halls in the palace, still survive.

On the banks opposite the palace sat the Louvre, which used to be a military fortress, then the royal residence. But as Paris grew and experienced peace and prosperity, France's Kings decided that living in a converted fortress wasn't comfortable enough, hence the construction of the palace on the *Île de la Cité*. And now those lucky enough to visit Paris can look at art from the medieval era in the Louvre museum!

By all accounts, Philip V was a smart and amiable King. He became King when his older brother, Louis X, died unexpectedly in 1316. He did indeed feud for several years with Edward II of England, for Edward refused to pay homage to Philip for lands he held in Gascony. Though Philip had his hands full with matters in his own country, he did support Robert the Bruce and allowed the Scottish envoy to pass through France to reach Avignon.

And here is where the history gets really juicy.

Patrick Dunbar, Earl of March, who was another member of the envoy delivering the declaration to Avignon, returned to Scotland before reaching the Papal court. Apparently he learned somewhere in France of a conspiracy against the Bruce and rushed back to Scone to warn the King. Though William de Soules (a real historical figure) wasn't present amongst the envoy, Dunbar apparently learned of a connection between de Soules, who owned land in the Picardy region of France, and Edward Balliol, who was residing at Château de Hélicourt in the same area (which was where Edward Balliol's father, John Balliol, died in 1314).

De Soules had been given the position of royal Butler of Scotland by Robert the Bruce in 1318 (not a butler like we'd think of today—this was actually a hereditary court role of honor). All outward signs indicated that de Soules was a loyal supporter of the Bruce. He was even one of the signatories on the Declaration of Arbroath. But in fact de Soules deeply resented the Bruce.

De Soules believed the Bruce had unjustly usurped the throne from the rightful line of successors, the Balliols. He also believed himself slighted when the Bruce redistributed lands and titles won back from the English as his campaign for freedom gained victories. De Soules began plotting to overthrow the Bruce and replace him with Edward Balliol, the son of the one-time puppet King for the English, John Balliol.

He gathered a group of like-minded nobles who all felt similarly overlooked for the Bruce's favors, as well as supporters of a Balliol King who would kowtow to

England. Because of his position as Butler of Scotland, de Soules was close enough to the Bruce to formulate a bold assassination plan.

Interestingly, despite fairly good record-keeping within the Bruce's court at Scone, there are no records of what de Soules's specific plan was, or just how close he got to executing it. Historians believe this is because the Bruce wished for the details to remain secret so that his opponents couldn't replicate de Soules's scheme. Therefore I fictionalized all the specifics of the attack, but the names I used for de Soules's conspirators are historically accurate.

In addition to William de Soules, Sir David de Brechin joined the conspiracy, along with Countess Agnes of Strathearn and Sirs John Logie, Gilbert Malherbe, Richard Broun, and Roger Mowbray. All of the co-conspirators had connections to both John Comyn, who had been a Balliol supporter and whom the Bruce had killed in a church, earning him his excommunication from the Pope, and Balliol himself. All had at one point or another supported either English rule over Scotland or Balliol's puppet reign. The Bruce had been generous with pardons for those who had once been loyal to Balliol, Comyn, and even King Edward of England, yet his leniency didn't prevent them from plotting against him.

Once captured, Countess Agnes of Strathearn cooperated, resulting in her punishment of life in prison rather than death. De Brechin, Logie, Malherbe, and Broun were all beheaded. Mowbray did indeed die in custody before he could be executed, though judgement was passed on his remains. The Bruce still allowed him to receive a Christian burial, however. The judgements were passed down at what came to be infamously known as the "Black Parliament" in Scone in August of 1320.

Like the countess, de Soules was also granted life in prison despite the fact that he was the architect of the conspiracy. This may have been because he cooperated and revealed the names of his co-conspirators, or maybe the Bruce thought it was a more fitting punishment to make him live out his days in a dungeon, as I portray it in my story. Either way, history was not quite through with de Soules, but I won't say more, because it will play a part in the next book in the series, Kieran and Vivienne's story!

Edward Balliol, too, hasn't reached the end of his story yet. He spent much of the first half of his life petitioning King Edward II to give him money, protection, land, and more based on the fact that his father and Edward's had had an agreement. But after the Battle of Bannockburn, which proved Edward II to be ineffectual against the Scottish, and the death of Balliol's father that same year in 1314, Edward Balliol shifted his attention from winning King Edward's favor to eyeing the Scottish throne that had once been his father's.

It's unclear exactly how large a role he played in the plotting of de Soules's conspiracy, or if he expected to simply be installed as King once de Soules and his co-conspirators got rid of the Bruce. Either way, when the Bruce was made aware of the plot against him and captured de Soules and his allies, Balliol fled his estate in France and took refuge in Edward II's court in London.

Edward II could have been behind the entire scheme. Because of a treaty with the Bruce made in 1319, he couldn't openly strike against the Scots. His direct attempts to defeat the Bruce—at the Battle of Bannockburn and in multiple attempts to retake Borderland strongholds like Berwick Castle—had been utterly disastrous. Still, he would have benefited immensely from the Bruce's assassination and the installation of an English-sympathizing Balliol King.

But thanks to several loyal Scots, de Soules's conspiracy was foiled and the Bruce lived to rule another day. What was more, the Pope received the Declaration of Arbroath in June or July of 1320, just before the Black Parliament, and decided in the Bruce's favor, reversing his excommunication, recognizing Scotland's independence, and writing personally to Edward II urging him to end his war with Scotland.

Yet those familiar with Scotland's history know that peace is always short-lived. Still, it was a joy to breathe life into the fascinating events of this time and layer them with my own fictitious tale. Thank you for journeying back to medieval Scotland with me, and look for more riveting history and unforgettable romance in the eighth book in the Highland Bodyguards series, Kieran and Vivienne's story, coming mid-2018!

Make sure to sign up for my newsletter to hear about all my sales, giveaways, and new releases. Plus, get exclusive content like stories, excerpts, cover reveals, and more.

Sign up at www.EmmaPrinceBooks.com

Thank You!

Thank you for taking the time to read *Surrender to the Scot* (Highland Bodyguards, Book 7)!

And thank you in advance for sharing your enjoyment of this book (or my other books) with fellow readers by leaving a review on Amazon. Long or short, detailed or to the point, I read all reviews and greatly appreciate you for writing one!

I love connecting with readers! Sign up for my newsletter and be the first to hear about my latest book news, flash sales, giveaways, and more—signing up is free and easy at www.EmmaPrinceBooks.com.

You also can join me on Twitter at @EmmaPrinceBooks. Or keep up on Facebook at https://www.facebook.com/EmmaPrinceBooks.

TEASERS FOR EMMA
PRINCE'S BOOKS

Highland Bodyguards Series

The Lady's Protector, the thrilling start to the Highland Bodyguards series, is available now on Amazon!

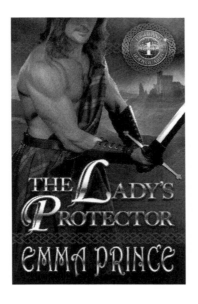

The Battle of Bannockburn may be over, but the war is far from won.

Her Protector...

Ansel Sutherland is charged with a mission from King

Robert the Bruce to protect the illegitimate son of a powerful English Earl. Though Ansel bristles at aiding an Englishman, the nature of the war for Scottish independence is changing, and he is honor-bound to serve as a bodyguard. He arrives in England to fulfill his assignment, only to meet the beautiful but secretive Lady Isolda, who refuses to tell him where his ward is. When a mysterious attacker threatens Isolda's life, Ansel realizes he is the only thing standing between her and deadly peril.

His Lady...

Lady Isolda harbors dark secrets—secrets she refuses to reveal to the rugged Highland rogue who arrives at her castle demanding answers. But Ansel's dark eyes cut through all her defenses, threatening to undo her resolve. To protect her past, she cannot submit to the white-hot desire that burns between them. As the threat to her life spirals out of control, she has no choice but to trust Ansel to whisk her to safety deep in the heart of the Highlands...

Meet Elaine Beaumore for the first time and read Finn and Rosamond's story in *A Warrior's Pledge* (**Highland Bodyguards, Book 3**). Available now on Amazon.

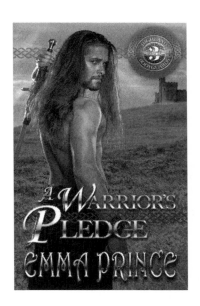

Her Warrior...

To forge an alliance between the English and the Scots, Lady Rosamond must marry a Lowland stranger. But when a mysterious attacker threatens the engagement and her life, Robert the Bruce assigns one of his most trusted warriors to protect her. Finn Sutherland's brooding gaze is almost as dark as his heart, yet Rosamond finds herself captivated by her Highland bodyguard. Now she must choose between responsibility and the searing need Finn ignites within her.

His Pledge…

Finn is honor-bound to swallow his hatred of the English and serve as bodyguard to Lady Rosamond. He never expects his charge to touch his scarred heart with her warmth and kindness. Worse, her honey hair and violet eyes bring him to his knees with lust. When the threat to Rosamond spirals out of control, Finn does the only thing he can think of to protect her—he stands in for her betrothed as a proxy husband. As desire clashes with duty, Finn's pledge will be tested like never before.

Meet Jerome Munro for the first time and read Graeme and Anna's story in *A Highland Betrothal* (**Highland Bodyguards, Book 4.5**), available now on Amazon.

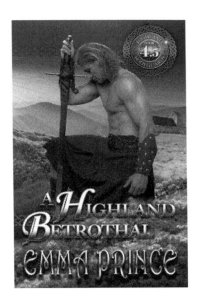

How can he protect the woman he loves when she is engaged to another?

Graeme MacKay returns from the siege on Berwick Castle a changed man. A wound to his leg has left him hobbled, but his injury is nothing compared to the blow his heart receives when he learns that Anna Ross, the only woman he has ever loved, is engaged. When Graeme is ordered to serve as Anna's bodyguard on the journey to wed her fiancé, he is tested like never before. Though he tells himself to feel nothing for her, his heart has other plans.

As the daughter of a Laird, Anna Ross has always known that it would one day be her duty to marry a stranger for the betterment of her clan. Though resigned to her fate, she owes Graeme, the Highland warrior who stole her heart, an explanation—she has never stopped loving him, despite being forced to wed another. But when a shocking truth about her betrothal is revealed, she and Graeme must embark on a perilous flight from her fiancé—or risk losing their love forever.

The Sinclair Brothers Trilogy

Go back to where it all began—with Robert and Alwin's story in ***Highlander's Ransom***, Book One of the Sinclair Brothers Trilogy. Available now on Amazon!

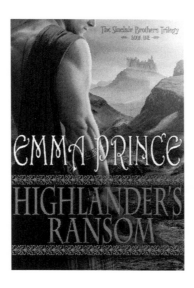

He was out for revenge...

Laird Robert Sinclair will stop at nothing to exact revenge on Lord Raef Warren, the English scoundrel who brought war to his doorstep and razed his lands and people. Leaving his clan in the Highlands to conduct covert attacks in the Borderlands, Robert lives to be a thorn in Warren's side. So when he finds a beautiful English lass on her way to marry Warren, he whisks her away to the Highlands with a plan to ransom her back to her dastardly fiancé.

She would not be controlled...

Lady Alwin Hewett had no idea when she left her father's manor to marry a man she'd never met that she would instead be kidnapped by a Highland rogue out for vengeance. But she refuses to be a pawn in any man's game. So when she learns that Robert has had them secretly wed, she will stop at nothing to regain her freedom. But her heart may have other plans...

Viking Lore Series

Step into the lush, daring world of the Vikings with
***Enthralled* (Viking Lore, Book 1)**!

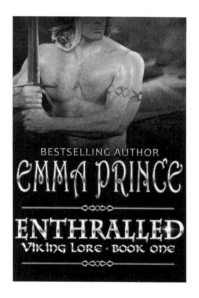

He is bound by honor...

Eirik is eager to plunder the treasures of the fabled lands
to the west in order to secure the future of his village.
The one thing he swears never to do is claim possession
over another human being. But when he journeys across
the North Sea to raid the holy houses of Northumbria,

he encounters a dark-haired beauty, Laurel, who stirs him like no other. When his cruel cousin tries to take Laurel for himself, Eirik breaks his oath in an attempt to protect her. He claims her as his thrall. But can he claim her heart, or will Laurel fall prey to the devious schemes of his enemies?

She has the heart of a warrior...

Life as an orphan at Whitby Abbey hasn't been easy, but Laurel refuses to be bested by the backbreaking work and lecherous advances she must endure. When Viking raiders storm the abbey and take her captive, her strength may finally fail her—especially when she must face her fear of water at every turn. But under Eirik's gentle protection, she discovers a deeper bravery within herself—and a yearning for her golden-haired captor that she shouldn't harbor. Torn between securing her freedom or giving herself to her Viking master, will fate decide for her—and rip them apart forever?

About the Author

Emma Prince is the Bestselling and Amazon All-Star Author of steamy historical romances jam-packed with adventure, conflict, and of course love!

Emma grew up in drizzly Seattle, but traded her rain boots for sunglasses when she and her husband moved to the eastern slopes of the Sierra Nevada. Emma spent several years in academia, both as a graduate student and an instructor of college-level English and Humanities courses. She always savored her "fun books"—normally historical romances—on breaks or vacations. But as she began looking for the next chapter in her life, she wondered if perhaps her passion could turn into a career. Ever since then, she's been reading and writing books that celebrate happily ever afters!

Visit Emma's website, www.EmmaPrinceBooks.com, for updates on new books, future projects, her newsletter sign-up, book extras, and more!

You can follow Emma on Twitter at: @EmmaPrinceBooks.

Or join her on Facebook at: www.facebook.com/EmmaPrinceBooks.

Made in the USA
Columbia, SC
21 February 2018

ROCKY AND BULLWINKLE

and the

Metal-Munching Mice

SIMON SPOTLIGHT
An imprint of Simon & Schuster Children's Publishing Division
1230 Avenue of the Americas, New York, New York 10020

Manufactured in the United States of America
First Edition   10 9 8 7 6 5 4 3 2 1
ISBN 0-689-82145-X
Library of Congress Catalog Card Number 98-60149

ROCKY AND BULLWINKLE

and the
Metal-Munching Mice

Adapted by CATHY EAST DUBOWSKI
from the script by BILL SCOTT

Simon Spotlight

A Note to Readers

Not too long ago, before cable TV, strange things appeared on the roofs of houses and apartment buildings—kind of like the antlers on Bullwinkle! These strange things were made of metal. They were called TV antennas. You've seen antennas on radios and cars. Well, TV antennas worked pretty much the same way. They received signals from TV stations and sent them into the TV sets of people's homes so everyone could watch programs like *The Rocky and Bullwinkle Show.*

Every house and building had an antenna, and everyone watched TV until one fateful night in the tiny town of Frostbite Falls. . . .

Chapter 1

TROUBLE IN TV LAND

It was an ordinary night in Frostbite Falls.

The streets were quiet. The shops were closed for the evening.

Blue light flickered from the windows of all the houses. Everyone was home watching their favorite shows on television.

TV was big in Frostbite Falls. *Really* big. In fact, it was the only town in the United States with more TV sets than people.

Until one terrible day when all the TV screens in town suddenly went blank!

The townsfolk were stumped. There was only one thing to do. They called on their heroes—Rocky and Bullwinkle.

Rocky was a small gray squirrel. He was known for his heart of gold, his aviator goggles, and his ability to fly with great skill and grace through the sky.

Bullwinkle was a very tall brown moose. He was primarily known for blocking the screen at the movies with his gigantic antlers. But he was a loyal sidekick. He could always be found at Rocky's side.

Quick as a flash, Rocky and Bullwinkle hurried to where a crowd of worried citizens had gathered in the street.

And that's when the sharp-eyed squirrel made a startling discovery.

"Hey! Look up there!" Rocky pointed

past Bullwinkle's antlers to the rooftop of the nearest house. "There's your answer."

"What do you mean, Rock?" Bullwinkle asked. "There's nothing there!"

"That's just what I mean," Rocky said. "Where are all the TV antennas?"

Sure enough, all the TV antennas had disappeared. There was nothing left but pointy metal stumps.

"We've got to do somethin', Rock!" Bullwinkle said.

And in a dazzling display, Rocky the Flying Squirrel soared into the air with an armload of new antennas. One by one he zoomed over rooftops and speared them into place.

Then Bullwinkle climbed up to fasten the wires. But when he got there, he found something surprising—nothing!

The antenna that Rocky had put there just moments ago was gone.

Bullwinkle climbed down and Rocky flew to his side. "There's only one thing left to do," Rocky said.

The moose thought hard. "Buy a book?"

"No!" said Rocky. "Call the sheriff!"

When Sheriff Wright arrived, he climbed up on a rooftop to study the evidence—and gasped.

"Were they sawed off, Sheriff?" Rocky called up.

"Nope," the sheriff replied.

"Chopped off?" Bullwinkle guessed.

"Nope."

"Busted off?" Rocky suggested.

"Uh-uh." The sheriff climbed down. His

face looked as grave as a tombstone. "I don't know quite how to say this, boys."

"Try it in English first," said Bullwinkle.

"Those TV antennas," the sheriff announced, "were all bitten off. With big, sharp, wicked teeth!"

Chapter 2

TO SET A TRAP

Bullwinkle gulped. "You mean there's some metal-munchin' monster loose in this town?"

"Now, let's not jump to conclusions," the sheriff warned. "There's probably some logical explanation. Any ideas, Rocky?"

Rocky nodded. "I think we should set a trap."

And so they did.

First they picked a house in the middle of town. Then they set up a special king-sized TV antenna on the roof.

Now all they had to do was guard the antenna day and night. Sooner or later, they were bound to see who—or what—was destroying the town's antennas.

Bullwinkle got first watch.

While Rocky and the sheriff dozed nearby, Bullwinkle patrolled his lonely post.

Then, just about midnight, Bullwinkle heard something.

It sounded like a strange, metallic chatter.

"Halt!" Bullwinkle hollered into the darkness. "Who's there?"

CH-Ch-CH-Ch-CH-Ch-CH-Ch-

"Uh, I didn't quite catch the name," Bullwinkle said.

CH-Ch-CH-Ch-CH-Ch-CH-Ch-

Bullwinkle struck a match and held up the tiny flame.

And standing right in front of him was a *six-foot-tall* metal mouse!

Bullwinkle tried to call out to his friends. But the giant mouse raised its heavy, metal fist—*Bonk!*—and knocked Bullwinkle out.

Chapter 3

A TALL MOUSE TALE

The next morning, as the sun rose, Rocky and the sheriff woke up to find what remained of the decoy antenna—a tiny stump.

And there, beside it, lay Bullwinkle. Fast asleep.

"Bullwinkle!" Rocky exclaimed. "You went to sleep at your post. How could you do it?"

Bullwinkle rubbed his eyes and stumbled to his feet. "Easy. I just closed my eyes and—"

Then he felt a huge lump between his antlers. "Hey, wait a minute. I didn't go to sleep. I was attacked and *put* to sleep!"

Rocky's eyes widened in surprise. "Really? Who did it?"

Bullwinkle started to tell them. But then he stopped. Would Rocky and the sheriff really believe he'd been attacked by a six-foot-tall metal mouse?

Not likely!

Bullwinkle sighed. "I'm sorry, Rock. I can't tell you—because I don't believe it myself!" he said.

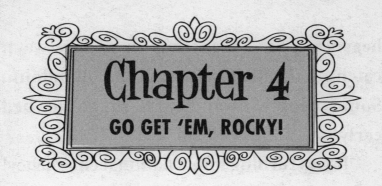

Chapter 4

GO GET 'EM, ROCKY!

The days passed. The people of Frostbite Falls struggled to come up with things to do in their TV-less town.

Some planted flowers in their useless TV sets. Some turned them into aquariums. Others filled them with wood and used them like fireplaces.

Even worse, the problem began to spread to nearby towns and cities. Even to nearby states.

Suddenly people all over the country

began to spend their time in strange ways: catching fireflies, playing the mandolin. Some people even began to go to bed early!

It was turning into a national emergency!

Something *had* to be done.

And so Senator Shunpike called a press conference on the steps of City Hall.

"Truly this is a task worthy of the greatest mind of the country!" announced the senator. "The most courageous heart. The most stalwart champion of the people. . . ."

"Yes!" the senator shouted to the crowd. "I mean Rocket J. Squirrel!"

Rocky proudly flew to the steps of City Hall and waved to the crowd. "Don't worry, folks," he said. "I'll do my best to track down the culprits."

Strangely enough, at that very moment, a tall iron lamppost began to tremble as if someone were shaking it. Then it started to fall—right on top of Rocky!

Chapter 5
MONSTER MOUSETRAP

Fortunately for Rocky, Senator Shunpike shoved him out of the way, and got hit instead. The wounded politician was whisked away on a stretcher. Rocky and Bullwinkle examined the fallen lamppost.

"No doubt about it, Bullwinkle," Rocky said. "This lamppost was bitten clear through! Who could have done it?"

"A beaver?" Bullwinkle guessed.

"Through an iron post?"

"An *eager* beaver!" Bullwinkle suggested.

Rocky shook his head. "No, it had to be some unknown creature."

"Yeah," Bullwinkle mumbled. "Like that six-foot-tall metal mouse I saw the other night."

Rocky stared at his pal. "A six-foot-tall mouse?"

Bullwinkle sighed. He decided to risk being made fun of and tell his pal the whole story.

"But why didn't you tell me before?" Rocky asked.

"I didn't think you'd believe me," Bullwinkle explained.

"I don't," Rocky admitted. "But it sure helps the plot."

So now they had a suspect: a giant metal mouse. How could they catch him?

"How about using a little mousetrap?" Bullwinkle suggested.

Rocky shook his head. "Too small." But Bullwinkle's suggestion had given Rocky an excellent idea. "Come on, Bullwinkle!" he said excitedly.

Together they quickly built a giant mousetrap, one big enough to catch a mouse as tall as a moose.

At last they wheeled the monster mouse-trap to the outskirts of town, right up to the front of a huge old house surrounded by a high brick wall.

It was Bleakly Mansion.

"Nobody's lived here for years," Bullwinkle reminded Rocky.

"Exactly," Rocky said. "So it ought to be full of mice. And maybe one of 'em is six feet tall."

Then Rocky produced a snack for the

metal-muncher—a two hundred-pound dumbbell!

"A metal-munching mouse won't be able to resist it," Rocky said.

Bullwinkle picked up the heavy dumbbell to put it in the trap. Suddenly he tripped over his own feet. "Look out!" he yelled.

As he fell, the hefty dumbbell flew through the air. It landed on the spring of the mousetrap.

Boing!

Rocky was sent flying through the air, straight through a window and into the top story of the deserted mansion.

"Rocky!" Bullwinkle cried. "Are you all right?"

His only answer was silence.

Chapter 6

BULLWINKLE TO THE RESCUE

Bullwinkle had to save his friend!

Without thinking, he hurled himself at the high gate that surrounded Bleakly Mansion.

Clang!

Hmm. That didn't work.

Then, without thinking again, he chopped down a small tree and made himself a long, thin pole. Then he tried to leap over the wall.

But the pole sank into the marshy ground.

Bullwinkle decided to stop and think.

Smoke poured from his ears from the strain on his brain!

Finally he got an idea. Maybe he could get in the same way Rocky did!

In a twinkling, the mighty moose reset the mousetrap. He perched on the crossbar. Then he tossed a rock at the spring.

Boing!

It worked! Bullwinkle flew through the air!

Meanwhile, Rocky had been creeping through the rooms of the dark, gloomy mansion.

Suddenly a huge shape loomed before him.

"Is—is that you, Bullwinkle?" Rocky whispered into the darkness.

CH-Ch-CH-Ch-CH-Ch-CH-Ch-

"Your teeth are chattering, Bullwinkle," Rocky said. "You got the flu?"

The big shape didn't answer.

Rocky lit a match. That's when he saw who his buddy really was.

"Hokey smoke!" Rocky gasped. "It's a six-foot-tall mouse!" It was just like the one Bullwinkle had described. And it was trying to catch Rocky!

It chased Rocky from room to room, and finally had him cornered.

The mouse came toward Rocky. Closer and closer. Then suddenly it turned away! Was it leaving?

No such luck!

The metal-muncher had turned around and was beginning to back up, straight toward Rocky. It was going to use its sharp metal tail as a spear!

Rocky stood helpless as the terrifying tail came toward him. At the last second Rocky jumped aside and the mouse's pointed tail stabbed the wall.

Just then Bullwinkle flew in through the window. "Rocky!" he said. "Are you all right?"

"I'm okay, Bullwinkle," Rocky said. "Let's get out of here!"

Together they ran through the mansion. But they seemed to run into a metal-munching mouse at every turn.

"How many of these things are there?" Bullwinkle gasped.

At last they came upon a secret passage. Maybe this was a good way to sneak out without getting caught.

They scrambled quickly through the opening in the wall. But as soon as they were inside—*clank!*

The opening closed behind them. They were trapped in the dark!

Then they spotted a tiny light off in the distance. Light shone through a crack in a door.

Rocky and Bullwinkle hurried down the passage toward the light. Then they froze. They could hear strange voices! Who could it be?

"Put your ear to the door," Rocky whispered.

Unfortunately there was only one way a moose with huge antlers could do that.

He put his antlers *through* the door.

Crunch!

The moose couldn't get loose, even when

someone yanked the door open. Bullwinkle was dragged into the room.

"Hokey smoke!" Rocky cried as he stared, horrified, at the scene before them. "Look!"

Chapter 7
BIG SECRET AT BLEAKLY MANSION

The room was *filled* with mice. Metal mice. And every one of them was six feet tall!

The rodents grabbed Rocky and Bullwinkle and took them to see their leader—the Big Cheese.

There was something strange about the Big Cheese. He had metal ears and a metal body like the other munching mechanical mice.

But his face was more humanlike, with dark eyes and mean-looking dark eyebrows, a fiendish smile, and strangest of all, a tiny black mustache.

"Now, where have I seen that face before?" Rocky wondered.

Little did our heroes know, the Big Cheese was in fact their worst enemy, the notorious Boris Badenov!

"What are you trying to do?" Rocky demanded.

The Big Cheese chuckled evilly. "Our big plan is to take over the whole U. S. of Hay!"

Rocky and Bullwinkle listened as the Big Cheese outlined his shocking plan.

The mechanical munching mice were going to eat up every antenna in the country, leaving the entire nation without TV!

"Everybody goes to some other country where they got television," the Big Cheese went on. "Country is left deserted. Then we move in and take over!"

Suddenly the Big Cheese sent the biggest, wickedest-looking mouse to get rid of Rocky and Bullwinkle.

Our two heroes ran faster than they had ever run in their lives!

All the TV screens in town suddenly went blank!

CH-Ch-CH-Ch-CH-Ch-CH-Ch

People all over the country struggled
to come up with things to do.

The metal-munching mice could no longer
bite anything, after chomping on sticky candy.

A strange spaceship landed
in a field nearby!

Scrooched!

What was in front of them was actually
a cardboard cutout of Boris Badenov.

Boris was winding up more mechanical mice for another attack.

Rocky and friends headed the mice off at the pass.

Hurray for Rocky and Bullwinkle!

Chapter 8
SOMETHING'S COOKIN'

Rocky and Bullwinkle dashed across the courtyard toward the wall—toward safety.

Suddenly the squirrel stopped short. "Bullwinkle, we're not running away," he said firmly.

"We're not?" Bullwinkle frowned. "Then how come I'm out of breath?"

Rocky shook his head. "What I mean is, we can't just run away. It's our job to find out who's in back of these mechanical mice."

"I'm more worried about who's in front of them," Bullwinkle replied. "Namely *me!*"

"Well, you go on if you want to," Rocky told his friend. "But I'm going back to Bleakly Mansion."

Bullwinkle gulped. Sometimes it wasn't easy being a loyal sidekick to a hero. "Okay, Rock," he said at last. "Anything you say."

And so the courageous squirrel and moose turned around. They sneaked back into Bleakly Mansion and found themselves in the kitchen.

CH-Ch-CH-Ch-CH-Ch-CH-Ch-

It sounded like a whole army of metal-munching mechanical mice was just outside the kitchen door!

Bullwinkle cracked open the door and tried to jab them with a metal poker.

CH-Ch-CH-Ch-CH-Ch-CH-Ch-

But in an instant they had chomped it down to a metal stump.

Bullwinkle slammed the door and braced himself against it. "Those monsters will eat anything!" he gasped.

Suddenly Rocky's eyes lit up. "That's it, Bullwinkle! They'll eat anything!"

Bullwinkle looked around. "Do you notice a kind of echo in here?"

"Hold the door, Bullwinkle!" Rocky ordered. "I'm going to cook up something special!"

Bullwinkle stared at his friend. "Have you flipped your goggles? Rocky, they're going to come busting through that door any minute!"

"Don't worry, Bullwinkle, we'll be

ready." Rocky tossed on an apron and set to work in the kitchen.

CH-Ch-CH-Ch-CH-Ch-CH-Ch-

"Hurry, Rock!" Bullwinkle hollered. "They're munching right through the door!"

Chapter 9

SWEET REVENGE

"Hold on, Bullwinkle," Rocky said cheerfully. "The caramels are almost cool!"

"Caramels?" Bullwinkle shrieked. "I always knew you were good-hearted, Rock. But this is ridiculous!"

"Okay, Bullwinkle," Rocky called. "Stand aside."

Instantly the pack of six-foot-tall mice swarmed into the room and headed toward Rocky. With a grin, Rocky began to toss caramels at them.

"My plan *is* working!" Rocky cheered.

"Tossing bonbons to mice?" Bullwinkle said nervously. "That's a plan?"

"Sure, Bullwinkle. Look!"

And sure enough, the plan was working. The metal-munching mechanical mice chomped on the sticky candy. And their mouths gummed up!

Soon they could no longer bite anything—including our heroes.

"Look, they're leaving," Rocky said.

Just then Rocky and Bullwinkle heard a strange whirring noise outside the mansion. They stuck their heads out the window.

A strange spaceship had landed in a field nearby! Slowly the door opened. And dozens of mechanical mice began to march down the ramp!

Meanwhile, in another part of Bleakly Mansion, Boris and Natasha had also spotted the spaceship.

Slipping into his disguise as the Big Cheese, leader of the mechanical mice, Boris hurried out to meet the ship.

Unfortunately Rocky and Bullwinkle had decided to sneak up on the spaceship too. So everyone arrived at the same time—just as a strange-looking weapon popped out of the spaceship.

Zzzzap!

"They got me, Rock!" Bullwinkle croaked, clutching his chest.

Chapter 10

SCROOCHED!

Rocky put his hands on his hips and shook his head. "No they didn't, Bullwinkle. They got *him*!"

Sure enough, the mysterious spaceship ray had zapped the Big Cheese. He stood frozen like a statue. Birds came to rest on his head and shoulders.

And weird as it was, Rocky knew he'd seen handiwork like this before.

"Bullwinkle!" Rocky said. "He's been SCROOCHED!"

And our heroes knew that only moon men can scrooch people.

The aliens from the spaceship turned out to be Gidney and Cloyd, their old friends from the moon.

"What are you doing down here?" Rocky asked.

"We just brought another shipment of metal moon mice," Gidney said proudly.

Rocky's and Bullwinkle's eyes bulged. Could their friends be the ones behind this whole fiendish plot? They didn't think so.

Rocky and Bullwinkle quickly explained what the metal mice had been doing on Earth.

"That's dreadful!" Cloyd exclaimed.

"We had no idea the mice were going to be used this way!" Gidney added.

There was only one thing to do.

"Let's go talk to the Big Cheese, Gidney," Cloyd said.

"Don't you remember?" Gidney said. "You scrooched him."

And so our friends settled down next to the Big Cheese, to wait for him to get unscrooched.

Little did they know, however, that the Big Cheese they had scrooched—also known as Boris Badenov—was safe and sound. What was in front of them was actually a cardboard cutout.

Boris and Natasha were just then winding up more mechanical mice for another attack.

"What city do we black out tonight, dahlink?" Natasha asked.

"Let's pick one scientificably," Boris said. He flung a dart at a map of the United States that hung on a wall.

Thunk!

Natasha clapped her hands. "Podunk Junction, dahlink!"

"Perfect!" Boris exclaimed.

Moments later, Rocky and friends were stunned to see a huge army of metal mice streaming out of the mansion.

They trampled on the Big Cheese as they headed for Podunk Junction.

That's when Rocky and his friends realized that the Big Cheese they had been waiting for was just a cutout.

"Come on!" Rocky called. "We'll take the shortcut and head 'em off."

"Where do we head 'em off?" Cloyd asked.

"Where does anybody head anybody off?" Gidney said.

"At the pass!" the others shouted.

Chapter 11

THE PIED PIPER OF FROSTBITE FALLS

A short while later, a short squirrel, a tall moose, and two short moon men stood shoulder to knee to shoulder across the narrow pass.

And then they heard a heart-stopping sound.

The sound of thundering metal footsteps. A stampede of metal-munching monster mice was heading straight toward them.

At the last minute something odd happened: The mice turned!

"Doggone it," Bullwinkle cried. "It never happens like this in the cowboy pictures."

Sure enough, the moon mice had taken the expressway instead of the pass. And with no one to stop them, they soon stormed into the little town of Podunk Junction.

CH-Ch-CH-Ch-CH-Ch-CH-Ch-
Chomp, chomp! CHOMP, CHOMP!

One by one, all the TVs in Podunk Junction went out.

Back at the pass, Rocky and his friends were out of ideas.

"We sure could use one of them pied piper fellas," Bullwinkle muttered.

"Bullwinkle, that's it!" Rocky cried. "We'll advertise for a pied piper to get rid of the moon mice!"

A short time later an ad appeared in *The Frostbite Falls Picayune Ledger:*

WANTED

PIED PIPER TO GET RID OF MOON MICE

MAKE BIG MONEY!

WHISTLE WHILE YOU WORK!

A piper showed up right away to interview for the job.

"Allow me to introduce myself," said the short man with the small black mustache. "I'm Rough-on-Rats Chasemoff at your service."

The man looked an awful lot like Boris Badenov. But our trusting heroes didn't suspect a thing.

"Okay, Mr. Chasemoff," Rocky said. "We'll pay you a dollar for every metal-munching mouse you pipe away from here!"

Dollar signs swam before Mr. Chasemoff's eyes. "All work guaranteed," he said. "Just leave it to me."

Soon our heroes were surprised and pleased to see Mr. Chasemoff piping away a whole line of moon mice.

Or at least, it looked that way.

The piper was really just marching the mice in a big circle. He took the same ones by again and again. But our heroes did not know that.

At the end of the day Rocky added up the bill. "Gee, we owe him close to six thousand dollars!" he exclaimed. "But it's worth it if it means the end of the moon mice."

Rocky and his friends were thrilled to have finally solved the country's biggest problem.

As the citizens of Podunk Junction cheered, our heroes quickly put up another TV antenna.

CH-Ch-CH-Ch-CH-Ch-CH-Ch-Crunch!

The celebration lasted about ten seconds before a huge metal-munching mouse chomped the whole thing off.

"I thought you said your work was guaranteed!" Rocky complained.

The mouse piper shrugged. "But I didn't say positively!"

Now Rocky and Bullwinkle were really down. It looked as if there was no way to win.

"Why'd you fellas bring all these mice down here, anyways?" Bullwinkle asked his moon friends.

"It wasn't our idea," Gidney said.

"Mr. Big said they were going to be used as messengers," Cloyd explained.

"Mr. Big!" Rocky and Bullwinkle exclaimed.

"You know him?" Cloyd asked.

They sure did. Mr. Big was Boris Badenov's boss!

Rocky and Bullwinkle told Gidney and Cloyd of their terrible experience with the sinister Mr. Big. The last they had seen of him, he had tried to steal a chunk of the anti-gravity metal Upsidaisium.

And then he fell into outer space.

"We know, Rocky," Cloyd said. "He made a dead-center hit on a moon crater! He's been running things up there ever since."

Now things looked hopeless. How could

they fight somebody on the moon?

Bullwinkle whipped out his ukulele. "Maybe a little music would cheer us up."

Then he began to play. Seconds into the song, Gidney and Cloyd secretly wished *they* were back on the moon—Bullwinkle was awful!

But suddenly Bullwinkle's concert was interrupted.

Our heroes and the moon men found themselves surrounded by thousands of mechanical mice!

Chapter 12
MOOSE MUSIC

And what was more shocking, the mice began to clap. They loved Bullwinkle's singing!

"Bullwinkle," Rocky exclaimed, "you're an honest-to-goodness pied piper! Sing some more!"

"I don't know any more tunes, Rock."

"Well, you'd better think of some fast," Rocky said.

The mice began to get mad at Bullwinkle for stopping.

"Quick, Bullwinkle!" Rocky cried. "Sing *something*!"

The flustered Bullwinkle blurted out the only song he could think of: "Three blind mice, three blind mice, see how they run—"

"Not that one, Bullwinkle!" Rocky whispered.

"How come?" Bullwinkle whispered back.

"Don't you remember the middle part?"

Bullwinkle thought a minute. "You mean the part about cutting off their tails?"

CH-Ch-CH-Ch-CH-Ch-CH-Ch-

"Uh-oh," Cloyd said. "Now you've done it."

"Pick another song before we're munched!" Gidney cried.

Under normal circumstances, Bullwinkle's brain ran a little slow. When he was terrified, it ground to a stop. He couldn't think of a thing!

"We sure could use a smart manager along about now," Bullwinkle moaned.

Suddenly a man dressed in a country-western outfit and cowboy boots strode up to the boys. "Hey, y'allski!" he said in a weird accent. It sounded like a mix of Southern and Russian. "Allow me to introduce myself!"

The man had a small black mustache. And he looked an awful lot like Boris Badenov. But Rocky and his friends didn't seem to notice.

He handed Rocky his card, which read:

COLONEL TOMSK PARKOFF.

SHOW BIZ MANAGER.

TEENAGE IDOLS A SPECIALTY.

And most important:

AUDIENCES CONTROLLED!

Our heroes hired him on the spot.

Colonel Tomsk stood up in front of the mad mice and waved his arms.

"Now lookahere, all y'all music-lovin' rats! We're all gonna hold a great big ol' concert in Colossus Stadium. And all you mice get in fer *free*! How about that?"

The mice clapped, whistled, and screamed.

Boris chuckled. There was more than one way to catch a mouse!

Chapter 13
TAKE IT AWAY, BULLWINKLE!

Later that day, when Colonel Tomsk and our boys arrived at the huge saucer-shaped stadium, it was already jam-packed with moon mice.

"And now, Mr. Golden Throat, a present from your fans." Colonel Tomsk held up a ukulele with a long electric cord hanging down. "Electric ukulele," he explained. "Plays twice as bad, twice as loud!"

Bullwinkle was touched. "Gee, thanks."

Boris struggled to hide his giggles. "Let me plug it in for you. Is the least I can do."

As Colonel Tomsk walked away with the electric cord, Natasha whispered, "Boris, dahlink. You've flipped!"

"Don't you believe it," Boris whispered back. Then he showed her what he had planned.

He opened a small door in one of the columns that supported the stadium.

Natasha looked inside. "Dahlink! Is full of TNT!"

Boris explained that every column in the stadium was full of the same explosive.

"Whole stadium is regular living bomb!" he added cheerfully.

"How is it wired to go off?" Natasha asked.

"How else? Look! Moose's electric ukulele. The first chord he hits—*Boom!*—will be his last."

Natasha's eyes sparkled. The raven-haired villainess adored the idea. "But won't we blow up all the metal-munching mice, too?"

Boris shrugged and glanced at the moon. "There's plenty more where they came from."

But unknown to Boris, an important decision was being made up on the moon at that very moment.

Mr. Big had just gotten some startling news.

"We've run out of materials, Mr. Big," said one of his moon men assistants. "There's not another moon mouse to be made."

Mr. Big thought a moment. "Oh, well, it really doesn't matter. There's a hundred thousand of them down there on Earth already. And they should have finished their terrible task by now. I think I'll go down and check up on them."

Mr. Big boarded a spaceship and blasted off toward Earth.

Unaware of their boss's approach, Boris and Natasha watched the stadium from a safe distance, and with their fingers in their ears.

Bullwinkle was about to go onstage to play his electric ukulele for a stadium full of metal-munching mice.

Would his performance blow them all away?

Chapter 14
ROCK 'N' ROCKET

"Bullwinkle, wait!"

Rocky stopped his starstruck friend before he could enter the stadium. "Did you tune your ukulele?"

"Shucks, no!" Bullwinkle replied. "I'll do it right away." He cleared his throat and flexed his fingers. Then he plucked the strings. "My dog has—"

Boom!

"Well, that's that, Natasha." Boris smirked.

"Not quite, dahlink," Natasha pointed out. "Look!"

The stadium didn't blow up!

Instead, the TNT in the columns of the stadium acted like a series of giant rockets, and the enormous bowl of the stadium rocketed into space!

Unfortunately, at exactly the same time, another spaceship was headed toward Earth.

Crash!

High above Earth, the stadium full of metal-munching mice crashed into Mr. Big's spaceship.

And amazingly, the stadium saucer made it through and landed safely on the moon.

Back on Earth our heroes watched it all.

"Bullwinkle, you did it!" Rocky cheered.

"They're back on the moon!" Cloyd cried.

"Oh, pfooey!" Boris spat. His wonderful awful plot was ruined.

Just then Natasha poked her comrade in the ribs. "Hoo-boy! Look who's here, dahlink."

Boris's eyes nearly popped out of his head. "M-M-M-Mr. Big!"

Mr. Big glared back. He had popped down to Earth, expecting to see that Boris and Natasha had taken over the whole U. S. of A.

Instead, he'd been run over in space by a flying stadium full of mice. And then he had crashed to Earth. He was not a happy boss.

"You know, Badenov," he said, "a funny think happened to me on my way to Earth this evening."

And so he dragged Boris and Natasha off

to tell them all about it.

"Well, Bullwinkle," Rocky said with a smile, "the moon mouse caper is over."

"The country is saved!" Gidney cheered.

Everyone was happy.

Except Bullwinkle. In fact, he was pouting!

"How come you're so sad?" Cloyd asked.

"Well," Bullwinkle said, sulking, "I never did get to sing my song."

Rocky patted his friend on the kneecap. "Well, go ahead, Bullwinkle. We'll listen, won't we, fellas?"

"You bet, Rock," Gidney said.

"Are you crazy?" Cloyd hissed.

Gidney grinned and showed his friend his secret. "Look. Earplugs!"